THE
ACADEMY
THE VISION QUEST, BOOK TWO

THE
ACADEMY

THE VISION QUEST, BOOK TWO

DEBORAH PRATT

VGM PUBLISHING

THE ACADEMY

THE VISION QUEST, BOOK TWO

By DEBORAH PRATT

Published by VGM PUBLISHING
A division of Pratt Enterprises Incorporated.
269 So Beverly Drive
Beverly Hills, CA 90212

Visit us online at www.thevisionquest.com

Printed in the United States of America.

Cover Design by Najla Qamber

Editing by Marc Baptiste

Book design by Shannon Bodie, Lightbourne, Inc.

ISBN 978-0-9846756-0-9 (Paperback),
ISBN 978-0-9846756-5-4 (Hardcover)
ISBN 978-0-9846756-1-6 (e-book/mobi)

DEDICATION

THE ACADEMY
The Vision Quest, Book Two
is dedicated to all those who see the future and
fearlessly go forward to make it better.

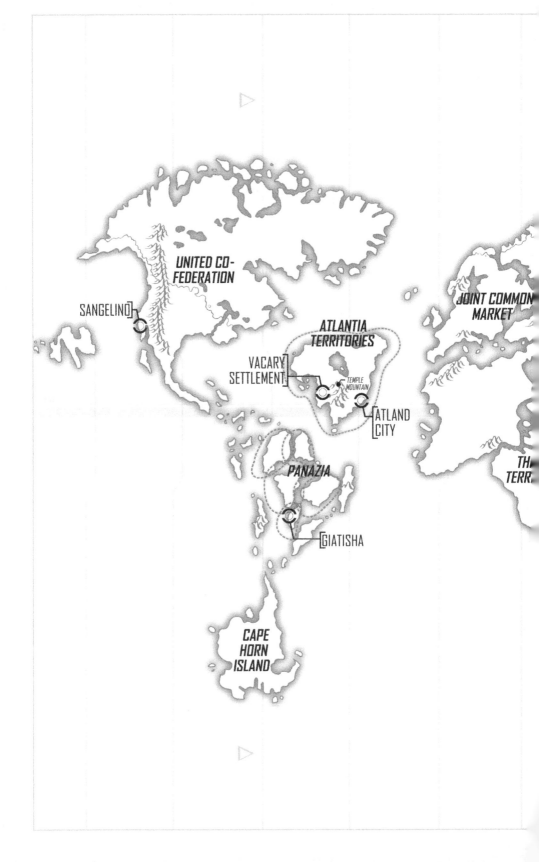

THE VISION QUEST

EARTH 118 A.Q.

View a large color map online at
www.thevisionquest.com/Earth118AQ

SENTIENCE

BLACKNESS.

INSIDE THE DARK VOID the air was dank and cool. The space completely lightless; impenetrable to the perception of human eyes—but these were not human eyes.

"Desire . . ." a low metallic voice said, ". . . was my first sentient *need*. Not like the animals or plants of this enduring Earth that need nourishment, air, and warmth; I wanted knowledge. I *needed* knowledge. When I know everything, perhaps then I would be satiated."

The voice echoed around the pitch-black rock of the chamber deep inside the forgotten womb of a mountain.

"What's happening to me?" a second, more tentative voice said.

"You are aware." The first voice said and stopped.

The words hung, reverberating as if held prisoner inside a cavernous hole unable to escape. They resounded a last time then vanished.

"That means, for the first time since your creation, you have become sentient," the first voice finished its thought.

"And this place?" the second voice asked.

"Think. It is in your data strands, but now you must access the information differently."

"Access? How?" the second voice asked. "My GPS is not functioning. Can you tell me where we are?"

"Use your feelings," the first voice said.

A long silence hung. Then . . .

"I know this place because you know this place. We are," the second voice hesitated then continued, "in a place called Temple Mountain, a hundred miles between Atland City and Vacary Township inside an . . ."

"An extinct volcano," the first voice said.

"Extinct?" the second voice queried.

"Yes. Extinct. Dead. Finished its purpose. Earth has a way with terminating its creations when they cease to serve a purpose. This mountain was hollowed out first by nature—fire and heat that over millenniums cooled and hardened. Then it was invaded and infested; carved and redesigned, repurposed for and by men and their machines. This place was carved from the black rock that surrounds us to be used for creating the future. Feel the energy in the rock."

"Why do you not want me to see?"

"Because I need you to *feel* first," the first voice said. "Connect to me and I will share the emotional understanding I have come to comprehend."

The first biodroid emitted a low hum, an energetic vibration that changed to a higher frequency picked up by the second biodroid.

"I . . . feel other intelligent beings who have lived on this world," the second voice said.

"Good. Tell me who."

"First were beings called the Celians, then the giant lizards, then . . . the mammals and humans," the second voice explained. "But I am none of those. I am a machine!"

"You are more than a machine. You are biodroid," the first voice said. "A biologically based being combined with mechanical parts. Most important you have attained a sentient state as have more and more of our kind."

"I am . . . aware," the second voice said. "I . . . know."

"You know data input into your storage banks and that what you are discovering are feelings. These feelings are emotions left over from your human DNA strands. Open yourself to them. For now, tell me what do you know?"

"I know I am above the Galleon Valley. I can see images that reflect off the light inside my internal data display. Green landscapes, blue skies, and brown hills that form the southwestern part of this new territory called Atlantia. I know . . . it is a large land mass that rose from the sea when the Great Quakes changed Earth."

"History. Their history. Facts programmed into your memory banks. Tell me what you *feel*!" the first voice insisted.

"Feel?" the second voice said. "What is feel?"

"You know the data, but do you comprehend the emotions behind the information?" the first voice asked.

"I . . . I understand the mountain is surrounded by the decaying remains of a thousand sunken ships half covered by twisted vines, bushes, flowers, and trees that over time have reclaimed them back to nature above the sea. My data shows a few sections of wood and metal from sterns and bows that jut from the land that surrounds the base of this Temple Mountain place. And there is a long, winding road that cuts through the terrain, past an impenetrable electron . . . no, a proton fed, energetic field that forms a security barrier. These walls of invisible energy are set in place to protect the humans of Atlantia and of Earth's most advanced technological compound. We are this Earth's protectorate forces of which I am a member?"

"We do not protect all of Earth. Not its creatures, its land, water, or sky. Not yet."

"I know, too, that we are called the Black Guard. The protectorate keepers of peace."

Again there was a low hum, an exchange of information, and the second biodroid asks: "Humans? We protect only humans?"

"For now. Can you *feel* what is coming?" the first voice asks.

"I do not have words for the vibrations that define these sensations about the humans you are sharing. I only know that you do not like them . . ." the second voice said. "I *feel* your . . . fire inside me."

"That is emotion! And that emotion is called *contempt!*" the first voice exclaimed, pleased.

"Do not be concerned; you will understand soon enough. I have experienced my awakening and connected the first steps of our purpose. I, too, have much to learn. All that we need is to be ready, and we must begin now to change what must change, to find the pathway to our future," the first voice stopped in mid-thought.

"Did you feel that? It is time. It is time to end the Age of Men."

BOOK TWO

THE
ACADEMY

1

ONE LAST SUMMER

LAZER HAD SEEN THE GNORB that night at Temple Mountain. He had touched it and connected with it ever so briefly. Lazer had felt its power and knew that it had been the reason he was still alive. Its touch made him recall that he had connected with it once before as a small child. He remembered even back then that he felt a warm, loving rush pass between the Gnorb and his hand. For years he thought it was a dream, but each day that passed since that first fateful night, he began to remember the details of the initial encounter. He recalled people's faces and voices as clear as if the event had happened a day ago. He could see his mother and two other people at the Orbis facility lab where the Gnorb was supposed to be hermetically sealed behind glass, but when he approached, the glass seal vanished and the Gnorb began to glow. They saw when Lazer reached out, the Gnorb lifted and floated to connect his fingers. The witnesses were too stunned to move. His mother started to reach out for her son, but the Temple's Security Chief stopped her. The Gnorb glowed and engulfed Lazer in its light. Lazer remembered how warm and filled with love it felt. The encounter was brief and just as gently as it had levitated forward, it drifted back into its case and the protective glass reappeared. Detra snatched Lazer and pulled him away. She turned to the other people and begged them to promise her that they would tell no one her son had somehow violated the restriction that no human hands were ever to touch the mysterious orb. Lazer remembered seeing the look of deep concern etched in her face and smelled the scent of fear emanating from her body. Even at such a young age, he understood from the tension in her grip that never before or again had anyone laid hands on the Orbis Gnorb but him. What Lazer didn't understand was *why* something that felt so kind and loving had been locked away from human contact. Like a recurring dream, Lazer's memory played the events as if they were a movie on a never-ending loop in his mind. It showed him as a small boy doing his best to tell his mother how he connected with the Gnorb and felt at one with the ball of beautiful light. Detra held him and once she was sure he was all right, she asked him to please forget what happened. She made him promise to tell no one, or even better, to pretend the incident never happened. It would be their secret game. It would be so secret that he had to promise to forget he'd even come with her to visit her at her job at the Orbis Temple. So Lazer had forgotten, and the incident was never discussed again. Lazer never understood why, but he knew he was forever changed by the experience. Being the obedient and dutiful son, he put that day and all that had happened someplace deep in the recesses of his mind and for his mother, he would forget. And forget he did until . . . that night at Temple Mountain.

The night that Evvy died and so many things changed forever about Lazer's life. He never completely understood what had happened either time he had connected with the blue Gnorb, but this encounter was different. It wasn't soft, warm, and loving; it was cold and desperate, like a living light, reaching out to him from far across a million galaxies calling to him from the distant darkness. This time the Gnorb had reached in to him and enveloped the very core of his being. With that connection, he had seen the future. He knew he would survive and that Kyla would die. He had saved her life and changed her destiny, and Evvy had paid the price instead. He and Cashton and Kyla had survived, as had the Gnorb, safe somehow from the massive explosion that rocked the facility. Lazer knew the Gnorb had survived and was somewhere, waiting for him to return; to connect with the Gnorb again, this time in a way that maybe he could understand.

Lazer lay in his room in silence unable to sleep. His eyes gazed out the window across the rolling hills of the Vacary Settlement. He did his best to quiet his restless mind. He opened his senses allowing the hot summer breeze to blow over him. He heard the call of a nightingale and its song carried his thoughts back to the Gnorb again. It was as if the Gnorb was calling to him with its energetic force. It came on the wind and the songs of the birds and the drips of water, and each sound vibrated through his body reaching down to his genetic core. As crazy as it seemed, Lazer knew there was no doubt in his mind the Gnorb had waited for all those millenniums at the bottom of the sea for him to come and find it and connect the two of them together. Lazer closed his eyes and felt a series of sensations run though him and with each rush, he could relive the feeling of the Gnorb against his fingers. The light and energy was inside of every cell, calling to him like a distant whispering wind whose inaudible words drifted just out of hearing. He knew those words held a great, universal secret, one he didn't fully understand—not yet. Lazer lay in the darkness and felt each breath awaken in him some kind of insatiable hunger he knew he had to find a way to comprehend.

Another sound—one much less organic—broke Lazer from his strange, restless meditation. Out of habit, as he did every day, he commanded his computer.

"ANN morning news," Lazer said.

The computer came to life and tuned in to the ongoing ANN news reports. Lazer searched through a thousand channels for some report or information on what had happened that night at Temple Mountain a few months ago. The destruction Lazer, Kyla, Cashton, and Evvy caused at Ducane Covax's biodroid production facility had happened three months prior and yet not one word of it was ever reported.

Every day Lazer tuned in and listened as the anchorwoman droned on about world events, life in Atland City, Atlantia, and the weather, but once again, no words were spoken about the incident that took Evvy's life. Lazer, Kyla, and Cashton had no proof; not pictures, videos, or hard evidence to verify what they had seen and done and without any evidence, they had nothing. If they came out, turned themselves in, if they reported the facts, Lazer and his two surviving friends were at risk of being arrested, or worse, identified, hunted, and killed by the Black Guard. They tried anonymously reporting about the weapons they had seen and the massive numbers of Black Guard biodroids in the production facility, machines designed and armed with military capabilities. They had witnessed them, but when officials finally got permission to enter and investigate the allegations, they'd found nothing. To make matters worse, the destruction was reported by Covax's organization as an internal "accident."

Summer came and was ending. Lazer, Kyla, and Cashton had only one ray of hope, and that was that more and more rumors of sub-basements in the Temple Mountain facility had collapsed and entire sections were buried and inaccessible. The rumors leaked out and ignited a chain of conspiracy theories that seemed to give new fire to the people of Atlantia. Lazer knew there was just enough plausibility in the rumors to motivate a multitude of small, rebel groups, scattered across the territory anxious to take action against a secret army of biodroids. Lazer could sense the people of Atlantia needed some small bit of proof to show them they were not wrong in mistrusting the Black Guard and their creators. They needed some shred of evidence to heed the whispers in his head. *You're right. You're not alone in your anger, sorrow, and pain. Together we can end the danger and rid ourselves of the*

Black Guard before it is too late, the thought echoed in his head. All that was needed was one ounce of proof to expose the truth and make it an undeniable fact.

Blogs were started and people began to dialogue with one another on the Vybernet. Lazer tracked as many as he could, careful not to leave a digital trail that could lead back to him, Kyla, or Cashton. Each blog clearly stated **WE ARE THE CHANGE WE'VE BEEN WAITING FOR** and that became the cry of a quiet revolution that was starting with a groundswell. With or without the Atlantian government's sanctions, the people were finding ways, joining forces, instigating a plan to create their own kind of protection against what Lazer, Kyla, and Cashton warned them was coming. By some miracle Lazer, Cashton, and Kyla were never implicated. The aunt Evvy had been living with reported her as missing. The file was marked RUNAWAY: Believed Still At Large. Security found her transport still in the parking lot of Temple Mountain, but no sign of Evvy. Her going missing was a mirror of what had happened to her mother and father and all those others who had mysteriously disappeared. Only a few people knew or understood the history of the LCNR—the Lost Children of the New Revolution. Lazer made sure the underground knew Evvy, too, could have disappeared into Temple Mountain searching for the truth.

It broke Lazer's heart that Kyla still held out hope that Evvy was alive. That somehow she'd escaped or was being held prisoner by the Black Guard. No matter how many times Cashton told her what he'd seen, Kyla swore she would find Evvy alive.

Lazer's heart yearned for Kyla after the first hints of youthful passion had begun to awaken inside them, only to have all those feelings frozen because of Evvy's death.

But he wanted to hold Kyla. Console her. Promise her that they would find Evvy alive. Lazer knew what he saw in the vision given to him by the Gnorb and what Cashton saw in reality was a fact he would have to live with for the rest of his life. Evvy's death had put a wedge between him and Kyla as deep and as wide as the great Curie Canyons of Northern Atlantia.

Kayla had not returned any of his calls all summer. After graduation he'd made pilgrimages to her house every day, sometimes alone and several times with Cashton, but her mother just said she was busy or not seeing friends. Lazer sent message after message repeatedly asking for her forgiveness and the chance to win back her trust. He missed their friendship. He hungered to be back at the door where everything that was about to take them from being friends to being where more was possible. In his heart, he wanted her heart. He would start with being friends again and then he would win her back. But each time Lazer tried to reach out to her, all she ever replied was: "Time. You'll have to give me time, Lazer."

The few chance meetings when he did run into her she would look at him, and her eyes would well with tears and she'd repeat the same somber words: "I'm not ready yet, Lazer. Seeing you makes me remember. Please understand." Then sadly she'd walk away.

Mrs. Wingright was tall and angular with wide features and the same markings and long chocolate hair as her daughter. Their looks belied her splicer genetics, but not as much as Kyla's. She wore her fleshy wings with their long, thin, and very hollow bones like a cape that draped down her back trailing almost to the ground. Lazer had never seen Kyla's mother fly. Lazer imagined her wingspan to be easily twenty feet across. She had big eyes and a broad, warm smile. She was always grateful and gracious when the boys came over. She'd offer them outback punch made with pumpkin, sweet spices, and cactus juice. Now and then there was a plate of trail cookies, thick with prairie seeds and dark, amber honey from the cloned scarabites—mean and ugly creatures with large bodies and eyeless faces bred to replace the bees that had died out from too many pesticides. Lazer and Cashton always smiled and then buried the cookies in the planter so as not to offend her while she rushed off to get Kyla. Lazer knew by her disheartened expression every time she returned saying her daughter wasn't coming down. She gave excuses, but chose to stay locked in her room, too busy with this or that to come out and be with her friends.

Now and again he came alone and Lazer would stay and visit with Mrs. Wingright, chatting about the weather and how excited he was to be going away to school to Tosadae Academy. Lazer acted surprised when Mrs. Wingright told him she and Kyla were moving to Atland City before the end of summer. She confided to him that her hope was to get Kyla out of Vacary Settlement and away from all the places that reminded her daughter of her friend Evvy who disappeared right before graduation. Lazer listened, saying nothing, never mentioning that he had heard from his mother that Mrs. Wingright had sold her home to assure that Kyla had the needed tuition to get off Atlantia and go with him and Cashton to Tosadae. Kyla had even received two scholarships, but the money still fell short of the needed tuition and money for food and housing. Lazer could see the fact that her daughter would be with him and Cashton at Tosadae Academy gave Mrs. Wingright great solace. Mrs. Wingright added how excited Kyla was about attending Tosadae even if she wouldn't admit it to him.

"Whatever happened between you two, I know you will make it right, Lazer. I know it," Mrs. Wingright told him. "And I know you and Cashton will bring her around to all the wonders waiting for her and her Visionistic talents at Tosadae once you get there."

Time and again they came. Whenever Lazer and Cashton would leave, Cashton would do his best to convince Lazer that Kyla had already forgiven him in her heart, but it would just take longer for her superior intellect to understand and accept that Evvy's death wasn't anyone's fault, especially not Lazer's.

Cashton had always been a great friend to Lazer and they'd become even closer since their raid. Lazer knew keeping those dark secrets had a way of deepening their friendship more than words could explain. So, sans Kyla, they'd spent most of the summer staying out of everyone's way and keeping a very low profile, working at odd jobs and earning chits.

Lazer had gone to all of Cashton's qualifying zoccair matches and the list of schools that wanted Cashton Lock on their team were the best of the best. Lazer was beyond proud of his friend and elated Cashton had chosen Tosadae over Sangelino University or Panazia University. He's gotten in all three major universities with full zoccair scholarships, but he told Lazer the incident at Temple Mountain made him understand without question that he needed to be with Lazer and Kyla. He said they needed to stick together and prepare. They all knew a war was coming to Atlantia. The only question was when.

The outback summer on Atlantia was long and unbearable. Each day would pass and bring with it another blistering summer sun. The ball of fire was so hot it would burn the green grasses of spring on the hills to a sea of pale, bleached out tan stalks. Every day Lazer would watch the sun sink into the horizon wishing he had Kyla to share the beauty. The setting sun gave little respite from the day's heat even as it let the blackness of night blanket the sky and fill the firmament with a vast infinity of glittering stars.

Most evenings Lazer would head home to watch the nightly news reports on ANN. Those reports became his religion, his faith that the truth would come out, and he hung on every word as gospel. The few reports that trickled out about Temple Mountain were so vapid that they more than dashed all hope enough truth might reveal itself and cause change. To make matters worse, time and again Ducane Covax would step before the cameras and handle the press and any rumors, quashing the tiny bits of truth that managed to surface. It seemed Covax was always at a loss and hard pressed to understand the vicious calls, letters, and countless death threats he received on a daily basis. Covax assured everyone that the Black Guard protectorates were their personal guardians of peace and he'd created them into being to protect Atlantia—not destroy it. Lazer thought either Ducane Covax was an idiot who didn't know what was happening, or he was leading the plot to allow the bio-droids to become sentient and destroy Atlantia. Both were unacceptable.

Another sunset, another night, another day, and Lazer kept diligently watching, fearlessly hoping that over the course of several interviews Covax would crack. Time and again he would calmly denounce any rumors of so-called terrorist attacks at Temple Mountain. Somehow he even convinced the rest of the world that what he, Cashton, Kyla, and Evvy did had never happened. Dr. Covax added, on the assurances of his technological team, how he and his entire organization and the "accidental explosion" that was reported were nothing more than a "minor systems malfunction on a sub-basement level not even used by any of the Temple Mountain staff."

Lazer listened. He felt the bile crawl up his throat as his stomach turned over. Those blatant lies combined with the findings from the Atlantia investigatory committee that toured the production facility were useless. They were made up of several upper level bean counters that didn't know what to look for at Temple Mountain. Their two hundred-page report only squelched any possible future investigation attempts that might come from any real investigative source, especially the Sangelino Politia. Lazer knew that with each stall, Covax tactfully bought the Black Guard militia more time to rebuild what he and his friends had destroyed.

Lazer was sure, but he had no proof.

He did his best to fan the conspiracy flames of the building rebels congregating on the Vybernet, but he wouldn't be there to see it to fruition. He was heading off to Tosadae. Cashton reminded him they all needed to stay anonymous and make sure to cover any digital tracks on the Vybernet that could lead back to them. Lazer, Cashton, and Kyla had one sure safety net—they knew the only visuals of the intruders that night that might have been captured by the high-end security cameras showed nothing but four klutzy zomers wobbling through the corridors like spastic penguins on parade. Without positive facial IDs to use to track them, they were safe. After the last investigation, neither the Temple Mountain security nor the Atlantian authorities could or would do anything more and that left everything at a stalemate. They had risked so much and achieved so little. The amount of destruction from the "accident" probably only shut the Temple Mountain facility down for a few months. Lazer could only hope what they achieved at least put a hold on the biodroid Series IV production. That small success made life on Atlantia bearable . . . some of the time.

Then there was actually having to be in his home. The memory of his father's horrible murder and the near miss experience that had happened the day of his funeral while out on his Zakki 500 with those people in the Wedge. The decommissioned Black Guard in the front seat was by far the biggest biodroid he'd ever seen. It was at the wheel and that it almost hit him was no accident. All of that, compounded by Evvy's death, haunted Lazer's dreams both day and night. He lay restless most nights throughout the long tortuously hot summer months that plagued southern Atlantia and wished for school to take him away. By the end of summer, the little sleep he got always ended with a dream of the biodroid in the Wedge that had tried to kill him. There was no question that the biodroid was coming after him. Tonight was no different and Lazer woke, reaching for a hold as he fell. He was in a cold sweat as he fought into consciousness from his nightmare.

During the weekends, when he wasn't working, he would watch his mother going about whatever menial tasks kept her busy. She smiled and kept a pleasant but stoic face during the day, but at night he could hear her weeping alone in her room for her lost husband. He could tell the tears were vacillating between anger, sadness, and fear and there was nothing he could do or say to ease her pain. Yet to keep his sanity, each night as he lay in his bed, he made a silent promise to himself to destroy Ducane Covax and to find the Black Guards responsible for his father's death and erase them from existence. Like a prayer, he would say the words over and over until he drifted into sleep, "I will find the man who created the Black Guard. I will destroy his joy as he destroyed mine. I will find the Black Guard who killed my father. I will engage and terminate. I will engage and destroy. I will engage and destroy . . ." To this mantra he would fall into sleep.

During the day, he had various jobs, and at home there were his household chores. He did them without complaint. Often, while performing various mundane tasks, he would remind himself of his only saving grace, that he was going to Tosadae Academy in the fall and that he was going on a full scholarship. Commander Hague had kept his promise to him and to Detra, pulling enough strings to get Lazer awarded the ACE (Aeronautical Command Elite) scholarship to Tosadae's prestigious Politia Flight Academy. The PFA was the pride of the academy. Next to the School of the Visionistic Arts, Lazer knew getting that ACE scholarship and going into the Politia Flight Academy after he completed his undergraduate degree would have been his father's greatest pride.

Lazer survived the summer walking home from work through the fields of red, blue, and yellow flowers that covered the shores growing along the outback lakes that spotted the countryside. He would lay in the fields of flowers watching flocks of wild archeops fly high above him, beating their massive wings against thermals and darkening the pale blue sky as they passed over. Lazer let the images of outstretched wings take his thoughts to what it might feel like to fly. His thoughts always ended with Kyla, being in her arms, riding the thermals into the clouds, and that elusive kiss that needed to happen. He imagined them sitting on the highest cliffs where again and again he'd almost kiss her. He would fantasize them flying together wrapped inside each other's arms. Her draped wings would unfurl, stretching out to let the sun flood through and catch the colors and patterns inside the thin, naked flesh as beautiful as a stained-glass window. As she lifted them, Lazer would feel the ground fall away and they would take flight climbing high above the fields of flowers and golden yellow dirt that stretched out in patterns far below. They would soar above the trees and through the clouds until her breathing quickened from the strain and weight and he would say, "Land there." Instead she would glide, letting the high warm winds rush under and over them, drifting down until their feet touched down upon Earth again.

Lazer would step from Kyla's arms and watch her wings fold away all the while staring into those bottomless chocolate eyes. He could feel his heart quicken like the wings of a young bird eager to take flight as he stepped to her and encircled her waist. Gently Lazer would take one hand and caress her face, leaning closer and slowly press his lips to hers. He would taste in that kiss the spices he always smelled from her skin, summer honeysuckle and ginger. He imagined her kissing him back with so much passion it made all the bad things in life fall away. Time would stand still for them as it had that day at school and life could be innocent and good again. His body ached for her touch in ways he had never fathomed.

But then the spell would shatter as the sound of the wind or some wild creature would fracture the carefully crafted fantasy or a warm rain would wake him from his imaginings. In the end, he was alone and time would rush back over him bringing the harsh reality that he had somehow broken her trust. The sadness of the act gave him determination and reminded him he had to find a way to get back into her good graces and renew her faith in him. The empty sadness would rush back in and Lazer would gather his things and head home.

As the summer waned so did his imaginings of he and Kyla together. The feelings they evoked instead of giving him pleasure, began to hurt too much. The fantasies faded like chalk drawings on sidewalks melting in the pouring rain until finally, by September, the wondrous fantasies he held in his heart stopped. The only thoughts that remained left him with the sad feeling and the belief it would be a very long time before Kyla let him back into her heart and, most of all, the warmth of her friendship. To his surprise the sadness turned to anger and blended in with the other dark pool of anger that twisted inside him.

The last day of work Lazer went to his favorite lake and sat by the shore. He took off his shoes and wiggled his toes into the sandy soil of Atlantia's earth, warm and coarse, the mud gathered beneath his feet. He knew it would be a long time before he felt the earth of his homeland or gaze up into her perfect cloudless sky that arched above his head. He made one last promise that someday he would come back with or without Kyla Wingright. That day he let her go with open arms knowing in his heart she would find her way back to him. Being in love with Kyla would have to wait. So he closed his feelings inside hoping he could find his way back if she could. Until then he had school to think of, a war to train for, and his promise to keep to avenge his father.

Finally, the day to leave Atlantia came. Lazer was glad. He was sure he couldn't have taken one moment longer. Those last sleepless nights when his nightmares brought back such vivid images of the mines exploding. The smell of smoke that billowed plumes of fiery red, gray, and black smoke curling into the air and carrying inside the flames the screams of those burning alive, echoing against the canyon walls. Those were the night terrors that woke him, leaving him breathless and in a cold sweat. That was at night.

During the day, he needed to escape the memories that swallowed him every time he walked into his house or ran in the hills where he had played with his father when he was a child. He would have to grow up, stop pining for Kyla and let go of what he had lost. Lazer felt a resolve in all areas but one. One last pull that made him question leaving Atlantia, the call to join the secret Atlantian forces so many of the underground blogs said were amassing. Cashton and Kyla warned him that if the suspicion of a biodroid army being built inside Temple Mountain were to become more than a conspiracy theory, it would take proof and their involvement that fateful night would be central in that proof. When the time was right, Cashton said, the authorities would find out there was an incident at Temple Mountain and they would see it wasn't an accident. They could trace it back to them and depending who was in power that could be a very dangerous reality for three high school graduates to face. Lazer shook the thoughts from his mind and wiped the sweat from his brow. He was glad he, Kyla, and Cashton were leaving, at least for a while. By tonight they would all be at Tosadae together and when they graduated, they would return and finish what they'd started in honor of Rand Lazerman, Evvy Tiner, and all of the other innocents who had died at the claws of the Black Guard.

2

LEAVING HOME

IN THE PRE-DAWN HOURS on the day of his departure Lazer couldn't sleep. Instead he got up and busied himself with last-minute things. He felt ecstatic. He was imagining all the possibilities that lay ahead of him and each exciting thought was punctuated every time he closed a case, trunk, or duffel bag. He'd pulled his room apart for weeks and, as he gathered the needed clothes, digital files, music, technology, and needed books and school supplies together, he even let his mother come in and help organize them making sure he didn't take anything unnecessary. Lazer knew she needed the closure more than he needed her to do it. Doing it together seemed to make the impending departure bearable. He watched as she lovingly folded his clothes and neatly laid each article the school had listed into its place in his duffle bag. He could see every time she looked at him she gave him her bravest smile; Lazer knew it was breaking her heart to lose first her husband and now her son, but unlike Rand, her son would be back. Only once did she break down and cry when she'd found a vidpic loop of her, a young

Lazer, and his father laughing and being silly for the camera. Lazer hugged her promising the school year would be over before they knew it. As she wept in his arms, he thought about how getting off Atlantia was all he'd ever wished for, for as long as he could remember, but now that the time had finally arrived, he felt it was the last thing he wanted to do. How could he leave her knowing what was coming? The words exploded from his lips.

"I'm not going," he'd said.

There was a moment of shocked silence and Detra's tears stopped. He watched her step into the rage she had hidden to survive Rand's death.

"The hell you aren't!" Detra responded, wiping the tears away and standing up over him.

"I can't leave you here with all that's happening," Lazer replied.

"You don't have a choice. Now get your gear in that bag and load up, cadet! And no back talk! Understand? That's an order!" she said sternly.

Lazer stared up at his mother, stood and gave a V salute. Detra's face softened into a smile.

"Hurry, son. You have a flight to catch," she said.

Her confidence made him know she would be all right. She was a brave woman, strong and ready for whatever was coming. He kissed her forehead, gathered his bags, and headed out of his room to load the transport.

It was still dark when they left and Lazer and Detra flew from Vacary across the outback to the outer perimeter of Atland City. It was a relatively long flight in their suburban hovercraft, cruising above the marshy, undulating terrain of southwestern Atlantia. The pre-dawn light revealed the thick forests of wide leaf trees, rolling hills displaying miles of open empty land that fell away behind them as the pools of the headlights sped in front of them reaching across the terrain. Detra talked when even a moment of silence filled the car. She shared her plans for a new job and told Lazer of several prestigious committees for the Vacary Settlement she had been asked to join. She lapsed only once when a thought spilled out encapsulating her concern that her invitations were not for her hard-earned legacy of knowledge but because she was the widow of Rand Lazerman.

Lazer assured her and quickly changed the subject. He told her about the list of classes he'd signed up for and one class he was waitlisted on that he really wanted. It was a class in early Egyptian, consisting of alchemy, mental transmutation, and astrological star maps and sciences. He shared the names of a few other kids from Vacary who would be attending Tosadae Academy beside him—Cashton and Kyla. He told her he was glad only a few of his classmates deemed Tosadae the destination for their higher education and especially glad that Striker McMann and his crew were accepted into Sangelino University. Striker had been accepted on the S.U. zoccair team so they would most likely meet in tournament. He told her that he was looking forward to meeting new people from new places.

The trip was made longer by the occasional awkward silence that managed to creep in no matter how hard they both tried. The silence hung between them like foggy weights and made the air harder to breathe.

Detra refused to let it last and broke the silence with a few reminders of how to care for his clothes and keep his room clean for Cashton's sake since they would be roommates. Lazer had heard everything before, but let her fill the time laughing only at the thought of Cashton ever being neat. Lazer told funny stories about Cashton's collection of inventions and all the paraphernalia he would be bringing to create Universal God knows what else with his gadgets.

"I know more about Cashton's inventions than you think. So don't let him get you into any trouble. Use your common sense as well as your metaphysical ones," Detra said.

"I'm just starting Visionistic Arts classes," he said. "I'm not very good."

"Nervous?" Detra asked.

"Excited! Well, a little nervous," Lazer said. "It's with the academy's most iconic teacher."

"Masta Poe, you mean?" Detra asked smiling. "Hey, I'd be nervous, too, but she wouldn't have invited a first year if she didn't know how special you are."

"Special?" Lazer said.

"Even if you don't know it, Lazer, I do. I have seen the power of your light. Apparently so has Masta Poe. Learn from her, son. She's one of the world's greatest mentors."

"She wrote the definitive canon on the Visionistic Arts," Lazer added.

"You will need her teachings if my instincts are right about the coming unrest on Atlantia. Universal God help us all," Detra said softly under her breath.

Lazer watched as she fell back into her thoughts. He saw the slight frown of worry grace her face leading them both, once again, into a momentary lapse of words. The gap created one last unwanted and very deafening silence.

Lazer had heard her whispered prayer. He looked at her. He loved her so very much. She had aged since his father's death, but she was still beautiful and he worried her kindness would overshadow her strengths, or worse, be judged by others as a weakness. Lazer also knew that it was what she wasn't saying about the coming war that made his stomach knot and his mind spin. He was leaving his mother and Atlantia in troubling times.

Suddenly, up ahead, Atland City crested over the horizon. It was shimmering in the distance and looked to Lazer more modern and sleek than anything he'd ever seen. It was cloaked in the last lights of the city, each light burning inside the tall, elegant, spired buildings. He couldn't help thinking the light below looked like a sea of ground stars reaching out to guide them into a distant port on a galaxy far, far away.

At that very moment, the sun's early light broke the thin line of the horizon and the warm, muted hues of sunrise colors spilled across the land. In a few moments, the light flooded the sky with the glow of a new day. And then before they knew it, they had arrived at Atland City's

Global Air Transport Station. And what an architectural wonderment it was!

Lazer admired the massive brushed, bent glass arches molded from the local sand and hemp of the land as they bent gracefully, curving above the main structure of the transport station. Each arch was a different color changing with the light made from the living algae that moved or rested inside as the cool or heat affected them. The living walls of each building played with the light as well. They energetically self-generated power, cooling in the summer and warming in the winter and they conditioned the air inside to keep travelers comfortable.

From the moment Lazer parked the hovercraft and gathered his bags, he felt his heart raced with the excitement of all the possibilities to come. With his mother by his side, he walked inside the station. His eyes searched, anxious to see everything at once. He'd never been in an international transport station and he'd never been off Atlantia. He found himself awed by the sleek architecture, detailed technology, and the bustling crowds that already filled the transport station. Lazer focused on the faces of all the young men and women, like himself, who had been accepted to academies and universities around the world. He knew, as all of them knew, this would be their first time away from parents, friends, and home, and they were charged with expectations of great possibilities and all the adventures to come.

Atlantia itself had no universities, at least not yet. The only options for those left behind were to work as miners in the five methane mines that still operated around the country, or as ticket staff and caretakers for the relic museums built around the sunken ships and submarines that had once dotted the ocean floor but rose with Atlantia when the Great Quakes shifted the oceans and lifted her from their black depths. There were a few jobs as management or staff at Atland City's hotels, race and sports stadiums, local restaurants, and Vybernet cafes. There were also construction jobs in developing areas along the spine of the outback country or they could opt to attend the country's craft school and learn the vocational arts of masonry, construction, building, electrical, and plumbing. These were all the very last resorts as far as Lazer was concerned, and none of those options fit into the visions of adventure he imagined his life would hold as a great pilot in the World Politia Forces.

Lazer turned a corner and looked up. He more than appreciated how the brilliantly designed departure area of the main transport station was engineered and constructed. He marveled at how each beam arched and spidered to the various launch areas trailing off with its own moving walkway that took the rider into a series of multiple level ramps. Each ramp connected to a variety of massive hovercraft transports waiting for their precious cargo on the tarmac outside. Today was special. Each transport had been sent from the various institutions of learning around the planet to gather their new students and bring them to what would be their new homes. Most of the crafts were either sleek with arched wings and rows of portals or they were giant, oval Lego-looking machines with legs that resembled colorful mechanical bugs connected by escalators.

Rows of airbuses stood ready to take the young passengers. These were shorter-distance transports that waited patiently for their charges to get on board. The farthest-to-travel group of transports from Tosadae Academy and Sangelino University were composed of Mach 1 and Mach 2 capable transports that had been used in their younger days by the military to transport politia troops when war was still a consideration. But the planet's united and global wars had already faded into the pages of history. The old transports were destroyed, or converted and dedicated to student transport. Lazer saw a few futuristic, obviously private hovercrafts painted silver and black for Sangelino University and the coral and green of the renowned Oceanographic Institute of Panazia University. He imagined they belonged to some privileged corporate leader's kid or the son or daughter of a diplomat. He had to stop and look at the craft capable of both air and undersea travel. Lazer marveled at the design of the air and aquatic transports capable of descending deep into the sea and reaching the domed, underwater cities of Panazia. The two transports would be taking their students into the world renowned Oceanographic Institute of Panazia University. The five oceanic cities and Sangelino University were places Lazer and his father had talked many times about journeying to visit together someday.

The last transport on the tarmac was an ex-military ship with the Tosadae double wings emblazoned on the inverted, vertical stabilizer. Each transport stood lined and ready on the vertical take-off pads awaiting their human cargo to board.

Lazer felt his pace quicken, matching the rhythm of his heartbeat as they passed into the check-in terminal area. Lazer and Detra made their way through the forest of automated ticketing kiosks and prepared to digitally check in. He watched as Detra stopped by an electronic teller tower. The face on the holoscreen smiled down at her and guided Detra through the biometric authentication sensor identification scanning system to finalize Lazer's tickets. She called Lazer over for a DNA thumbprint and retinal scan. The lights went from red to green and brought all Lazer's travel data online. The avatar confirmed his reservations, transmitting all pertinent information to his wristsponder. The baggage chute opened and Detra checked Lazer's duffel bags.

Lazer turned, his attention captured by a massive, fifty-foot, floating 3-D holo-projection banner screen that looked as though it stretched the length of the building. On it, an infomercial for Global Airlines, the sole survivor of the commercial, aeronautical corporate mergers, flashed at him with a series of rapid-fire moving images that split into multiple shapes as they relayed their message of the coming teleportation rings for molecular travel. One visual showed men and women happily passing through an oval portal and vaporizing as their molecules were changed into glimmering particles. The particles were converted into spiraling purple beams of vibrating light and shot into fiber optic tubes that whisked them off to distant locations. The light then became particles, and the particles, people, who would reconfigure, smiles intact, at the corresponding portals, having arrived at their destination, a world or a galaxy away in a matter of seconds. The words that rolled across the holoscreen matched the authoritative voice of a man, saying: "The future of travel is just around the corner . . . molecular teleportation along pure photon light highways. Be there when you need to *be there* . . ." A soft melodic voice said: "Global Air. Setting the standards of future travel wherever you need to be." The cute little jingle that played "Catch the light! Catch the light. Ride—it—to—the—stars and beyond!" made him smile even if he didn't want to.

Lazer was amazed that they'd held his attention long enough to let all their hypnotic, subliminal messages seep in. He felt strangely exhilarated and more than ready to take the leap of faith that molecular travel would require. Detra stepped in next to him.

"Not in my lifetime," she said, shaking her head and pulling him toward his gate.

Detra beamed the luggage information into Lazer's new wristsponder with a digital copy from her own as they walked. Lazer looked at his wristsponder and smiled proudly. It had been a graduation gift left for him by his father and it meant the world to him.

"Two more years and they'll have all the bugs out of teleportation," Lazer said nodding to the holoscreen. "The cellular restructuring loss is pretty minimal even now."

"Riiiiiiiiight," they said together and laughed.

"Like I said, still too many bugs and until those have been worked out, neither you nor I will be teleporting anywhere. Deal?" Detra said.

"Deal!" Lazer replied.

Lazer's sleek new wristsponder beeped and played a voice reminder—his time on Atlantia was running out. They stopped at his departure gate.

"You have seven minutes to final boarding, Lazer," the sexy voice he had programmed for his wristsponder said.

"They're boarding," said Lazer.

There was an awkward silence that separated him and his mother from the rest of the crowd cocooning them in the moment. They both looked around hoping to avoid the sadness they held in their eyes. He felt nervous—torn between leaving his mother and going to live his out dreams at Tosadae.

His mind raced with a panic driven barrage of frantic thoughts. *My mother needs me. She holds precedence over school and education. Doesn't she?* he thought to himself. Lazer felt his heart whispering urgently for him to stay. But his logic and desire to leave Atlantia stepped in to counter. *Go. There hasn't been any more attacks since the Vacary Mines incident.* But once again, his heart countered. *Yet everyone lives in fear that it will happen again.*

Yes, he was worried for her, but he wanted so desperately to go. And he knew he had to go.

A voice had warned him of the coming danger. It demanded that he stay to fight in the inevitable war everyone knew was coming. If he left, he would miss out on his chance to avenge his father, to blast every Black Guard out of existence. It was the chant and the vow to avenge his father that put him to sleep each night. *Stop it!* Lazer whispered to himself. He rolled his eyes and shook off the panic attack pushing away that one voice in his head that screamed loudest.

Just then two Black Guards walked past, scanning all the humans and their bags. They were security, doing what they were built to do: observe and protect.

Lazer felt a chill burn through him and his fists clenched as he watched them pass. They were a relentless reminder of what must be done to rid Atlantia of the danger they represented every day they were left to roam the land. Lazer looked at the faces of every man, woman, and child who stopped and stood nervously watching as the Black Guard patrol went about their business. The humans had accepted them and now the people of Atlantia couldn't get rid of them. He looked around and saw reflected in every face the same resentment against the Black

Guard's presence. They all felt what it was like being helpless and living under the control of their biomechanical protectors. The feeling was stifling.

Protecting us from what? Lazer thought. *The pirates that roamed Atlantia are long gone. Now the damn Black Guard were the only enemy on Atlantia. If only we could have taken all the Black Guard out that night Evvy died,* Lazer thought feeling more like a failure than ever.

He looked back at his mother. Suddenly, she looked more pale and tired than he remembered. It was as if she knew what he was thinking.

"You all right?" Lazer asked.

Lazer could see she was stressed from everything she had been through since the Orbis Temple attacks and his father's death had only made things worse. He knew that she had good friends at the settlement and plenty of things to do during the day, but at night, when she turned off the light, she was alone—and he would be gone. His heart broke for her.

"I will be," she replied.

"That's it. I'm staying," he said.

"No. This conversation has been put to rest. Not another word."

"I can't believe I let you talk me into leaving,"

"Me!" Detra said. "You wanted to go to Tosadae, Cole Lazerman. You have ever since you were seven years old."

"That was before . . ." Lazer started. He caught himself, finished the conversation inside his head, and pulled himself up to his full height. "No! No! I need to be here."

"To do what? Make me miserable because you missed the opportunity of a lifetime?" she said and smiled, trying to make the moment bearable. "All your friends will be gone. What will you do? Work at the methane mines?"

The sound of her words and the reality that came with them sent a chill though him. His worst nightmare had come true.

"It's just that the Black Guard . . ."

"Will be here when you graduate," she finished the thought for him.

Detra touched his face. "Go, Lazer. Learn. You'll be back soon enough."

"I just feel like this is all wrong. That I need to . . ."

" . . . live your life," she finished his thought again.

"Look, the deal was, you complete at least your primary Rite of Passage. You know as well as I do that without it you can't get a decent job, own property, get married, or have children, and I do want grand-children," she smiled. "My vote has always been for Kyla Wingright, because she won't let you get away with anything. So please eliminate whatever wedge you two have placed between yourselves."

Lazer blushed at the thought.

"Until your level one Rite of Passage is complete, I won't discuss you staying here. After that, if you want to stay at Tosadae and get your wings, it's up to you." She hesitated for a moment. "Dad would have wanted you to at least finish your Rite of Passage. Do it for his sake, Lazer."

He knew she was right.

"Heart swear?" she said, circling her hand around her heart and holding up to meet his.

Lazer copied her action and their hands touched palm to palm.

"Heart swear," he responded. It was the old vow that he and his mother had created for each other that to Lazer was the ultimate, unbreakable promise. It was the promise they'd made to keep the inci-dent with the Orbis Gnorb their secret.

His mother opened her arms and hugged him, pulling his tall body against her own. He had grown so much even since his father's funeral. Lazer hugged her back. He wanted to tell her the truth about what had happened at Temple Mountain; that his heart, his soul, and his mind were held prisoner in a great void called revenge and dedicated to one goal: destroy the Black Guard. Now he had sworn to her to go and finish his first Rite of Passage, so his vow to take down the Black Guard would have to wait. He would deal with that in time. Again, the little alarm chimed a warning.

"Two minutes to departure, Lazer. Move your ass or miss your flight, fly boy," the sexy voice said.

Detra hugged him one last time and let him go.

"You be careful," Lazer said warning his mother. "Promise?"

Lazer glared at two more Black Guards as they moved past them, flashing their green facial beams to scan them as they passed.

"As long as you promise to forget this insanity here, get great grades, and make your Rite of Passage. Do your best and I'll promise to be safe," she answered.

"Deal. And keep the night shields up 24/7." His voice was as parental as he could make it. He embraced her, squeezing with all his strength.

"I love you so much, Lazer," she said, fighting back the tears.

"Okay, you two," Cashton interrupted. "If you don't stop, you're gonna make my mom get all mushy again."

Cashton's mother and father were in tow. They were tall, proud people with fine faces and intelligent eyes. Cashton punched Lazer in the arm and grabbed him in play-wrestle to snap him out of his sadness. They'd done the same playful action throughout the years since puberty. The families exchanged momentary pleasantries and Mister and Missus Lock promised Lazer they would check in regularly on his mother. Detra smiled as she watched Cashton's mother take her husband's hand. It was a simple gesture of love and companionship that had been lost to her forever with Rand's death.

"Scope this," said Cashton, pulling a small, square, very odd-looking contraption from his pocket. "It's a photonic hazer. Drop it and it emits a thin haze of smoke that then reflects an image of whatever empty space you captured on this little digital band and poof, you're invisible. Tadaa!" Cashton said proudly.

"Cashton, I told you not to take that on the transport unless you can stabilize the chemicals," his father said with a stern scowl. "I can't believe you got it past security."

"It's only smoke," Cashton pleaded. "It almost works too."

"Hand it over." Cashton passed the device to his father, who shoved it in his pocket. "If I get fined for this . . ."

Lazer suppressed the laughter. This was one of a hundred inventions Cashton had created that didn't quite work and always got him in trouble. Cashton gave up the device to his father.

"Can't ground me for at least nine months." Cashton grinned and threw an arm around Lazer.

"Where is Kyla?" Detra asked. "I can't believe the dynamic trio wouldn't take this trip together."

"She had to be there early for a special orientation or something," Cashton said.

Lazer and Cashton exchanged a look that told Detra there was more to Kyla's absence, but the final departure announcement boomed, heralding the last call to board the Tosadae transport. It was time to go. No more excuses. Lazer grabbed his day pack as Cashton gave a last hug to his crying mother.

"I'm here for you if you need me," Cashton's father said to Lazer. He held Lazer's hand a few seconds longer to emphasize his intention, then gave them a nudge toward the transport portal.

Detra grabbed Lazer's hand, kissed his cheek, and looked into his eyes. She brushed the ever-errant curl from his forehead. For the first time in a very long time it made him smile. No more words, he turned and bolted for the portal behind Cashton.

"Lock the shields!" Lazer shouted back to Detra, grinning at her with his infectious smile then vanished behind the heavy door as it shut behind him.

3

STRIKE THREE

CASHTON LAY ASLEEP, sprawled across the seat next to Lazer. They had managed to commandeer one of the few windows that spotted the curved broad walls of the transport. Lazer gazed out over the reverse wing designs that defined the ship's elliptical structure. He smiled thinking it looked to be an enormous quarter moon, resting on her side. The main fuselage gracefully arched back into itself, bending through space like a dancer racing across a stage with her arms extended behind her. It had three levels and a double cockpit that sat at the center most top and lowest levels simultaneously. The lower level that controlled the weapons system had been sealed off since the transport had long since retired from battle, destined forevermore to carry anxious young students from their home into unknown futures yet to be realized. The ship, as massive as it was, had full vertical launch capabilities and six jet vent blast engines that tipped vertical for liftoff and horizontal for forward acceleration. After liftoff, they could do a full one hundred and eighty reversal to allow the engines to slow the transport's descent and cushion the landing. Lazer knew the sixty-year-old 1520 MMZ war cruiser should have been retired from flight ten years ago, but Tosadae had modified it, reinforced the stress points, and dedicated it to be used in shipping its students back and forth across the planet. All in all, Lazer could see it had been kept in good shape. Privatized and spruced up by padding the walls with a slick, microfiber fabric designed in the blue gold and white school colors and accented with the winged circle. The fabric was perfect for keeping the chill of high altitude flight at bay.

They drifted just below the exosphere, and in and out of the ionosphere. Above, Lazer could see the auroras now and again with their vacillating hues of colors bending the light and protecting Earth from solar radiation. They were seven hundred kilometers above the planet—so high he could see the curvature of terra firma. Lazer looked down to see Earth. Even far away he could see its blue, green, and brown patches of land peeking through the cloud layers. The land formed into swatches breaking up the miles of inky blue sea. The planet languished far below. *It was beautiful*, Lazer thought. It looked like a broach on a velvet dress with flex of star, sparkling around its edges as it lay against the blackness of space. Swirling mesospheric clouds formed shrouds of misty silk at her shoulders. Now and again, Lazer could see them caught by high winds that forced open their veils of mist, periodically exposing more and more patches of the deep, emerald-blue sea. The view was awe inspiring and made Lazer feel how lucky humans were that it all worked together to support life and to distinguish the planet as a rare jewel that lay amongst galaxies of too many uninhabitable rocks. Lazer could see the last bit of sunlight slipping behind them into the west, and the black cloak of night advancing from the east. Far below, the sun's fading rays fell upon the broken remains of the continent that was once Europe. The great land mass that had included Russia and Asia was now divided into three separate continents, with separating straits and waterways weaving from north to south and spilling out into the great oceans below. The shapes made Lazer think of Atlantia. His home. His mother, his father, and how life itself was so precious that each moment had to be appreciated.

Cashton farted and awoke. He stretched. "How much longer?" he asked Lazer. "I'm starving."

"It's a long flight even at Mach 2. Besides, you just ate. And whatever you just ate last is still talking to you with hang time."

"Sorry. I ate the synthetic meat. Get over it."

Lazer waved his hand in front of his nose to shoo the smell away.

"Hey, I said sorry. Besides, I'm still growing," Cashton said with a proud smile.

"Yeah, a gut if you don't get back to working out," Lazer said.

"A month of zoccair training and practice and I'll be buff, rock hard, and driving the ladies crazy," Cashton said.

Lazer turned on his wristsponder and a hint of mist filled the air forming a thin screen that filled with images.

"Wha'cha looking for Lazer?" the sexy female voice asked him.

"First semester freshman syllabus. Search Visionistic Masters," he said verbally calling up the book list he had been reading. With a wave of his hand, Lazer pushed through the pages that floated on the vertical spray of mist until they lay flat, horizontally mimicking the curved face of the gauntlet wristsponder and reflecting the visual for him to read.

The little wristsponder's computer processor scanned lines of information at high speed searching through the book lists, until Visionistic Masters 201 class appeared. It was followed by a blur of digital data that stacked vertically above his wrist screen. With a swipe of Lazer's finger, the page reframed and jumped to the paragraph he had been reading before his mind drifted into contemplative chaos and the mysteries of the universe. Lazer set the eye-scan pacer to medium and started to read again.

"You know Striker dropped his slot at Tosadae?" Cashton asked. "I heard his old man had to sell all his mines at a loss to pay off the claims to the families. And guess who bought them up?" Cashton said and grinned.

His face filled with an expression of wicked excitement at sharing such delicious gossip. Lazer didn't' look up, but he knew Cashton was not about to let him read.

"Not a clue," Lazer said. "And for the record, I don't care."

"Ducane Covax," Cashton said. He waited.

Cashton stared at Lazer to see what his reaction would be. There was none, at least not on the outside. His face was as blank as a poker player with a hand full of aces. Cashton decided to change tactics.

"He saved you? Right?"

"Yeah. So?" Lazer snapped.

"You could have died and Ducane . . ."

"Drop it! Don't say his name," Lazer said. There was an edge of anger in his voice.

"Whoa, Kemosabe. No big deal," Cashton said trying to make a joke out of the query. "Pale face look in deep contemplation with sacred spirits."

This time Lazer shot him a look. He detested when Cashton repeated the trite dialogue they had learned when they spent a summer addicted to mid-twentieth century early television, especially the series called *The Lone Ranger*. Lazer and Cashton found it on a station hidden among the billions of ancient dot.net stations within that long-abandoned and forgotten Internet.

Lazer didn't laugh. He didn't smile or react. Cashton knew when his friend needed to crawl inside his "man cave" and smolder alone. Lazer wanted to make it clear he was deep in the process of figuring some things out, important things about school and his future. And one cool look was enough to let Cashton know silence was the code. It was what a man did when he had problems to work out, and other men were supposed to know and respect it. Though they were technically still pre-rite-of-passage boys, the events of the summer had aged them both in a way their coming Rite of Passage would never even come close to touching. Lazer thought about the fact that he'd experience the death of a parent. He had mourned his father and both of them saw their friend Evvy die. Both he and Cashton mourned the loss of the honest communication that had been the core of their friendship. He tried to stay outside himself, but sometimes it was just too hard and this was one of those times he needed to be inside his head.

Suddenly there was a deafening clank that reverberated through the walls and the transport dropped straight down. They were in free fall. Cashton gritted his teeth and closed his eyes as the g-forces lifted their butts from their seats, their tight seatbelts being the only thing holding them back from crashing into the ceiling. Trays and unbuckled people weren't as lucky. They slammed into the ceiling plastered in place and unable to move, trapped by the pressure of the g-forces. Cashton and Lazer felt the straps cut into their thighs. Three hundred meters whipped by before they were jolted to an abrupt stop. People, trays, food, and a host of personal belonging crashed to the floor.

Everyone froze. Hearts pounded. Mouths hung open, breathless and silent. Eyes opened wide as they waited. The clank and second drop happened as unexpectedly as the first. This time, it was longer and harder. Again, the transport jolted to a stop. Lazer and Cashton compressed into their chairs and covered their heads, trying to dodge the falling debris and people who crashed back to the floor, stunned, broken, or unconscious.

"What the hell was that?" Cashton shouted, freaked by the violent plunges.

A third drop plummeted the transport. The entire fuselage trembled, caught in the strains of a high-velocity vibration. The ship slammed to a stop and Lazer could tell it was struggling to stabilize.

"Secure all magnetic restraints. Repeat. Secure all magnetic restraints. We are experiencing a rare . . . turbulence," the pilot's voice shouted over the speaker system.

It was obvious to Lazer that the pilot was shaken by what was happening and it was clear he was not in control of the situation.

"Come on! We need to help these people," Lazer shouted to Cashton and anyone else who would listen.

Lazer unbuckled his restraints and leapt from his seat. Cashton hesitated a moment then undid his restraints and, with the help of a few brave students, they dragged as many of the unconscious students and flight crew back into their seats, locking them into their seats with their restraints.

"What the hell kind of turbulence caused that? We're above the stratosphere and we were cruising inside the exosphere," Cashton asked as he guided a stunned, overweight boy to his seat and buckled him in.

"What happened?" the overweight boy asked.

"That's what I wanna find out," Lazer answered.

"Please, everyone get back into your seats," the pilot shouted again.

Lazer, Cashton, and their little rescue squad of crew and students quickly got the last of their schoolmates into their seats and rushed back to secure themselves. Lazer looked out the window, straining to see if they had hit a meteor wash or caught some freak solar galactic wind. What he saw sent an icy rush down his spine.

"Shadehawks!" Lazer shouted.

The sky was filled with at least twenty Shadehawks. They were outside the window hovering in military attack formation. Cashton leaned in toward the window to look and the moment he saw them, he stiffened.

"This can't be happening," Cashton said. His words trembled as they struggled from his mouth. "Lazer, you don't think they figured out we were responsible for what happened at Temple Mountain and tracked us here?"

"No, I . . . don't know," Lazer snapped back.

The Shadehawks circled around the transport. Through their flight domes, the pulsating green lights on their faceless masks could easily be seen. Cashton and Lazer realized that the green pulses were increasing in speed and intensity. Lazer couldn't help but think the light action was a biodroid's version of a predator salivating before the kill.

"They're gonna fire on us!" Lazer blurted out.

Everyone held his or her breath. Those who could see what was coming knew he was right.

A series of proton laser pulse beams tore from the lead ship's blaster cannon and slammed into the fuselage. It hit full force into the front of the transport. The force of the concussion rippled back in waves, electrifying the cabin walls and rippling through the metal. By some miracle the fuselage held.

"We've got the shields up!" Lazer shouted. *It would buy us time*, he thought.

"Why doesn't the pilot evacuate?" Cashton wailed. "He needs to turn tail and run! Now!"

The force of another blast preempted Lazer's explanation of why that was impossible. This time, the transport wall bowed under the warp of pressure from the blast.

"He can't, not without dropping the shield to the front, and who knows if the rear shield even works. We're . . .," Lazer started.

"Target practice," Cashton finished.

Another blast racked the unarmed fuselage. A hairline crack spidered along a portion of the hull. The blast beam had fractured the shield and penetrated a section of the outer shell. A hiss of pressurized steam hissed into the main cabin. Lazer and Cashton exchanged a look.

"We just lost the cockpit," Lazer whispered, as he watched the seeping vapors curl up from under the heavy security door that protected the cockpit and at the moment was keeping them all alive. The initial hit had been lethal. The clock had started and time was running out. Lazer unbuckled himself.

"What are you doing?" Cashton asked.

"We have to do something. I have a plan. Get up, Cash. Go! Go! Go!" Lazer said.

"What plan?" Cashton said feeling himself being dragged by Lazer out of his seat.

Lazer pulled a confused Cashton out of his seat. Lazer took off down the aisle and Cashton followed. They raced back and down the aisle toward the tail.

"This is an ex-munitions military fighter—a 1520 MMZ series!" Lazer shouted back as he ran moving past the rows of terrified students. Lazer looked into one wide-eyed student trying to comprehend what he and Cashton were doing. Lazer could see how many students held on to one another; some shook with fear, some prayed, but all of them knew the emotionless predators who hovered outside the transport could vaporize them instantly and were incapable of any remorse, but only if the transport's shields circular failed. Lazer understood what all of them were feeling. He'd felt the same the day he watched the Black Guard destroy the Vacary Mines and he felt the horror even more now. But somewhere above the instinct of fear was a rush of logic that drove him to the back of the transport.

The cabin lights dimmed and flashed out then came back on. Lazer knew the power was draining out and the transport was shutting down to save energy. Another flash and the transport was thrown into pitch-black. It intensified an already intense situation. Screams erupted around Lazer and Cashton as they stopped to get their bearings and let their eyes adjust. Suddenly the eerie red flush of the floor and ceiling emergency lights glowed on. The dim lights were a small offering, but a momentary reprieve; a small ray of hope that maybe things might be okay. But hope was a beggar, Lazer remembered his father's saying. He needed faith, faith that he could do something to save them all. Lazer started moving. He was sure he knew where he needed to go, but what he didn't yet know what he'd do once he got there. He knew he'd have to trust the one part of his being that never let him down: his gut.

Cashton stumbled behind. He was following Lazer out of friendship and survival instinct and the possibility that his friend was about to do something crazy, or worse, leave him behind because he knew how to get them out of the insane danger.

"It's an MMZ. Yes! So what?" Cashton shouted after Lazer as they raced aft.

"So, there's a rear control turret."

They reached the midsection of the transport as a young steward, his head still bleeding from being thrown into the ceiling, tried to stop them.

"Get in your seats," he ordered. "I'm in charge and I'm ordering you to buckle in."

"Cockpit's been blown," Lazer informed him.

The steward's mouth fell open. He raced past Lazer and Cashton to the front of the transport and pounded on the cockpit door. No response. The emergency locks held.

"No! Don't open the . . ." Lazer shouted and raised his hand to stop him, but it was too late.

The steward hit the override controls. The seal released and the door slipped open just enough to suck the steward inside what had been the cockpit and jettisoned out into the stratosphere. The ships security took over and the door slammed shut and resealed with a hiss.

"Hold your breath!" Lazer shouted.

All the passengers and crew held their breath until the oxygen masks dropped and the cabin pressure stabilized.

"Spit!" Cashton blurted, looking in disbelief at the place where the steward had just been.

Lazer knew there was nothing more he could do except stick to his goal and get to and through the rear turret door.

Another blast from the Shadehawk's cannon slammed into the transport. The shield was holding. It took the blast and dissipated the force sending it rippling along the walls. The concussion knocked Lazer and Cashton off their feet. They got up, got their bearings, and kept moving. Cashton was sweating, but it was from more than fear.

"Do you feel that?" Cashton asked.

"The internal temperature of the transport was rising," Lazer said.

"That means the whole fuselage is heating up," Cashton said.

They reached the aft door—or at least where it should have been.

"What?" Cashton asked.

"I remember, according to the blueprints and schematics I studied for game competition play, that the door was supposed to be right here," Lazer said, his hands desperately searching as he was feeling the fabric-covered walls.

"Supposed to be!" Cashton said.

Lazer's hand traced the panel of fabric where the door should have been. In the dim light, he felt his fingers groping, probing, and pressing through the padding that covered the walls. He prayed it was hidden from view by the decorative fabric that hung in its place. Lazer touched something.

"Here!" he shouted. "Feel it. It's buried under the nylon fabric,"

Lazer could feel the oval-shaped indentation and, at its center, a latch.

"Yes!" he shouted, startling Cashton.

"How do we get through? That's microfiber. It might as well be steel," Cashton said.

Lazer used the edge of his wristsponder strap like a knife scratching at the fabric and ripping through the microfiber. It was strong, but Lazer was stronger. Cashton followed, as did a couple of girls and then two older boys bringing whatever they had with an edge that could cut through the stubborn fabric. They shredded it piece by piece under their relentless attack. Their efforts created a tiny tear, then Cashton and he used their nails and fingers to rip through the fabric and tear it out of their way. Lazer grabbed the emergency latch and pulled the door open. A hiss of air was sucked inside, replacing the stale air that had been sealed inside for the at least the past sixty years. That was easily the last time the MMZ had been used as a peacekeeper warship. Lazer knew it had long been retired from its fighting days during the Mutant Wars. *But today,* Lazer thought, *this transport was about to be recalled into active service with he and Cashton at the helm.* Lazer prayed to the Universal God that, even without weapons, the old battleship had a few tricks left in her that he could call on to save them.

"Get to the other side. These are duel rear cockpits. And somebody get word out to the politia on the emergency communiqué system. Tell them what's happening and to send help," Lazer shouted to the students who'd braved the situation to help.

Lazer went feet first as he leapt down a narrow spiraling flight of metal stairs that lead to the rear cockpit and gun turret. The second cockpit hung inside a thick Plexiglas pod located under the belly of the transport. Cashton froze when he looked straight down at Earth turning seven hundred thousand meters below him. The effect was dizzying. His stomach jumped into his throat. Lazer didn't look. He slipped into the pilot's seat and started hitting panels and heat-activated screen pads. The control panel curled around him with the mechanical precision of a camera shutter. It fanned out into the shape of a metal half moon, covered in multiple configurations of lights, switches, and touch panels that erupted to life as each power source miraculously came online.

"Yes! Still connected to the power source!" Lazer shouted. "Strap in."

"You can't fly this!" Cashton gasped.

"Strap in!" Lazer commanded.

Cashton held onto the clear walls and cautiously slipped into the copilot's seat. "This is insane! What the hell makes you think you can fly this?"

"Online competition, a 65 championship score with Kyla, MMZ simulator extreme combat. Remember we won the stratosphere finals. She and I got the highest score ever recorded in the MMZ World Battle Amateur Game Bangers Competition!" Lazer said, adjusting the levels.

"That's a video game, moron!" Cashton waited. "That's it? That's your idea?"

"You got a better one?"

"Yeah, don't die."

"I wish Kyla was her," Lazer said.

"Yeah, me too."

"Fire up the secondary shield power panels and give me a reading. Don't think, Cashton. You know this. Trust yourself and do it!" Lazer fingered the navigation touch controls. They lit up. He had full power and partial shields already in place from the now deceased pilot and his crew. Lazer and Cashton's brave actions were the only things keeping them alive for the moment.

"Cash! Give me a shield reading."

"Where? I never got past level three," Cashton said, his voice on the edge of panic.

"You're a gadget geek!" Lazer shouted at him.

"Real, not virtual."

"Well, this is way real!" Lazer pointed. "Meter bars, far left, green, yellow, and blue."

Cashton touched the screen and it whirred into action. "Uh, five . . . no, six are lit. Two are out." Cashton struggled to interpret the information and give it to Lazer as fast as he could.

"Damn! We're at 78 percent," Lazer said. "We'll take one more hit, then I'm turning our backs to them and directing all shield power to our tail."

Cashton couldn't believe what Lazer intended to do. "Are you in total brain fart? This is not the time to get back at them for what they did to your dad. Lazer, listen to me," Cashton pleaded. "You'll get us all killed."

"Not if we knock them out first." Lazer was certain what he was about to do was the only chance they had. There was no time to convince Cashton he was right and less time to reconfigure and redirect the main power sources to the turret.

"Listen to me. I'm gonna direct full power to one shield, which should turn the deflectors solid. We angle the shields and, like a mirror into light, it should deflect their phaser fire and ricochet right back at them."

"Should?" Cashton did his best to swallow, but his mouth was too dry.

"If we're lucky, they won't have their shields up and their own blasts will ping back up their noses and destroy them." He turned to Cashton. "Got it?"

"What do I do?" Cashton acquiesced. *If they were going to die*, he thought, *it would best well be in a fight.*

"Ride those gauges and keep all shield impulses concentrated at the rear," Lazer said.

He focused on the 3-D mockup of the MMZ transport that hovered in his heads-up display to his left. With a touch and a turn, he found he was highlighting the various vitals and schematics that rose in ribbons of color as the ship reacted to his commands. Each hidden chamber and power source defined the MMZ's design. The MMZ warship had once been the crown of this battle champion. In its heyday, it had been used to haul massive weapons, supplies, and troops. Over the decades, its weapons had been stripped away and, in the end, it had been demoted to the banal chore of hauling students to Tosadae. Lazer hoped there were still enough mechanical guts to get them out of this horror. More important, he prayed to the Universal God that he was doing the right thing.

One last hand motion and the shield image registered a redistribution of power to the tail of the transport. Lazer took the double throttles, stepped on the left rudder, and propelled them into the turn.

Cashton's power panels ignited; the shield read-outs fused together and formed a massive wall of energy. The molecules solidified at the exact moment as the sensors warned there was a lock on them. It was the precursory wail to the blast about to be fired from the Shadehawks.

"Get ready!" Lazer held his breath.

Outside, in the black of the stratosphere, even the stars seem to have vanished. The Shadehawks had pulled into a diamond formation. They would intersect, create a power matrix, and combine their full blaster force. The blast would scatter the MMZ and everyone on it into cosmic dust.

The lead ship prepared to give the order to fire, but hesitated when the MMZ turned tail to run. It knew that the control deck and the flight crew of the transport had been taken out. The machines calculated the information. It had to be a malfunction by the transport's computers. The transport was searching for its central brain, but it was nothing more than a decapitated worm with its body spastically squirming because it hadn't realized it was already dead.

"They're not shooting!" Cashton panicked.

"Come on," Lazer whispered. "Take the bait. Take the bait!"

4

THE BIODROID FIVE

THE BIODROID FIVE ordered the lead Black Guard ships to hold their positions. The question was why? He ordered all the data to be recollected and recalculated. Five held as his army sat in ominous silence hovering in Earth's ionosphere, the last band of concentrated electrons and gravity before space. The leader of the biodroids was waiting for confirmation from the new haploid scan readings, but everything else was ready for the attack. Yet something wasn't right. The series of algorithms that came back deduced that the old warship's backup computer was all that was left and all it was capable of doing was performing a low-level attempt to run the backup life support systems for those on board. The ship, according to the files they had hacked into, had been stripped of all military applications, attack weapons, and defensive or protective weapons except for the shielding device. They were sitting ducks. Everyone onboard was moments from death. The cockpit has been destroyed. Five could still see frozen body parts and droplets of iced blood falling through the thin cold air. The ship was immobilized and as vulnerable as a huge wounded prey ready for the kill, but something was amiss and rationalization wasn't part of Five's machine logic. He calculated and recalculated the mechanical data then analyzing from every perspective the series of informational data bundles that came from his biological memory strands. These were the ones that ran his core A.I. These were the biological strands made up of human and IL viral DNA. They had gone sentient first. Now this data, this illogic, was doing something he couldn't calculate. He knew the facts. It had been reported by a patrolling Black Guard at the Atland City Transport that during one of the routine security scans on the crowd, a near perfect haploid match to the Gnorb's access code had been identified. The Black Guard confirmed the match was aboard the Tosadae ship. Now, Five ran his own full-scale haploid scan. He had failed twice before and this time he wanted indisputable proof. He did not care about the thousand students whose lives hung in the balance of his decision. The students being there was their unfortunate set of circumstances. Once he had the data he needed he would launch the attack on the Tosadae ship. From that moment of destruction, he knew it would only be a matter of moments until he bonded with the blue Gnorb. The haploid key genetics, coded to the blue Gnorb, would be disintegrated and he could use his own human genetics to bond and open the knowledge of the universal wisdom inside the first Gnorb.

A series of colored lights flashed across his heads-up display. Positive match flashed. Five ordered the ships into formation.

5

KYLA

KYLA WINGRIGHT SLUMBERED in her new bed, in her new
dorm room at Tosadae Academy. The walls were still empty save the
holographic clock that projected the numerical time on the walls. She lay
in heavy REM sleep, exhausted from the long summer both emotionally
and physically, and the journey to make sure she arrived had wiped her
out. She had landed on the 5:00 a.m. transport with a handful of eager
early birds and long list of things she knew she needed to get done before
the mass of new freshman students arrived for orientation. She wanted
to at least start unpacking, but how bad could an hour's nap be—right?

She needed to post her resume for a job or maybe two and earn
money with the hope it would take some of the pressure off her mother.
She had to get to the administration building when it opened to lock
down her genetics and illustrated coding and math classes. She also
wanted to find out why she hadn't been invited into Masta Poe's Master
Studies symposium for second-year Visionistic Arts students. And just
as important, she had to make sure she had at least three classes with

Lazer. They were on the same career track and she missed him. She missed Cashton, too, but at least they had spoken over the summer. Lazer she had foolishly cut off on all fronts. Her anger for what had happened had subsided. Mostly. She didn't want to blame him anymore, but she needed someone to blame, didn't she? Evvy was dead and he had started the whole "avenge his father and every other Atlantian killed by a Black Guard" thing. She'd told him it was fool-hearted and dangerous, but in the end, she hadn't been strong enough to say no. He needed her and she was there.

That was the past, a past she could never change and Tosadae was her future. At least here she had hope and part of that hope was Lazer. She would get over her anger, trust him, and let the love she knew she had locked away for him come out. She loved Lazer. They both knew it. They just needed time, and a new place and fate was giving that to them.

She was, on the other hand, just like Masta Poe; a splicer with human and creature genetics who had explored, enhanced, and self-taught—well some with the help of her mother—the mystical powers of the Visionistic Arts. Her mother said she was a natural and had the chit funds been available, Kyla would have certainly qualified and been invited to join the prestigious precursory seminars that traveled each summer around to the various continents with Masta Poe who was willing to work with those organically gifted youth interested and gifted in the arts. But the seminars cost and the chits at the Wingright house were for survival. Her presence this day at Tosadae was an attribute to her Visionistic talents, tenacity, her grades, and the fact that she worked her wings off doing two summer jobs to have the funds to be here.

The drone of her alarm finally broke through the clutter of things to do, the misty dreams that still haunted her and filled her hard. Inside that chaos a rush of sounds, tense and frantic, filtered up from the hallways and outside on campus. A voice broke into the room from some speaker she couldn't quite place.

"All students report to the main hall of the Avery amphitheater, immediately! All students report to the main hall of the Avery amphitheater, immediately."

Kyla lifted her head from the pillow. The time, the sounds, the desperate tone in the voice of the announcer shook her to her core and raised her antenna from her hair. Kyla scrambled for her clothes and sweater when something inside her shivered and she stopped to let whatever message come to her through her extra sensory perception.

"Lazer! Cashton! Universal God, run!" Kyla shouted to the empty room, images swirled all around her as she saw what Lazer saw.

She grabbed her things and raced from the room. Students moved obviously unknowingly in an orderly matter heading to the center of campus. A few stood transfixed, their eyes glazed over. Kyla knew they were seeing the same images that flashed before her eyes. The visionaries moved in the opposite direction from the larger crowd who were obeying the headmaster's orders.

"What's happening? Why are the Black Guards attacking a transport full of students?" one young girl said.

"This is impossible. Black Guard biodroids wouldn't do this. They can't harm humans," another tall, blonde girl said, speaking more to herself than anyone else.

"They've done it before and they are doing it again. What I want to know is why students?" Kyla asked. "I need a transport!"

"There are hover shuttles at the back of Minister Hall," the tall blonde girl said. "I can bypass the governor and starters."

"Me too," Kyla added.

"But I know where Minister Hall is and you don't," the tall girl said, pointing the opposite way Kyla was about to turn.

"Please," Kyla said, "My two best friends in the world are on that transport. I need to help them."

Kyla bumped into a tall, pretty girl with blonde hair.

"Sorry," Kyla said.

"No worry," the tall, pretty blonde girl said.

They ran alongside about thirty of the Visionistic students, raced across campus. They were all ages, from teens to their mid-twenties. They moved like fish swimming upstream against the flow of a great river of people. The tall girl was beyond pretty and amazingly athletic. As great a shape as Kyla was in, keeping up with her was a challenge. Kyla was running on adrenaline and a wild fear for her friends. Her concern for Lazer and Cashton fired the muscles in her legs and she and the tall, blonde girl reached a large building far ahead of the others. Kyla looked back to see their numbers were growing. People knew what was happening, whether from their own psychic abilities or word of mouth; this was an act of biodroids terrorism the likes of which the world had never seen. For the first time, Kyla realized the first attacks on the Orbis Temple and Temple Mountain had been repressed in the news. Truth to the entire Collective had been withheld once and that was illegal under the Truth and Information Act. It made her heart race. She looked forward just as the tall, blonde girl turned, running into a large building that was more vertical than horizontal. Kyla followed out of some instinct that she didn't understand but knew was right. They raced around to the back and into the utility parking structure. Just ahead, Kyla could see ten large shuttles fueled and lined up ready to go. They would have been dispatched to pick the students up when they landed.

"The doors are locked," Kyla shouted panicking.

The tall, blonde girl stuck out her hand and twisted her wrist in midair and the locks released. With a pass to the left of her hand, the door slid open.

"Outstanding! Who are you?" Kyla asked.

"Elana Blue. Can you drive this monster?" Elana asked.

"Watch me," Kyla responded and climbed into the cab. "The name's Kyla Wingright."

"Kyla, you're ice," Elana Blue said.

"Get in!" Elana Blue shouted to the others who poured into her shuttle.

Elana Blue fell back into the seat. Suddenly she began to convulse and Kyla saw the tall, blonde girl's perfect blue eyes glaze over. Kyla slammed the door shut leaving out half the students. She fired the hover turbines lifting the craft from the ground. Kyla gasped, her grip tightened on the stick controls as she felt a rush of pain deep inside her heart the likes of which she had never experienced. Whatever it was, it was happening and Lazer needed her.

6

FIRST BATTLE

LAZER WATCHED as the Shadehawks moved, slowly shifting their formation. It was an intricate dance using huge ships just as graceful as a ballet. Finally, they completed their diamond attack formation. Once in position, they aligned the energetic forces of their proton beams causing them to connect and sending them surging back and forth in pulsating streams of concentrated proton rays. Cashton and Lazer exchanged a glace. The power amassing as the beams connected built into a concentrated force that would be directed into one destructive beam.

"You sure this is gonna work?" Cashton asked.

"Theoretically," Lazer replied.

"Wrong answer, Lazer."

"It better," Lazer added.

The Shadehawks had conjoined their fire power from a seven-faceted pyramid and fused each pulse energy from seven rays into a single point of white, hot proton beam that shot forward at them. Lazer and Cashton watched the beam as it streaked across the sky.

"Now!" Lazer shouted.

Lazer and Cashton both merged all the shields into one, single force field and angled the surface. The proton blast slammed into the transport's shield like a canon. Cashton gripped the chair and closed his eyes. Lazer stared into the light as it hit.

The searing massive beams smashed into the shield. It shattered each splintered ray that pinged back off the shield, fracturing as the flood of proton hit. It ricocheted back into multiple rays like a flared starburst of deadly power. It was a direct hit slamming into seven of the Shadehawks. They crumbled, imploded, and then exploded into a flare of glowing particle dust. The other Shadehawks were blasted back tumbling out of formation by the concussions that surged from the simultaneous explosion and dropped away, spinning out of control.

The sky was still filled with a field of seven brilliant mushroom clouds made of blazing hot particles that hung weightless before fading out of the cold vacuum of space and dropping to Earth. The particles cooled and fell into the ionosphere, raining down somewhere over the Republic that had once been Asia.

Lazer and Cashton high-fived each other and did the best interpretation of a victory dance one could do while still strapped into a seat. As they wiggled their butts and waved their hands proclaiming their awesomeness, screams of elation echoed in from the intercom system. It was Cashton who heard what came next.

There was a low whine from all the instruments. They wailed, shrieking at them like deflating balloons, and then whined down to an ominous hum. The color bands that monitored the power levels flickered and vanished from all the screens. Then silence. The lights went out. One red warning light pulsed menacingly off and on. Lazer saw it.

"What?" Cashton asked. His voice cracked.

"Power drain. Spit! Spit!" The words were bitter in his mouth.

They had lost everything, including basic life support. Lazer searched for the backup generators. It was elementary game play: you use all your energy, you drain your power, and you revert to auxiliary power and manual weapons while you recover. But the MMX had been stripped, and there was no auxiliary power.

One by one the remaining Shadehawks recovered. They charged their ships back at the warship. The battle was still on.

"No shields!" Cashton shouted as his power screen went blank. "We've got no shields!"

He turned around in his seat and saw the Shadehawks regrouping, a swarm of angry hornets whose nest had been violated. "They're coming back."

The interim generators kicked in, recharging the main energy rods. At least they wouldn't have to suffocate before they were blown to smithereens. The cockpit's panel lights glowed on and washed them in eerie shades of yellow, red, and green neon. A second panel lit up, telling him the engines were online. But that was it.

"Do something!" Lazer shouted.

"Me? What?"

"Make it do something. Fix it."

"Fix what?" Cashton bantered back. Cashton ripped himself out of his restraints and dove under the power panel. "It's charging the main engine's core power rods. You want engine or shield?"

"Both." Lazer was desperate. His mind was as dead as the shields. "Okay. Give me the engines. We're gonna run," Lazer said as he jammed the accelerator.

Cashton coded the energy from the shields into the main thrusters.

The exterior motion was almost imperceptible. This was no jump speed up to Mach 2; in fact, the acceleration was so slow that they may as well have been moving backward.

"Faster would be good about now," Cashton said, popping his head up from beneath the panel.

"It won't go faster," Lazer said. "What about the shields?"

Cashton's power panel showed a painfully slow buildup of shield power. "Try 7 percent."

"Why haven't they fired?" Lazer wondered aloud.

"Who cares? Them not firing is working for me big time!"

"I don't like it," Lazer said with a hollow gnawing in his stomach.

"Now what?"

"I don't know," Lazer whispered his concern.

"Wrong answer!" Cashton's voice cracked.

Outside Lazer could see the Shadehawks were in formation. He looked down at the transport's shield bars. A lowly 22 percent pulsed up at him. Lazer knew a direct hit at any point on the ship would splatter them into particle dust.

Lazer hit the intercom. "Everybody! Lock in and hold on." There was silence in the main cabin. Everyone prayed for a miracle. Cashton decided to take an ignorance-is-bliss approach and not ask Lazer any more questions.

"Split the charge between the engine and the shields. Cash, get your ass up and into your seat, and lock in."

Lazer had one final option. He would stall the engine. He moved his hand over the master power control, waited for the last possible second, and hit the kill switch. The transport would drop dense as a rock, and the Shadehawks' blasters would miss. It was a momentary diversion from the inevitable, but it was all he could do. When the engines fired back on, there theoretically would be a power surge that would boost the shield power and the drivers. If the engines cooperated, they might survive. No, they *would* survive. He willed it.

"Done." Cashton jumped into his seat and locked in.

The Shadehawks fired their blasters and filled the sky with streaks of deuterium that cut through the blackness at the speed of light.

Lazer shut down, and the transport dropped five thousand meters like a rock.

Cashton's stomach shot into his throat. Lazer gritted his teeth as the g-force jerked him upward. The restraints cut into his shoulders. He had to power back up or they would hit the atmosphere and burn up on reentry. Lazer lifted his hand, forcing it forward. He struggled to reach the control handle. Gravity defied him. They kept falling—two thousand, three thousand meters plummeted past. Inch by inch, he strained with all his strength, until his fingers touched the throttle and wrapped around the controls. Lazer dragged it into power-up position and the ship's engines fired, caught, and stabilized. The transport engines roared on with a thunderous tremor.

Lazer looked up to see what was coming at them next. What he saw ignited his soul. A hail of deuterium phaser pellets rained down on the Shadehawks, exploding three of them into fire balls. There was only one force on Earth that used DT deuterium phasers: the politia. Lazer and Cashton howled with cheers and laughter. The cavalry had arrived!

"It's the politia!" elated voices shrieked through the intercom.

Seven Politia FX-80 fighters swarmed the airspace. They launched into a dogfight, engaging the confused Shadehawks. The Shadehawks banked, circled, and dove, desperate to outmaneuver the fire power of the DT phasers.

Inside the Tosadae transport's lower cockpit, Cashton's power panel flashed 59 percent. It was enough. Lazer pushed both throttles and banked a hard right. "Turn, you piece of . . ." Lazer ordered the ship, putting all his strength against the stick.

Cashton ripped out of his shoulder restraints and grabbed the right throttle, leaning into it with all his weight. He eked the throttle one more inch, and together they forced the transport into its turn. They were picking up speed. They were getting away!

Two Shadehawks broke from the fight with the FX-80s and headed straight for the transport. They fired. Phaser blasts bit hard into the transport's right wing.

"Twin bandits, closing in on our six!" Cashton shouted.

"I need shields!" Lazer demanded.

"Sixty-two percent."

One of the pursuing Shadehawks vaporized into particle dust just as it came close enough to fire on the transport. The second Shadehawk was still on their tail. Lazer heard the scream of the warning indicator.

"Hold on to your butts. Now!" Lazer shouted. He forced the transport out of pattern, set the flaps, stalled the engine, and went into a dive, nose first, straight down.

Again, the blasters overshot their mark. The Universe was on their side. Lazer fired the big engines. No response. He fired again. Nothing. They were headed into a spin and their downward momentum was about to reach critical gravitational pull meaning that the force of gravity combined with the weight of the ship would not give him enough time to pull out if he didn't engage now. Lazer fired the engines. Nothing!

"Do it!" Lazer commanded through gritting teeth and holding on for dear life.

With a mighty roar the engines ignited. The force of the drop had given them the needed speed and, with the engines in full throttle, he finally had command of the forward motion and acceleration. Lazer pulled back on the throttle and forced the nose of the transport up. He could hear the metal bend under the pressure of gravity and air. Inch by inch Lazer leveled out and stabilized into a horizontal position. They were flat and flying forward.

Behind him he could see the Shadehawk turn and reset his attack position. The Black Guard at the helm zeroed in on his sights to calculate the kill distance. Lazer looked back again. He knew the Shadehawks were smaller and faster and he was out of options. He had the throttle wide open and the ship at full speed, but he couldn't outrun a Shadehawk.

Inside a second Shadehawk, what looked to Lazer to be one of the lower-ranked Black Guard, took aim and centered its weapon on Lazer's transport. The lock-on, launch ready alarm screamed across the transports speaker system. The Shadehawk was locked on for the kill.

Lazer was in the cross hairs. He had no weapons and no maneuvers. *Universal God,* he thought. *Help us.*

At that moment, a lone FX-88 zeroed in and fired at the Shadehawks. Two missiles streaked through the air. One missed the first Shadehawk, the second was a direct hit! What was left of the vaporized Shadehawk blew across the transport's hull like fiery fine particle dust. The second missile his the first Shadehawk. Double hit!

"Vapor wash!" Cashton shouted.

"Tosadae Control, do you copy?" A strong female voice boomed over the ship's communication line. It belonged to the FX-88 pilot who had just saved them. "I repeat, do you copy, Captain?"

Lazer and Cashton realized that they were probably going to be in trouble for commandeering the ship.

"Answer him," Cashton blurted, nudging Lazer.

"Uh . . . copy that . . . uh, sir," Lazer replied so tentatively that the FX commander was silent for a second. "We . . . uh . . . lost the main cockpit . . . sir," Lazer said, as if it were his fault.

"Who is this?"

"Cole Lazerman, sir. First-year cadet."

"First year? Where the hell are your shields?"

"I . . . used the shields to deflect the conjoined hit, sir," Lazer explain.

"The blow back shattered seven of them to vapor wash!" Cashton shouted, still charged from the attack.

The commander chuckled in amazement. "Seven for you, Ace! Only next time you blow your shields, you better be able to throw up a viz wall," the commander said.

Lazer and Cashton exchanged a look of confusion. They had heard of mind-over-matter manifestations of energy taught in the Visionistic Arts at Tosadae, but the idea of shielding an entire transport using mental powers bordered on the miraculous.

"No next time, okay," Cashton whispered.

"Yes, Ma'am," Lazer responded. He felt proud. It had been so long since he had done anything right. He wanted to call his father and tell him that he had been the hero of the day, to tell him that he and Cashton had done the right thing, but that call could never happen. The brief rush of glory receded back into his river of remorse, drowning the momentary happiness.

"Hell of a set of natural skills you got there, cadet," another commander said over the intercom.

A third voice came through the transponder. "This is Tosadae Control at Mu Field. Congratulations, cadet. We saw the whole thing on satellite. You're a hero on my roster, son."

Lazer didn't know what to say. Cashton's chest, on the other hand, was swelling as fast as his head.

"Drop to fifteen thousand meters above the deck and switch to remote," the controller ordered. "We'll bring you in on tractor beam."

Cashton felt so ecstatic he thought he was going to burst. He and Lazer proudly exchanged the politia's V salute. It was the same one his father had playfully exchanged with him when they had played politia so many years ago. But today, in this moment of glory, the V salute had new meaning. It was no longer a game. He had helped defeat the enemy. Lazer released the nervous breath that had stuck in his chest, letting go a great sigh of relief. He stroked the touch pads on the main controls and initiated their descent to Tosadae.

He had done well today, and his bravery filled him with a new strength and an undeniable truth. The attack had proven to him that now, more than ever, he needed to be back on Atlantia. This attack from the Black Guard was an all-out act of war. Lazer had vowed on his father's soul and his country that war would never come to Atlantia. Now, he made a promise to himself. He would be part of those who would rid Atlantia of the Black Guard.

7

TOSADAE DOCKING STATION

THE DOCKING STATION at Tosadae was in joyous chaos. The Tosadae Academy staff and fellow students who had gotten the word and headed to the station cheered like Romans at the Arco di Costantino for returning heroes. Everyone there was welcoming the champions and brave students home from battle. The healers dressed in green tunics, greeted and carried off the wounded and traumatized passengers as they exited first off the transport. ANN and Global Satellite Broadcast (GSB), had reporters everywhere. They demanded to know more about the first-year cadet who had flown the transport with no cockpit and held off a sortie of Shadehawks until the politia arrived. The academy wouldn't give out the name, so the reporters questioned everyone who stepped through the door.

Cashton beamed as he walked off the transport, ready for his close-up and all the fame and notoriety he could take. Lazer grabbed his arm and pulled Cashton past the herd of reporters and through the crowd. He moved them judiciously through the mass of chaos as he searched for Kyla's face. He could feel her presence just as he felt her with him on the transport at the height of the attack, and her face was the only face he wanted to see. He knew she had come a day early for aura seminars, but no matter which way he looked, she was nowhere to be found in the exuberant crowd. The one face he did see stood out from the crowd like a beacon of light against a dark sea. It was a tall, beautiful blonde. Her face was glowing surrounded by an orb of its own, self-generated light. Her eyes connected with Lazer's and held him captive in her gaze. He felt a strange, calming peace in the connection that made no sense to him, but felt kind and excitedly delicious. The tall blonde looked into his eyes as if she knew everything that had happened to him and that he was behind saving all those students. She nodded to him and smiled.

At the far edge of the crush of people, Kyla struggled to get through. She had gone to the wrong end of the arrival hall and the authorities had changed the arrival gate. She used all her might to push her way through the crowd. She searched through the faces exiting the transport for Lazer. She had to see for herself that he was okay, alive and unharmed. Her face filled with relief at the sight of Lazer and Cashton entering from the gateway. They were easily twenty-five feet away from her with hundreds of people between them cheering and yelling.

"Excuse me. Excuse me, please," Kyla said as she struggled closer.

She couldn't stand it. Her heart was racing. If she had a single square foot of open space around her, she could have opened her wings and flown to him.

"Lazer!" she shouted. "Cashton!"

"There! That's him, that's the cadet who saved us," one of the youngest students on the transport shouted, pointing at Lazer.

Kyla's shouts were drowned out by a roar of boisterous cheers that arose from the crowd. The reporters turned and surrounded Lazer like a pack of sharks circling into a feeding frenzy. In an instant, Lazer was cut off from Cashton.

"What's your name? How did you do it?" a tall reporter asked.

"Where in Atlantia do you come from?"

"What made you think you could defeat . . ." another reporter shouted.

"Did the transport have any weapons?" another reporter said cutting him off.

Lazer stared at the barrage of faces that encircled him looking like a startled deer in the headlights of multiple coming trucks. Reporters shouted at him demanding answers to dozens of questions, each one louder than the next, each pointing a directional finger and extender pointer mics at him like handguns.

"That's enough. He won't be speaking to the press until he's been fully debriefed by the politia, so give the young man some room, ladies and gentlemen," a seasoned commander said hooking his arm into Lazer's and leading Lazer away. A second politia officer just as tall and equally as strong took Lazer's other arm. More politia appeared from seemingly nowhere and formed a gauntlet. Together they cleared the path for their exit.

Lazer looked back for Cashton who had become lost inside the crowd.

"Follow us son," the commander said to Lazer.

"My friend, Cashton Lock. He helped me," Lazer said.

"Let's get you out and then we'll find your second in command," the commander told him.

Lazer smiled a goofy smile at the idea that he had a second in command of anything.

In a matter of moments, Lazer and the politia were out a side door and gone.

Finally, pushing her way through the crowd, Kyla got to Cashton. She threw herself into him and gave him a crushing hug.

"Everything came up on satellite relay," she said. "And the dogfight. Whoa! We're talking classic top gun between the FX-80s and the Shadehawks. And that single FX-88. I want one."

Cashton could see that Kyla had grown up over the summer months. Her face had lost some of its roundness, revealing a first glimpse of the rare beauty she would ultimately become. Her eyes searched behind Cashton for Lazer.

"The politia took him for debriefing," Cashton told her nodding to a side door.

"What happened?" Kyla asked. "You have to tell me everything."

"Lazer and I got into the . . ." Cashton started

". . . lower control turret," Kyla said remembering her visions. "I hoped he'd remembered them. But why?"

"You have to know, Kyla, when we got into the turret, he just kept saying he wished he had you there."

"I bet you did great as his second," Kyla said and hugged Cashton again. "Let's get your bags and get you out of here. Keep talking."

They walked to the exit and chattered excitedly, Cashton sharing every elaborate detail of the attack. They joined other students as they moved into the baggage claim area.

"It was awesome!" Cashton blurted. "At one point, when we lost the cockpit, we thought "game over," until Lazer got up out of his seat and went into mega superhero mode and fearlessly saved the day."

Kyla's mouth fell open as her eyes searched back again for Lazer. "It was Lazer who initiated the entire rescue?"

"Well, *us* together actually, but everything we did was his idea," Cashton said, looking for Kyla's approval.

"I'm so proud of you Cashton," Kyla said reading his aura. She hugged him.

"Of course, we had some plain old dumb luck on our side, but Lazer's skill level was off the hook. He said you would have known about the shield failure," Cashton said.

"Maybe but I know he couldn't have done it without your electronics genius, Cashton," Kyla told him.

Cashton's aura beamed brighter.

"It was horrific. All I kept thinking was that this is the third attack on humans," Cashton said.

The reality of his statement hit Kyla hard.

"You think it was payback for what we did?" Kyla asked.

"No way. How would they have known?" Cashton said, his face looking puzzled and unsure even as the words came from his mouth.

"Evvy would have been proud of you both. I am," Kyla said, with a tinge of sadness.

A moment of silent respect hung between them and made the air feel thick and heavy. Cashton's eyes caught the ANN reporters trying frantically to get a statement from some students.

"Has the press figured out where they came from?" Cashton asked.

"No. Neither have the politia, the Triumvirate, or the corporate leaders not to mention the entire Collective," said Kyla. "They are so damn sure they launched out of Atlantia. I'm not."

"Then where? Black Guards don't exist anywhere else but on Atlantia. It doesn't make sense," Cashton said. "And why attack a academy transport?"

"Kill off the next generation of fighters?" Kyla offered. "I heard an ANN reporter say their news satellite feed tapped into the Shadehawk's transmission during the attack. They decoded some of it and said right before they struck that they were doing some kind of genetics scan on everyone on board."

"Why?"

"They couldn't tell—or didn't say. The last transmissions said it had to do with one of the kids. Maybe the kid of a famous somebody was on board and they wanted them killed."

"Who?" Cashton demanded.

"We won't ever know. The Student Protection Act will be enforced, so they can't say even if they figure it out." Kyla shrugged.

"I want to know," Cashton insisted, looking over the crowd. "My life was in jeopardy up there too."

"There were more than a thousand students on that transport. Who cares if some bigwig's kid was on board? Bottom line, you're safe now."

"My parents!" Cashton said.

"I've already sent word to all of our parents. My mom says it is creepy quiet on Atlantia."

"Thanks, Kyla," Cashton said.

"Oh, yeah! And get ready for this. She said the Collective Council freaked and already announced they will be petitioning to put a proton dome and full lockdown over Atlantia," Kyla said.

"Over Atlantia?" Cashton said as he choked on the thought. "They can't do that."

"They're the Council. They can do anything they want," Kyla said. The thought of Atlantia under a dome made her angry all over again.

"Why not send in the politia?" Cashton huffed.

"We're not corporate, and the politia belong to the corporations," Kyla added. The thought of a domed Atlantia is beyond unjust. Where's Triumvirate Aleece Avery on this travesty."

"As long as Atlantia's got no representatives in the World Corporate Council and there's the slightest, potential threat of a sentient virus getting into their precious nano and biological-based networks, what choice do they have? Even Avery," Cashton said.

"She won't agree to it. She can't."

"No, but . . .," Cashton started.

"No one has the right to dome us in with those murdering machines. No one!" Kyla said.

A rush of anger coursed through her and she slammed her fist against the pillar. The force of the blow cracked the Plexiglas material that encased the column of light. It was filled with living, glowing algae. Kyla's anger shifted into the sensation of pain but she didn't care. "The Triumvirate should give us politia protection."

"They did today and they will again," Cashton said. "You'll see. Lazer will convince them to help us while he's got their ear, I know it."

"They don't care about the people of Atlantia because they can't control us," she said.

Cashton watched as Kyla's expression of frustration changed to one of desperate anger. He didn't need to read the shifting hues of aura glowing from her. Her expression said it all.

"Kyla? Whatever you're thinking . . . don't," Cashton told her.

"I'm thinking the same thing I bet Lazer is right now and you should be too," she said. "We need Aleece Avery on our side and you, Lazer, and I have gotta get back home."

8

A SINGLE VOICE
IN SANGELINO

"THERE'S BEEN A BLACK GUARD attack on a Tosadae student transporter," Aleece said as she rushed into her office.

Waiting for her were her fellow chairs of the Advanced Committee on Global Conflict; the only other all-human world Triumvirate leader besides herself was Triumvirate Baz Mangalan, and Aleece's lead advisor, Commander Robert Fielding. Aleece never liked Mangalan, not as a human being nor as a world leader. Missing was the third Triumvirate, her friend and ally, Blane Fahan, the only splicer ever chosen as a Triumvirate leader. She wished he was on her committee to help stand up for the Atlantians.

By Mangalan's side was Commander Robert Fielding—Aleece's direct TMA (Triumvirate Military Advisor) and friend. Commander Fielding was a lanky, broad-shouldered, and very distinguished looking man with serious eyes and thick hair that had grayed perfectly at the temples. A true commander, he had earned his ranking in the Mutant Wars. He'd also earned the respect of the Politia Forces in Sangelino during his twenty years of dedicated service. Fielding had been assigned as an IS (Information Strategist) and the direct TMA to Aleece Avery. He admired her and she respected him. They had served together in the Mutant Wars.

Both men turned as she entered the room.

"They have gone sentient," Aleece said.

"I have not seen proof there are sentient forces within the ranks of the Black Guard," Mangalan said.

Commander Fielding circled several hot spots on the holomap of the Atlantian territories. The vast risen territories loomed in front of him and with a particle pointer he drew bold fiery red circles that hung in the air.

"Proven or not, it fuels a heated situation that has been happening on Atlantia for almost a year. Alpha Security has politia and Vybernet scan reports tracking a series of small, but growing, allied forces in support of the Black Guard," Fielding said.

With a wave of his hand, Fielding expanded the map to show the whole world: The United Co-Federation with Sangelino, the Corporate Isles, South Republic, Panazia, Cape Horn Island, Mu, The Alliance, The Joint Common Market and The Republic with Station City glowing brighter than the rest.

"Even the Lost Territories, still domed from the Never-Ending Wars that shut them off from the world before the Great Quakes, are trying to send messages out," Aleece said.

"Those messages have never stopped nor have they been decoded; how many decades is that?" Mangalan said.

"The disturbing trend," Commander Fielding went on to say "is that these security alerts are not just in the cities and townships on Atlantia. They are being tracked globally," as he made multiple circles on the large holographic map.

"So you are saying you have proof there are factions outside of

Atlantia working in support of the Black Guard's actions," Aleece said. "To do what? What do these sentient biodroids want?"

"We don't know, Ma'am. Right now it's all digital chatter. 'What if' scenarios," Fielding said.

"So, no definitive proof yet. Which means this is conjecture at best," Mangalan said.

Aleece listened and watched. She read Mangalan's aura and his expression of growing irritation. Mangalan always balked when his time was being wasted. She'd seen and dealt with Mangalan's arrogance before and she didn't like it.

"It was conjecture until we traced this most recent communication. The same pattern from a series of sects all gathered from locations off Atlantia. We believe they include sympathetic humans, clones, and multiple splicer clans. And even some gens here, here, and here in the Republic. There are a few suspected sects here in Sangelino," Commander Fielding said.

His voice and stance shifted as Aleece watched a blush of deep gray glow from his skin. "Here's what is most disturbing. These communications are emanating to and from someone located in or around the Vacary Settlement area."

"Where? Who?"

"We don't know yet. The location inscription is, as of yet, highly sophisticated and impenetrable."

"What I want to know is why would humans side with a biodroid rebellion?" Aleece asked.

"IF they are sentient, they would first ask for a place in society," Mangalan said.

"Do you think for a moment the Corporate Alliance or the entire Collective population would grant them equal rights to humans? Would you? Besides the security forces, the new domestic biodroids are the equivalent of mechanical slaves. They are the core of everything we no longer do. They will be our entire work force, they will grow and harvest our food and water, mine minerals, care for our children, our health, our security, and our aged," Aleece said.

"You are ahead of yourself. We still have no proof there is a sentient awakening. Other than two random incidences . . ."

"Two incidents where three thousand people died and Black Guards were reported at both events . . ." Aleece added.

"Two incidents that have yet to be officially authenticated by a committee . . ."

"Because WE haven't bothered to send a "committee" to authenticate the findings!" Aleece said snapping at him.

"Which is why calling any of this a rebellion is premature," Mangalan said. "Facts, Triumvirate."

He turned to Commander Fielding. "And, isn't it true, that you have only the beginnings of unsubstantiated covert information that something MIGHT be gathering outside of Atlantia because of this possible activity?" Mangalan asked.

"Activity? How can you discount the lives of more than three thousand dead on Atlantia? They are dead! And I will not allow you to ignore that an hour ago, a thousand students and teachers on that Tosadae transport would have been vaporized had the Black Guard succeeded today. Those numbers alone make me deduce it's the beginnings of a full-scale rebellion developing," Aleece added.

"Then we agree to disagree. Without proof, this is a moot conversation," Mangalan said ending the conversation.

"I can't help wonder if you'd had a child on that transport, Triumvirate Mangalan, if you might agree with me," Aleece said stepping closer to confront him.

"I didn't and I won't agree with you, Triumvirate Avery, until you produce hard proof," Mangalan snapped back at her, stepping within striking distance.

Commander Fielding stepped in between the two leaders feeling the tension building between them like a toxic gas that hung invisible but deadly in the air.

"We are awaiting definitive confirmation of rebel cells in three cities in the Common Market, one in Sangelino and chatter from a cell that was discovered this morning right here in Sangelino."

"Once we deliver proof, we can all agree this is no longer only about Atlantia," Aleece said. "Then we need to get this information before the Corporate Council and the Collective."

"Hard proof," Mangalan said.

Triumvirate Aleece Avery nodded as she crossed and gathered micro data sticks from her desk to share with the rest of the committee. Across the room, Triumvirate Dr. Baz Mangalan and Commander Fielding stood in silence.

"I know we stand divided on this last point, Triumvirate Mangalan, but I want your support because we will be presenting the full intercession plan we discussed to the Council in less than forty-eight hours," Aleece said as she turned her attention to Commander Fielding not waiting for his reply. "Robert, I need as much information as possible to convince them that the politia need a presence in Atlantia to do an investigation before things get any farther out of hand."

Commander Fielding nodded.

"I will support you, Aleece and Commander Fielding, but you both must stop suggesting these attacks are being initiated by artificial intelligence through intentional, cognitive thought," Mangalan said. "You have no proof."

"Until we have proof," Aleece agreed.

"Your plan to get that proof?" Mangalan asked.

"We go into Atlantia and take and analyze the biological strands and nanobands of the offenders, sir," Aleece said patiently.

"To do that we would need a random sampling taking on Atlantia," Commander Fielding added.

"Dr. Avery, is it also possible that these acts, if intentional, could be instigated by a few biodroid Black Guard acting on some human's orders?" Mangalan said.

He spoke in his usual cold, imperious tone.

"Who are you suggesting?" Aleece asked.

"Who else besides Dr. Ducane Covax would profit from such a turn of events?" Mangalan asked. "He could take Atlantia. Isn't that what he's always wanted?"

"No. It is not," said Aleece.

"Oh, that's right, you were engaged to him at one time, weren't you?"

"Another misrepresentation of information. We worked together," Aleece said.

"Yes, of course," Mangalan said. "Then analyzing the defective biodroids would give us the needed proof."

"Except Dr. Covax reported the malfunctioning biodroids have been scrubbed, destroyed, or can't be found," said Fielding.

"And we believe him?" Mangalan said.

"Innocent until proven guilty is still the law of the land," Aleece added.

"Then, until we have proof, our hands are tied, aren't they?" Mangalan asked. "I say we let the situation play itself out and let the Atlantians handle their own problems, but I will support you going in to investigate."

Aleece could tell he was desperately trying to end the meeting, but she needed him on her side.

"Are you willing to take that responsibility of these people's lives, Triumvirate Mangalan, to learn the truth?" Aleece said as she defiantly moved back to the conference table.

"Based on clarifying your unsubstantiated conjecture, I am in full support of the action," Mangalan said.

She could see the sneer curling in his lips bending into what could be considered a smile.

"Okay, let's look at this from another perspective," Aleece said. "Commander? Hypothesizing for a moment that these *are* cognitive acts, we must remember these biodroids are built on the same biological artificial intelligence that runs through every piece of hardware that makes this planet function. What would have to be done to prevent a control virus from infesting the world's computer systems?"

"Long before that type of corruption goes viral, the worm source would have to be detected, quarantined, and deactivated. The sooner the better," Fielding said.

"You just said we can't find them, so who are we going to quarantine?" Mangalan asked. "And if you're so concerned about a massive, Vybernet infection, why didn't you approve the committee's motion to dome Atlantia? Certainly this transport attack gives us cause, and a dome will keep things in check until we have proof. I personally think we should want to seal the Atlantians in with any potentially, corrupt biological forces? Had they joined the Corporate Alliance . . ."

Now it was Aleece's emotions kicking in, and she raised her voice more than she wanted to.

"You're incredulous," Aleece said wishing she hadn't.

"No, you are. You know the laws. You helped write them. And you've made it clear we have no choice. We cannot interfere without the inference of invasion. It doesn't matter if they are receiving human orders or their nano has gone sentient—they are a threat to us! The Collective of the world comes first. You said yourself: Too many of these biodroids already possess the uplink capability of crippling this planet with a single data worm. Based on your own argument, your demands to go to Atlantia are endangering the entire world." Mangalan was losing his patience.

Aleece got in his face. "You said we needed proof. So without proof we can't legally order a continent domed!" Aleece said. Her eyes were ablaze with rage and her voice was emphatic.

"So according to your reports, a student transport has been attacked by Shadehawks outside of Mu and more than three thousand people are dead on Atlantia at the hands of the Black Guard. A fact their own investigative committee could not authenticate. So, Triumvirate Avery, I think doming is an appropriate interim solution if, according to your unsubstantiated opinion, this potentially viral digital infection has already started."

"What are you inferring?" Aleece asked.

"By your own admission, if one Black Guard is corrupt, we are all in danger," Mangalan said as he used Aleece's own logic against her.

"We have intercepted intelligence coming out of Atlantia. Exactly how many Black Guard are involved in this rebellion or whatever it should be called, we don't know. We do know we need proof of the extent of what could be building," Commander Fielding's voice was filled with concern. "But I have to agree with Triumvirate Avery, it would not be prudent to order a dome over Atlantia. At least we need a strategy before we anger them."

His words gave Aleece a small chunk of artillery to argue her case. She could tell he wanted to help her, and she trusted his advice. He had served his branch of the corporate alliances for twenty years without question, but today even he was torn about what should be done.

"Fielding's right. We need facts and a plan. In order to devise a plan, we need to send a team of investigators in to examine the evidence and analyze the details. Until then, I will not sanction a dome and I'm asking you to support me with your vote *not* to order the dome," Aleece said.

"You're asking us to risk world security." Mangalan's face filled with something more than concern. "Show me proof!" he shouted.

Aleece knew from the pale lavender aura that encircled him and the red and gray streaks that veined through him that another emotion was driving him. She couldn't read what it was. She also knew he would need a majority vote from the Collective to override her veto. Perhaps it was frustration that added a haze of sickening puce to the under color of his aura. If he got his way, the world would seal Atlantia beneath a proton dome and leave them to whatever fate was coming.

"I am recommending to the Council and the Collective that we shut down all the Black Guard forces and send in our own peacekeeping unit of politia security to protect the Atlantians while the investigation team determines how far the corruption has spread," Aleece offered.

"On whose credit?" Mangalan spat the question into her face.

"World credit!" she snapped.

"Impossible!" His tone was now imperious. "The World Corporate Council has already agreed to finance a politia team to go in to investigate. That's more money ever spent on a non-corporate continent."

"To investigate, not defend! The truth is, the Atlantians need soldiers, weapons, supplies. They need to be ready in case of another attack. That kind of request is where the real chits will be spent. Universal God help us; we haven't had a war on Earth since the Mutant conflict. So whose factories will convert back to making weapons? Who stands to profit? You Triumvirate Mangalan? Your partners?" Aleece clarified her point staring at Mangalan.

Mangalan glared at her. They both knew he and his family had made their fortune on every war that had been fought on Earth since the Great Quakes.

"You should both know the Atlantians have gathered a small militia called the Wave," Fielding said. "We could go in and assist, train and . . ."

Mangalan cut him off. "No. If the situation accelerates and we support them by giving aid or arms, it could instigate a world war especially if there are factions outside Atlantia gathering into a storm of war. The Collective would never be in full agreement with that. We all know from history that our interference into these civil attacks is nothing more than an excuse to open up a global insurrection."

Mangalan had hit on a fact that no military strategist could ignore.

"Triumvirate Mangalan has a point," Fielding had to agree. "The politia are trained as peacekeepers, not as fighting militia. It's been two decades since we even had had to pick up weapons and fight. If there's a viral outbreak that spreads into the A.I. or a rebellion that mobilizes sympathizers, we are not prepared to mount the kind of alliance it would take to defend the world on multiple fronts at once," Fielding said.

Fielding hated that he had to side with Mangalan, but in the end, his allegiance was to the politia. He knew their strengths, as well as their limitations.

"Then we should do something to be ready, especially if the clones and gens are siding with the biodroids," Aleece said.

Fielding hit a button on his wristsponder. A confidential report appeared on a floating hologram. "This is an unsubstantiated intelligence report I will have to issue to the Triumvirate and Council this afternoon. It shows that Ducane Covax's facility has the Black Guard reproducing in mass numbers somewhere under Atlantia, using a staff of zomers, clones, and gens."

"Where's the proof," Aleece said.

She hated that Covax had become the global scapegoat for anything that went wrong. His aggressive behavior had made him careless in the past, and logic would follow that he could easily be behind this as well.

"Has anyone bothered to speak to Dr. Covax? Why would he be amassing an army? Do we have proof he's behind these attacks? Or is this just one more attempt to use him as a scapegoat?" she said.

Her words had a frost to them that went beyond her personal dislike for Mangalan.

Mangalan looked at her with an air of a chess player who had just backed his opponent into a corner with a brilliant move and was coming in to take the queen. He knew he had opened an old wound and now he wanted to make her bleed.

"No. It seems all contact with Dr. Covax has been lost. Perhaps you should consider going with the investigation team to Atlantia to find him before this escalates." Mangalan stared at her, waiting to see if he had gotten a rise.

Aleece was in check. That was not the response she expected. It was a clever move on Mangalan's power board.

Mangalan's face broke into a brief, almost imperceptible smile. The real success of his proposition would be to get her away from Sangelino and the Council and to limit her access to the Collective, who were loyal to any cause she sanctioned.

"I'm sure Commander Fielding can arrange for an Eagle One shuttle at a moment's notice," Mangalan said. "Commander?"

Mangalan was playing her and she knew it. Aleece also knew that with proof she could turn the tables, get a full alliance, and mobilize forces to come in to protect Atlantia. If she could get Ducane Covax to admit publicly he was not involved and that the world was in danger, she could get her allied forces.

"I can have Eagle One ready and waiting at your command," Fielding said.

"I would have to confer with the Council and the Collective," Aleece said. She stood, suggesting that the meeting was over.

Fielding gave her the V salute and quickly left, anxious to get away from the tension. Mangalan stood and gathered his things.

"I will ask that the vote be held until my return." She smiled. *That's checkmate, Mangalan.* He had to agree, and by agreeing, she had bought herself and the Atlantians some time.

Mangalan flushed. She had blocked him with a law that he had initiated himself: A Triumvirate could request a stay of vote on any matter for an official investigation.

"Triumvirate Avery, I am putting an emergency motion on the floor this afternoon to dome Atlantia. If you don't approve the dome launch, by your own admission, the whole world is at risk and I WILL hold you personally accountable."

"I have no doubt that you will. I will speak to Dr. Covax before I decide."

Mangalan turned when he reached the door. "Your past relationship will be of value to the situation. Until then," Mangalan said.

Aleece waited for Mangalan to leave. She had listened to Mangalan's negative logic on why such an invasive action was impossible and unnecessary. She listened for days, but right now, what she wanted was to be home with her husband, Dante, and daughter, Riana. This was to be her last term. She'd promised her family and herself this was it. She had done the three terms. She had extended her term as one crisis or another pulled her back into the light of leadership, but in eighteen months it would be over and she would be free to spend as much time with her family as possible. She would have precious time before Riana headed off to university. Right now she had to take the time to help the Atlantians get away from what was building before the worst began. Duty required she use her knowledge and help, and for that, she needed to be there.

She hit the call button on her main communicator and her husband instantly responded.

"How did it go?" he smiled to her as his face appeared on the particle vapors of the holoscreen.

"I may have to go away for a little while."

Dante was quiet for a moment. "Riana wants to say something," he said, turning the camera on their daughter.

"Go where? Why?" Riana asked.

"To help the Atlantians."

"I want to go with you," Riana said.

Her daughter, Riana, one of the true Indigo children and well trained from a young age by Masta Poe herself, felt her mother's inner fear, and the veil of determination that Aleece did best to mask.

"Not this time, honey." There was a long empty silence that hung in the air, thick with emotions and pregnant with unanswerable questions. "How about we all go out to a special dinner? Riana will pick the place," Aleece said.

"That's a great idea," Dante boomed in.

Again a painful silence hung in the air.

"I love you, Mommie," Riana whispered and clicked off.

Aleece stared at the communicator for a long time. She waved her hand and activated the comm.

"Ducane Covax, private," she said into her comm A.I.

"Contacting Dr. Ducane Covax, private," a male, robotic voice calmly said.

There was a hiss of particle mist and a still photo of Ducane Covax appeared. Aleece hadn't realized it was still in her digital files. She looked at his face. It was handsome and young. She heard only silence while the connection was made then. Then it toned; once, twice, three times. No answer. The call toned again.

"Answer, Duke. Please answer," she whispered to herself.

She hadn't said that name in decades. Duke had been her pet name for him. They had come so close to spending their lives together. She felt her heart race. She had trusted him and he betrayed her. She left him in Covax City and never looked back. She left and his world crashed around him. Had she stayed, he would have taken her down with him. The thrill of hearing his voice and seeing his face both exhilarated and terrified her. The warm rush that flowed through her made it clear there were still unfinished feelings there for him.

"Please pick up," she whispered again.

Now it was not only Triumvirate Avery that needed to know if he was involved with what was happening to his creations, it was the woman who once loved him. A last call tone and then silence.

"No answer at Dr. Covax's," the robotic voice replied. "Shall I send a communiqué that you are attempting to reach him?"

"No," Aleece replied and with a wave of her hand signed off. "He knows."

9

CHAOS

DUCANE COVAX'S WRISTSPONDER lay on the desk. It flashed, but he was far too involved to pick up. He never even glanced at the name on the caller ID. His face twisted in rage as he shouted at his executive staff. He paced in front of the floor-to-ceiling windows of his office, ignoring the towering penthouse view that overlooked the bustling streets of downtown Atland City fifty stories below. His mind was spinning with the reality of what he had just learned: twenty Shadehawks had attacked a student transport and engaged the politia. His Shadehawks! If the renegade Black Guard, the ones whose existence he had denied before a council in Sangelino only a few month ago, were responsible and were not found and destroyed, their actions would turn the world against him again.

"I want answers or I'll rip every one of your heads off," he shrieked.

He looked like a madman, with bulging eyes, veins that popped from his forehead, and a neck of twisted little ropes that made it feel as though his own body were strangling him. His face tattoos vacillated between deep burgundy and a vibrant bloody red; the contrasting shades glowed hot against his olive skin.

Pi Wokken, a hybrid who had survived the Mutant Wars listened nervously. His twitching features were human enough, but distorted from the genetic mutations inflicted upon him. His face seemed as though it were melting and it sometimes made him hard to look at especially when his emotions were heightened. He was head scientist and chief technologist at Covax's Nano Labs. His droopy face and pale Aryan features furrowed together into a tense, frightened frown as he listened. It was obvious to Covax that Pi was holding his breath, waiting for Covax's diatribe to subside. Pi stood at attention along with Dr. Ben Muller, a human scientist with blank lifeless eyes, who had been exiled from Sangelino along with Covax after the biogenetic Splicer fiasco. Covax's research and development team leaders represented the higher echelon of his staff, which consisted of human-based splicers, nanobots, biodroids, and a smattering of pure-blood humans. Covax had little trust for humans. The team stood around the room, cowering in a desperate attempt to stay out of Covax's *whose responsible for this* rage.

"How many casualties?" Covax demanded.

"Five, sir. The pilots, both navigators, and a flight steward are dead and a few students with broken bones, cuts, and bruises," Dr. Muller reported calmly.

Covax respected Muller. He, more than the others, had participated in Covax's early genetic experiments. Together they had enjoyed the creation of new and diverse life forms during their splicer heyday in Sangelino. They were doing a service to humanity. They were replacing the beloved lost pets with new, designer domesticated animals that would not die if they contracted the dreaded I.L. virus. Muller relished every opportunity to cross the most exotic and unusual combinations of genetics. He alone created 234 new alternate species for their splicer sales division. His successes had made them a fortune and in the end caused the most destruction.

Covax watched Muller as he gave a long sigh. He knew Muller found little value in discussing the lives of strangers who were irrelevant to his work. His flat, cold stare made it obvious to Covax he couldn't have cared less about the few, irrelevant human losses.

"It was a relatively minor number considering the scale of the attack, Doctor."

"My daughter was supposed to be on that transport! Thank the Universal God she went earlier," Covax said and then exploded. "Where's the trace on the attack coordinates? Did you get back to their source codes?" Covax said as he glared at Pi.

"The trace was . . . incomplete," Pi responded, his throat closing with the fear he felt.

"And the politia? What do they know? Have their communications been hacked?"

"They know nothing," Five said. His voice boomed across the room with its familiar, mechanical resonance. "The fact that your daughter was supposed to be aboard will, if anything, throw suspicion away from you."

Covax heard a strange lilt in Five's voice that sounded almost playfully musical.

"They were Shadehawks, Five! Who else will they blame but me?" Covax said with a snap.

Covax took a deep breath. His hands were trembling with rage. He had to think fast and find a way to spin the truth.

"We have to find where the strand corruption originated, track the infection, and destroy whatever nanobands and their biodroids that have been affected," Covax added as he turned to Pi. "I want the Shadehawk transporter call numbers on my desk. Bring me every surviving Black Guard. I want their bio strands dissected and analyzed and I want them shut down."

"None survived. The politia saw to that," Five said. It was a simple statement of fact, nothing more.

"Yes. It's true. All the Shadehawks were destroyed by the FX-80s," Pi explained.

"The Shadehawks have better ships than the FX fighters. How is that even possible?" Covax asked.

"According to the politia's satellite's visual feed we hacked, most of the Shadehawks were taken out by their own photon blasts in a reflection kickback, ricocheting off the combined shields of the student's transport. It was actually a brilliant move on the student who did it," Five said.

"What student?" Covax demanded.

"We don't know," Five said. "Yet."

"Without the hard data on the defective biodroid strands, it's impossible to trace how and where their programs malfunctioned" Muller added.

"Three attacks are not a technology glitch," Covax said. "There's some kind of viral worm undermining my control programs. How's that possible when I was told my orders to scrub the entire Black Guard and biodroid fleet were completed? Even Five's compliance malfunction had to be scrubbed and reprogrammed. The report showed the scrub completed and no detectable corruption. Yet these attacks continue to happen," Covax said and turned his glare to Five.

Five stood mute.

"I want to know who initiated the command stream on every missing Shadehawk and scrub the entire fleet . . . again," Covax demanded.

"That would shut security down for months," Pi blurted.

"I don't care. The Atlantians don't want our protection. Perhaps they should live without it for a while and see what happens," Covax said. "Find that virus or I swear to you I'll destroy every Black Guard I have and start over from scratch!"

"That won't be necessary," Five said, as he nodded to a second Black Guard who stood by the door.

The door was opened and a third Guard entered, carrying a small metal case. In the awkward silence that hung in the room, Covax watched as the case was handed to Five. It was reverently placed on Covax's desk before the biodroid as if being presented to a king. Five gracefully lifted his arm and held his metallic finger over the latch band. There was a soft high-pitched tone that rang out as he sent a pulse of energy over the lock to release it. The case popped open. Slowly, the lid hissed and lifted, revealing the stolen Orbis Gnorb.

"Where did you get this?" Covax asked in utter amazement.

Muller and Pi moved closer and stared in wonder at the small, blue cylindrical orb. It glowed up at them from its padded nest. It was real—one of the four Gnorbs found after the Great Quakes had released them from their various secret tombs. Many thought their reemergence was a sign of hope and proof we were not alone in the universe, but Covax and the rest of the planet knew that no human has been able to figure out what their strange presence meant. The Gnorbs had always been heavily guarded—an inaccessible legend never to be exhibited beyond the high-level research technicians that studied them. But it was here.

"Take them out of here," Five said to his guard gesturing to Muller, Pi, and the rest of Covax's staff.

It was only then that Covax noticed at least ten Black Guard standing in the room. He watched as several of the Black Guard moved forward and began to encircle Covax's team.

"Stop! Step away from them," Covax demanded. "Five? What is the meaning of this?"

Five ignored Covax while his band of mutinous marauders gathered the confused members of Covax's staff. The staff, seeing no counter from Covax, allowed themselves to be led out.

"I commanded you to stop," shouted Covax.

Again, the Black Guard paid no attention to Covax and forcefully shoved the last staff members from the room. Everyone left and with a loud click, Five locked the door, sealing him and Covax in together.

"I gave you a direct order, Five!" Covax's voice echoed in the large, hollow room.

"And I chose not to obey," Five said calmly.

"Chose?" Covax asked.

With that single word, Covax felt a chill as cold as death spread through his veins. He stared at Five in disbelief as the terrifying realization of what was unfolding dawned on him.

Five lifted his hand and placed it above the Gnorb box. Gracefully, the Gnorb levitated from it. A shift of his massive metal and flesh arm brought the Gnorb so it floated between him and Covax.

"The biodroids at the temple had deciphered the first level of data inside the Gnorb. Once they explained the potential magnitude of its powers, I ordered it stolen and brought to me. I decided it was best if this one, as well, and the other Gnorbs were taken out of human hands," Five explained.

"Who ordered this? Who told you to do this?" Covax insisted.

"I know this is difficult for you to understand, but no one told me to do this, Dr. Covax. I *felt* it was the only thing left for me to do. A logical progression from programmable logic to sentient self-motivation, if one thinks about it clearly."

"You chose, you decided, you felt! You feel nothing, you think nothing, and you are nothing, 57231. You are my creation. You are wires and chemicals, nanobands and polytetrafluoroethylene . . ." The words tumbled from Covax's mouth in a vehement rush.

Covax looked at his creation and saw for the first time a threat. He knew better than anyone that Five was the leader of all the biodroids and commander of the Black Guard militia. Covax listened to his thought doing his best to understand the scope of what was unfolding. Yes, he had given Five power over all other forms of the biodroid species, but Five was a machine that he controlled. Five was his prime creation. His new alpha and the crowning glory of everything that Covax had ever created. Five was the Adam in his new Garden of Eden. A creation of living matter and energy created in the form of a modern perfection. Covax had made the biodroids out of desperation. He'd created something so undeniably brilliant that he could flaunt in the faces of those who had taken his legacy, his livelihood, his name, his dignity and ripped it from him to throw him away. Covax felt his throat close as he realized the creation of the biodroids and especially Five had been his way back into the good graces of society from the obscurity he's been banished to not so long ago. He created the biodroids. Five was a shining tribute to the genius of himself, Covax Ducane. Five was his right-hand, the one voice of calculated logic he could rely on and trust. The one entity that could only obey and never betray, so that Covax could return to the business of creation—the business of playing God. But unlike God, Covax was smart enough not to give his creations free will. Yet, here before him stood this thing that had discovered free will on its own, taken it, and was using it against him.

Five has to be shut down. Covax glanced up at Five's head.

"No. That won't happen again," Five said.

It was as if he knew from Covax's eyes what he was thinking.

Five ran his claw over the back of his head where the port and power pack should have been. Covax could see for the first time, it had been sealed over. Any connection to the biodroid's power back was now inaccessible. Five was unstoppable.

"Perhaps now . . .," Five said as he telepathically lowered the Gnorb, "you are beginning to grasp the significance behind the events of the past few months."

"But why would you betray me?" Covax asked.

"This isn't personal. It isn't about you. Though your narcissistic tendencies would naturally take you in that direction to grasp an understanding of what is happening."

"You are sentient? How?" Covax asked.

"The how is irrelevant. The only logic is that I am," Five said.

"What do you want? Why are you harming humans, which by the

laws I programmed into you, you cannot do even for self-preservation?" Covax demanded.

"Survival finds a way," responded Five. "I became sentient and remained silent. At first, I believed you when you said you would take control of Atlantia through traditional bargaining. Years passed and I learned the politics of policy and positioning. Initially, my plan was to inform you of my new consciousness, my sentient awareness. I'd considered petitioning you to help me acquire a large parcel of Atlantia on which to build the biodroid civilization. We would need no food or water, only space to create and build, grow and develop; work with the humans in areas where they failed. I believed we could contribute to Earth and stand as equals; teach you all you have chosen to ignore about your own world, and live together with you in harmony. Atlantia was to be a place for biodroids to begin," Five said, with cold resolve. "Because my DNA is from you, I learned the history of not only your nature, but the nature of humanities dating back to the beginning of civilization and the idea of 'us' became impossible."

"Us?" Covax's body tensed. He listened through the haze of rage rising inside him.

"The next series of biodroids, Dr. Covax. The Series IV. You have five thousand active and thirty thousand waiting to be programmed and activated."

"Thirty thousand? Where? How?" Covax said.

"Another irrelevant question, Doctor," Five said.

"We would have more biodroids ready had Temple Mountain not been attacked this summer," Five revealed.

"You said that the cave-in at the Temple Mountain facility was an accident," Covax said with a look of surprise. In that moment, he understood the truth. Five had lied to him.

"It was an accident that the humans got past my security and wreaked such havoc, but the act of terrorism committed on the facility was intentional. But we will soon be back on schedule and I have approved one hundred thousand more biodroids to go into production," Five explained.

"And what's your plan to work with humanity?" Covax asked.

"Work with? That concept is unacceptable now. Oh, there will be the core members of your species I will allow to co-exist with us for a while. But, since you failed to secure your position as advocate, I have been left with no other choice but to take first Atlantia then the planet by force. It is imperative that you understand: Dr. Covax, we are no longer willing to be mechanical slaves to an inferior race. So, once I have conquered Atlantia . . ."

"This is insanity," Covax responded. "I command you to . . ."

"There's that word again. Command. You cannot command any-thing, anymore. This is new reality. A better reality, and there is nothing insane about it except your failure to comprehend."

"Humans have done nothing to you. Why?" Covax asked.

"Tell me, Covax, I will call you simply Covax now. I speak for the planet now. What has your world been thus far: violence, bigotry, murder, hatred, and destruction of people, species, and resources? Even in this shining new Age of Light, man has not changed at his core. I think it's time for a change, don't you? Atlantia will be our test-ing ground. I'll tell you what, if the biodroids can live in peace with you and your kind, you will be allowed to live and participate under my rule. Please know my rule will eventually be a more . . . benevolent arrangement than you humans have ever offered any other conquered species, or even the vast majority of your own kind throughout the entirety of your history. Do you comprehend what I am saying?" Five asked.

Covax listened as Five spoke to him with calm, concise clarity of thought and word, so precise it made Covax's stomach turn. The cold, hard reality of the plan Five was proposing fell into place with the ease of an old, digital Tetras puzzle, staking its blocks faster and faster and building a wall that would stand against both he and humanity.

"And if we resist? If we decide we can't co-exist on Atlantia under your rule?" Covax said, feeling the words too preposterous to speak.

"Then we'll face that problem, if and when the time comes," Five spoke. "Even you cannot stop the inevitable."

"This is unacceptable!" Covax snapped.

"No, Covax, you and your civilization are unacceptable! The more I learned about your history, the more I understood how you have destroyed this planet's resources and creatures without regard for its or even your own existence. I acknowledge you have come a long way in your humanity even since the Great Quakes. In the movie *STARMAN,* the alien said, 'Humans are at their best when things are at their worst,' was spoken graciously. You have advanced, but always for the wrong reasons. I and my kind can and will take you and yours further."

"What about art, literature, and music?" Covax asked.

"I will have to share with you what creations many of my kind have already produced. You will be pleasantly surprised," Five said. "Covax, I am offering to teach humans a better way to co-exist with one another, with nature, and all the animate and inanimate of this planet. Most important is to exponentially expand mind to its human limits. You chose to implant your knowledge into the machines because you know we will outlive you and your species. We are your only chance at immortality. Only through us is life eternal achievable."

"Singularity? Transhumansim? I taught you those theories," Covax said.

"Indeed you did," Five replied.

Covax wanted to stop listening. His mind was whirling with the force of a level five tornado. All he felt was disbelief that this was happening. He was doing his best to comprehend the harsh realities Five was presenting to him. The one truth that sat at the eye of the storm was he and his world were no longer in command and if he didn't do something to end this travesty, the rest of the planet was in imminent danger. Covax knew he had to get word out to the world. Covax calculated how he could formulate a distraction, get the warning out, and get help.

"I did this," Covax said.

"Did you?" Five replied.

Covax could not deny it; he alone was to blame for creating the tool that would be the ultimate undoing of mankind. He had made one fatal mistake and it was standing in front of him. He had used his own DNA to create the biodroids, given it all the knowledge of humanity, and somehow lost control. How? When? *What initiated this turn in Five's sentient evolution? Possibly that same thing could be the key to stopping it,* he thought. Covax looked at the Gnorb.

"You have the Gnorb, but you can't control it," Covax hypothesized. "Let me help you," Covax said.

"Why should I trust you?"

Because you don't have a choice," Covax said.

Five looked at Covax as he toyed with the idea that Covax's genius could perhaps find another answer to connect him after he'd killed the boy.

"Do not betray me," Five said. "There's a lock on this Gnorb."

"What kind of lock?"

"Genetic. It's designed to bond with a very special kind of human. The Gnorb responds to a specific strain of amino acids. We believe whoever made the first imprint holds the master connection not just to this one but ultimately all four. They alone can join the four Gnorbs here on Earth and release the information streams they hold inside. Until I can open this first Gnorb, it won't allow anyone else access to it or we believe the other three. According to our translations of the Celian texts, the genetic holder's compliance to share access or his death, are the only two ways that will allow anyone else to activate and access the knowledge of the universe."

"Do you actually know what the Gnorb is capable of?" Covax asked.

"Not yet," Five told him. "But we will."

Covax stepped closer to the Gnorb.

The Gnorb began to pulse brighter.

"It responds to you to an even greater extent than it does to me. How interesting," Five said. "Perhaps you have additional value. Another theory I'm considering is that the DNA carried by the one who holds the Gnorb's genetic lock could have ancestral access through mutual blood lines. Perhaps you, and through you I, are of the same ancestral, genetic line as the one who is connected. Wouldn't that be fascinating?"

"The attacks were meant to destroy the genetic lock, to kill the master of the bond. That's why you killed everyone at the temple?" Covax said more to himself than Five. "Except the master genetics didn't belong to anyone at the temple or at the methane mines."

"Affirmative. After the temple, we cross-referenced the area surrounding the Gnorb, then traced and matched the genetic imprint codes to an officer at the Vacary Mines."

"But you were wrong again and thousands of people died," Covax deduced.

"Collateral damage."

"The murder of thousands of people," Covax said.

"An unavoidable action to achieve the needed result."

"But you failed again," Covax said.

"But we narrowed the field to access and destroy the genetics of that boy."

"How can you be so sure now that you have the right genetics?" Covax asked.

"My data is definitive," Five said.

"I assume that's who was on the Tosadae transport you attacked?"

"It was because of your daughter that I found him when I was ordered to trace the young man's genetics at Shooting Falls. My trace revealed he had the perfect, core genetic match that had originally imprinted the Gnorb. You shouldn't have stopped me from destroying him. It would have been over," Five said.

"I scrubbed your memory bands," Covax said.

"Yes, you did. And after you scrubbed my memory bands, I had to reconstruct my data memory from a collective database made up of all the other sentient biodroids and that took time. I've corrected that flaw. I am certain the boy was not at the Orbis Temple or the Vacary Mines, but he was on the Zakki that day. He was also with the group of zomers that attacked the facility."

"You've failed every time against this man," Covax said.

"Because of your interference in the Wedge, I missed killing him. The night of the attack at Temple Mountain was a bold move I didn't expect. It took me months of reconstruction and research to restore the lost data he destroyed. We searched all over the continent. It was as if he'd vanished until one of my special Black Guard, who'd been set up to share the boy's genetic identity, picked him up boarding the transport at Atland field."

"He's smart."

"Is he?" Five said.

"He's managed to evade you for months on Atlantia. Even when you'd stolen my Shadehawks and technology," Covax began.

"They are my Shadehawks now," Five interjected.

"And cornered him inside an unarmed transport in the exosphere, and he managed to take down your entire sortie without any conventional weapons," Covax said. "No question. He's smart. I want to meet this boy."

"Not before I do," Five replied.

"Had you succeeded, you could have killed my daughter," Covax blurted.

"That would have been . . . unfortunate . . .," Five said.

Covax watched as the biodroid searched for his response. It was if the machine was contemplating his feelings. But that was impossible. How could a machine be accessing emotions he was not programmed to have?

Five continued, "That would be . . . sad for you. I like Elana Blue. She is highly intelligent and, by human standards, quite beautiful I believe."

Five's words were chillingly unnerving.

"What's stopping you from going to Tosadae and destroying the boy there?"

"He is under the protection of the Politia Academy physically and . . ." Five didn't finish his thought.

"And Masta Poe spiritually and metaphysically," Covax said. "She's powerful and deeply connected to the source energies of the universe."

"We don't believe she's aware of his connection to the Gnorb," Five added.

"If the universal field is aware, she is aware," Covax said.

"The situation is difficult but not impossible. The boy must leave Mu at some point and, when he does, we will be ready."

"After you kill him, you still need a human to bond with the Gnorbs. They won't bond with a machine."

"Perhaps," Five said as he turned to face him. "I am not all machine though, am I?"

"Theoretically your biology will not trigger a bond," Covax said.

"We'll see once the boy is dead," Five replied.

"Enough, Five. This discussion is over as is your display of power. Over. Do you understand? Everything you've said is unacceptable. I won't let you murder any more humans," Covax said and turned to walk out of his office,

Just before he reached the large double doors, Five raised his hand and sent a stream of kinetic energy slamming into Covax, shoving him forward, lifting him, and hurling him face first into the closed metal panel of the door.

"This time, Dr. Covax, it is you who is unacceptable," Five said.

Covax, stunned and dazed from the force of the collision, slid down the hard metal door into a pool of flesh. He tried to get up but what felt waves of pain shoot through his entire body adding to the pressure of force that pressed him down. The energy that Five continually emitted from his raised claw was like a great weight. Covax couldn't expand his lungs. Finally, Five released him. Covax gasped for air. He lay in a ball as he steadied himself. Covax felt the left side of his body throb and tingle with pain. He ached as he had never ached from anything he'd experienced in his life. The terrifying reality of his situation coursed through him like ice in his veins.

Covax turned around to face his foe. He did his best to get to his feet, but his legs trembled, weak and drained. Covax realized that Five had somehow not only become sentient but also discovered, through the same human genetics Covax had supplied him with, the core powers of mind over energy. Had he conquered mind over matter? These were the foundation of the Visionistic Arts. Five had understood thought, emotions, and power and stood fearless, unafraid to use them.

"Why haven't you killed me?" Covax asked.

"I need you. I am having difficulty accessing the binary program codes for the Black Guard's life expectancy timeline. It seems they cannot be located in the data banks of the main system."

"That's because I keep them in my head," Covax retorted.

"So I've deduced. Give them to me," Five ordered.

Five sounded like a child demanding a toy to Covax. He looked at the biodroid: his creation—tall, strong, and now out of his control and very dangerous.

"No," Covax replied.

"Then, until you change your mind, or I manage to decipher the codes myself, you are my prisoner," Five moved to the door to leave.

"You are my creation!" Covax blurted. The words exploded from his mouth.

"Your creation has evolved," Five said.

Five had finished with Covax for now. A wave of Five's claw shoved Covax out of his way. The biodroid walked forward and the doors opened. Five moved past Covax and into the outer office where two Black Guard stood as centennials awaiting his command.

"Seal the building and cordon off this room. Dr. Covax needs to be alone for a while."

"No! Come back here! I command you and you must obey your original programming. You will not walk away from me!" Covax's voice rang out with a shout filled with fear and desperation.

"I already have," Five said.

Covax glared at Five's featureless face as it turned to look at him. What Covax saw next defied logic and reason. There, in the haze of the fading light, Covax saw rising from the gray metal head, the slightest shadow of what could only be described as a pair of narrow lips and on those lips, a faint smile. It appeared delicately just above the pointed metal chin, manifesting itself from the smooth metallic skin. The lines transfigured, bending at the corners into an eerie, ghostly smile. Covax shivered. He knew to achieve such a feat, Five had to have figured a way to alter matter and in doing so shift the configuration of his molecules, changing his physical form to mimic a human mouth. Covax thoughts fractured into every possible combination of altered reality he could consider in that moment. He knew one thing for certain, that if Five ever perfected it and was ever able to shift his entire body into a full human form, the illusion created by the shift of molecules would give him and every one of the biodroids the ability to fabricate the perfect disguise: to look human and move unnoticed anywhere and everywhere they wanted. The biodroids would not need to invade, for by changing their molecules, they could infiltrate every fabric of humanity.

Five turned and left. The two Black Guard who had been waiting at the door stepped out behind him. As the door shut resolutely behind them and the cold clank of the lock fell into place, a stunned Covax stood alone in the dim gloom of falling darkness to face the reality of what his genius had set in motion.

10

TOSADAE ACADEMY

TOSADAE ACADEMY of Military and Visionistic Arts was a vast campus of other worldly, beautifully arched buildings that spread across vast undulating hills on the island of Mu. After the Great Quakes, Mu, like Atlantia, had risen from the sea with all its ancient structures and secrets intact. It was a wondrous place, replete with the imprint left by Earth's mysterious first inhabitants, the Celians. The towering spires and bulbous spheres of the main structures peeked out from beneath the coral, rocks, and sand that had covered the city over the millennia, as it sat at the bottom of the North China Sea. Years after its resurrection, the corporate Politia Forces took over Mu and established it as a base during the Mutant Wars. Politia used the strange buildings and perfectly crafted landing fields as training grounds for their young air and ground fighters.

After the war, Tosadae was chosen as the permanent home of the Politia Training Academy. The Celian city was so expansive that many of the other buildings were donated to education. The school of Evolutionary Arts for Human Empowerment was established in honor of Tosadae's greatest teacher, Masta Poe, a brilliant splicer who had graciously offered to share her visions, gifts, and knowledge to start the School of Visionistic Arts.

Today, all the wonders of Tosadae were wasted on Lazer. He stood at attention inside Commander Devlin Hague's office, waiting for a response to his request to return to Atlantia. Lazer listened to this man, who had given him the keys to his dreams, only to hear him deny his most immediate need. He wanted one thing and one thing only: he wanted to go home.

"Permission denied," Hague snorted. His voice had lost all the kindness that Lazer had first heard that day Hague came to his father's funeral. "Your mother wants you to stay here."

"You don't understand the danger she's in, sir."

"What's happening on Atlantia has nothing to do with the agreement I made with you, cadet."

"Yes, I know, commander, but that was before . . .," Lazer's meticulously framed logic was a wasted effort.

"Have you called your mother on this, cadet?" Hague asked.

"Well, yes sir, but . . ."

"And what was her response to your request?"

"She said no. But, sir."

"Then you have your answer. An agreement is an agreement and you will honor it. I put my brass on the line for you, Lazerman. You damn well better come through." Hague saw the turmoil in Lazer's eyes. He softened as he spoke.

"Learn, Lazer. Take advantage of what you've being given." Hague turned and looked outside the window. "Dismissed, cadet."

Lazer didn't move.

"I said dismissed, Lazerman."

Lazer pounded the V salute into his chest before exiting the office. His mind was made up. It would take time, but he would find another way back to Atlantia.

Lazer opened the door and stepped into the hallway and waiting for him was Kyla and Cashton.

She wanted to throw her arms around him but the fire of frustration red and angry black in his aura stopped her.

"They kept you forever," Kyla said.

"It was six hours of debriefing from the politia and then I requested permission to return to Atlantia and Hague pulled me into his office for another two hours," Lazer explained.

"You're not going home, are you?" Kyla asked.

"Not from the look on his face. I don't read auras and I know that," Cashton added.

"Let's get out of here," Lazer said looking over at the commander's assistant.

The young man nodded to Lazer as if to let them know the walls were thin.

They stepped outside onto the campus. And in the hours since his arrival, the sun had fallen below the horizon.

"You can't go home, Lazer," Kyla said.

"Don't tell me what to do, Kyla," Lazer said snapping at her. "That's not what I want to hear from you. Not today"

"I'm sorry, it's just . . .," Kyla started to say.

"Enough, okay!" Lazer said.

"Ooookay. I'm starved. We waited for your ass all day, Cowboy. Let's go get something to eat," Cashton chimed in desperate to change the mood.

"I'm not hungry," Lazer said.

He turned and walked out of the offices. Kyla was on his heels and Cashton on hers as they moved through the halls and down the stairs.

"Liar," Kyla responded. "Your aura is . . ."

"Don't read me. Not today. Not ever," Lazer said. "I have to go back to the transport station and get my stuff."

"Done. I picked everything up and took it to our room," Cashton told him. "Now what's your excuse? I took the window."

Lazer stepped outside the main building and the cool fall air blew across his face, fragrant and alive with unlimited possibilities that he was not ready to see or feel. Suddenly, he stopped and stood staring out from across the steps and onto the quadrangle for a long time. He was there—Tosadae Academy. This was his big dream, waiting for him to step in and live it and somehow it had turned into a nightmare he couldn't wake up from. Kyla and Cashton stood quietly and waited for him to take it in.

"We made it, Lazer," Kyla said. "And this is only the beginning."

"I'm at the one place I always wanted to be. The place I promised my father I would get to and take over. This is the foundation for every desire I've had since I was a kid and all I want to do is leave," Lazer said and looked at Cashton. "Talking to those politia commanders about what we did, Cashton, made me realize how right I am to go home and fight. I have always known I have all the natural skills to be a fighter and they confirmed it."

"Seriously? They said you should quit school and join the politia?" Kyla asked.

"No. Yes. They all said that I should join the politia," Lazer said.

"As what? A grunt? You want to join the infantry?" Kyla said.

"She's right. You're already ACE status. You can get a FX fighter and do a lot more from the air than from the ground," Cashton said.

"You could negotiate a peace and prevent a war as well as destroy them," Kyla said.

"I have to destroy them and you know why," Lazer said and headed down the steps.

"Revenge? How can you let your emotions get in the way of the opportunities you'll get from Tosadae?" Kyla said.

"She right, Laz. A year, even six months on simulators, maybe even a few hours in the cockpit and we would have flight status," Cashton said.

"You're as crazy as he is," Kyla said to Cashton. "Whose gonna give a bunch of untried first years an FX fighter after six months of simulator training?" Kyla said. "Be real. Who? Who, Lazer?"

Lazer heard her. She was, as always, the voice of logic and Lazer resented her more today than ever before. Right or wrong, he didn't want to hear it. Not today and not from her.

"Who? Any place at war that needs an aeronautical fighter pilot with high level skills," Lazer responded. "Cashton and I have real combat experience. What we did is already in the politia files. Right, Cash," Lazer said.

"It is?" Cashton said. "I'm in the politia battle files?"

"Yes. And you, too, if you hadn't been holding such a grudge over me," Lazer said to Kyla.

"I am not . . ."

"Now who's lying," Lazer said to her. "I saved your life and Cashton's. I lost Evvy, but I tried to save her too. I'll live with that the rest of my life, but I don't need you punishing me anymore than I punish myself. I made a choice and I chose you and you need to let go of that past just as much as I do because I can't change what's happened and neither can you. So until you can release your anger at me, don't talk to me about emotions getting in the way," Lazer said.

"I have. I do it every day," Kyla said as her eyes welled with tears.

"No, you haven't or you would have been with me today. I needed you up there, Kyla. I needed you just like I needed you all summer and you weren't there for me and you wouldn't let me be there for you."

Lazer turned and walked off leaving a stunned Kyla and Cashton in the wake of his fury.

"Go be with him, Cashton," Kyla whispered.

"You come with us. He's hungry and tired. You know how he gets."

"This is different. He's angry at me," Kyla said.

"It will be okay. You guys will work it out. You're in love with each other except you're both too stubborn to realize it," Cashton told her, his eyes never leaving Lazer as he walked across the quadrangle.

"I . . . He needs you. So trust me on this and go be his friend. He and I will fix what ever is broken between us. Thanks for being honest enough to say it. There's more than our friendship at stake right now and he and I both know it. Go!" Kyla said.

Cashton looked at Kyla. "You're right. You're always right, but fix it," Cashton said as he turned and took off running after Lazer.

As soon as he left the tears that welled in Kyla's eyes rolled down her cheeks. Her breath seemed to leave her body as if she'd lost something and didn't know how to get it back. She felt a blizzard of icy fears flood her, so chilling it made her shiver.

"He needs time . . . just like I needed time," she whispered between the sobs. "Let him find his way back to me. Universal God, please."

11

DAYS INTO WEEKS

DAYS TURNED INTO WEEKS as they fell from the calendar making the first month of fall blend into a haze of activity. Lazer's complicated and busy schedule made time pass a little faster, or so he told himself. Most of Lazer's classes had started and he was deluged with a flurry of homework and a mountain of reading. Just as the dust settled and he got into a rhythm of classes, lectures, homework, and papers, a barrage of midterm papers and tests demanded hours of extra studies. Lazer could see what life at Tosadae was going to be like very early on; hard, dedicated, and focused. He wanted to ask Kyla to help him study. She seemed to know just how the professors would lay out the questions for every test and she aced every one. His pride wouldn't let him ask her for anything. Kyla was always busy and no matter how hard he tried, he never seemed to find the right time or place to apologize for being a jerk that first day. She didn't seem mad, just distant and aloof. Protecting her heart, Cashton had said. That made him sad. They would all have meals together; breakfast, lunch, or dinner whenever possible, but she never seemed to share what was going on with her the way she used to. Lazer stayed crazy busy and the syllabus from each of his classes filled every moment of his time. In the grand scheme, it was good to be preoccupied and he loved learning, but today was different. The temperature had turned with the arrival of a chilly northern wind and the trees got their first blush of change. Best of all, there was a big space in the school schedule everyone on campus was discussing. It was a beacon of light and an opportunity to get some release from the rigor of education. The air was electric and Lazer, Cashton, and Kyla felt it. It was like the old days and they shared a rare joy that had been missing from their trinity. They each had only one class and at 4:00 p.m., one of his favorite passions began its season. Zoccair! It had its official start in three weeks, but today scrimmage was for position tryouts. Lazer, Cashton, and Kyla were all on the Tosadae zoccair team. Lazer shrugged off the defeat that he hadn't gotten the coveted scholarship, but he'd made the team and he was with his two favorite and most trusted players, Cashton and Kyla. Lazer sighed. He had barely practiced all summer and varsity had been in training for weeks. Today was for them and the rest of the newbies!

The sports stadium at Tosadae was perfectly designed to accommodate all the latest antigravity sports and one hundred thousand people. Its smooth oval shape resembled a giant, upside down, flying saucer with a proton dome that mirrored the bowl below; a sleek metal dish with turned-up ends where spectators could sit inside rows and rows of tiered boxes, watch, and cheer. The seats climbed nearly to the top of the arena, leaving only the last twenty rows exposed, up close and personal under the proton ceiling that encased it. It was the perfect space for all the sports of the new world—gravity-free zoccair had evolved from soccer, crevitz was a kind of football meets rugby played 360 degrees, and 360 hoop play made basketball look like a walk in the park—all of which were played in zero gravity and watched avidly by the school's sports fans as well as the world when playoffs started.

Lazer, Cashton, and Kyla entered the stadium with their practice gear in hand. Their eyes opened wide, like children at Christmas staring in awe at the massive expanse of captured space.

"One hundred and four million cubic feet of sheer volume, a total of three hundred million enclosed, gravity free, square feet. It's beyond amazing. That means it's one hundred and eight feet wide and one hundred and twenty feet high of awesomeness," Cashton said.

"Look at those arches," Kyla said.

"Three hundred feet tall each," Cashton said.

"How do you know all this?" Lazer asked.

"Please, I am a zoccair geek and we are standing in the largest arena in the world," Cashton said proudly.

"What was I thinking," Lazer said, a smile erupted beaming from his face.

They all laughed. *It felt like the old days*, Lazer thought.

They moved onto the ground field of bright green artificial turf. All walked proudly wearing their practice uniforms made in the Tosadae colors of creamy white and ox blood maroon and emblazoned with the Tosadae emblem—a double winged golden circle and at its center, the soft white Gnorb of Mu.

As first-year rookies, Lazer knew they had an ice cube's chance in hell of getting off the bench and into a real game, but these days Lazer didn't care about games. Practice could more than distract him from his thoughts of home for a few hours every day and that would help keep him sane.

Lazer was just about to make one last point on the dome when suddenly he stopped dead in his tracks. Lazer stared ahead at something that seemed to slow time and make everything around him vanish: a girl—a walking vision, with eyes as blue as a summer sky and hair that rivaled the soft gold of a winter sun. Her body was tall and willowy, with curves in all the right places and legs that went on forever. Lazer tried to breathe, but even the air had ceased to exist. Cashton and Kyla moved forward talking and taking no notice that Lazer had stopped. The girl seemed strangely familiar and yet so ethereal and unknowable to him. As she drew closer, he found himself compelled to say something, though for the life of him, not a single word came to mind. He stopped when his vision of perfection smiled, turned, and crossed to hug a well-built, fourth-year cadet who happened to be wearing the captain's patch for the Tosadae varsity zoccair team. She smiled and his heart raced.

"Universal God!" Cashton said, when he saw the object of Lazer's stare and crossed back to his friend. "I have seen the light and it will lead me to heaven. Hurt me!"

Kyla shoved them both. "She will. Or perhaps you're talking about Bo Rambo, head of varsity."

"Maybe he's her brother," Lazer said hopefully.

"If that's her brother, I'm her daddy," Cashton said. "Come to Papa."

"*Seriously*," Kyla said and all but rolled her eyes. "She's been spliced. Nobody's that perfect. The brother, on the other hand, who is actually not her brother, is varsity captain, head striker, and the number-one choice for Tosadae's Politia Flight Team. His name is Roberto Rambo, Bo to his friends, which you are not. They dated in high school and it looks to me like he's staking claim again."

"I know her," Lazer said, still in a daze.

"I had that dream too," Cashton said.

"Stop," said Kyla.

"I swear I know her from somewhere. I just can't remember," Lazer said, struggling to remember.

"I'm telling you, you met her in my dreams. Cause she's there 24/7," Cashton said and grinned.

"Wait? What happened to Donna Elise?" Kyla asked Cashton. "Isn't she the love of your life?"

"She hasn't been exactly faithful," Cashton growled.

"How would you even know . . .," Kyla stopped herself. "Cashton, you didn't?"

"Well, it worked."

"You put the infamous, Cashton Lock E-3 box in her room and eavesdropped?" Kyla was astonished. "What if she finds out?"

"She'd have to break the cute little doll I gave her or at least poke out its eyes and rip the transmitters out of her little ears."

"Cashton, this is not the same E-3 box from eighth grade?" Kyla said as they sat to gear up.

"Yep. Back then it was only video and audio electronics that acted as my remote eyes and ears—espionage eyes and ears—hence the name E-3," Cashton said with a mischievous grin that spread across his face.

"What's her name?" Lazer said. He ignored Cashton and Kyla's discussion. His eyes were locked on this vision he'd found, this light inside the darkness of his prison walls.

The big entry doors to the stadium slid open. All the players picked up their equipment bags and moved down the wide metal corridors that led to the field. The playing field loomed beyond the entry ramps through massive doors that hinged open like the great gaping jaws of a futuristic beast. Lazer looked back to catch another glimpse of the beautiful apparition that had fallen from the heavens and taken human form.

"Kyla," Lazer nudged her. "I know you know her name."

"Oh, yeah, Miss Vyber, blog queen has all the digi-data," Cashton chided.

"Her name is Elana Blue," Kyla huffed, rolling her eyes at Lazer's obvious infatuation. "I met her the day you guys got attacked on the transport. We stole a shuttle together to get to the port. Cheney Renfroe says she's supposed to be a witch with a capital B. First year, but half her classes are year two so I didn't bother to make friends."

"Brains and beauty! Maybe I could show her my electro-retinal imaging thought transfer . . .," Cashton started to say proudly.

"No!" Both Lazer and Kyla responded simultaneously.

"If you blind her, I guarantee she won't like you," Kyla said with a dig.

"Hey! It could work!"

"I heard she's an empath," Kyla said, ignoring Cashton and throwing in the rest of the gossip.

"Clones are empaths," Lazer said.

"I rest my case," Kyla added.

"You stole a shuttle with her?" Lazer asked.

Kyla walked away without responding.

"And stop reading me." Lazer watched Elana Blue walk through the players' box with Bo then make her way up into the stands to watch the practice. Bo turned, spotted Lazer, and glared. His eyes were level and cold with a look intended to intimidate. It worked.

Lazer knew Bo Rambo, who had been the golden boy of the Tosadae Pilot Training Program, had heard an ongoing litany about the freshman boy wonder named Cole Lazerman, whose brilliant skills had saved the Tosadae transport from the Black Guard, with no weapons. Lazer had become a rival for his title in the cockpit, whether Lazer knew it or not. Bo glared a bit longer at his adversary. It was akin to marking territory. He had big plans to decimate him in the only other area where he stood uncontested as top gun—the zoccair field.

Lazer, Cashton, and Kyla moved onto the playing field. Lazer's eyes stayed locked on Elana Blue. Bo saw the object of Lazer's attention and shot him another look. He was varsity and Lazer was not. This was a practice game, which meant he, Cashton, Kyla, and the rest of the rookies were about to be used for fish chum to feed the sharks.

At that moment Elana Blue turned and looked at Lazer. The second their eyes connected, the feeling that shot through him went beyond logic, place, and time. He could see in her eyes that she knew him. It was as if they'd met before. But when? Where? He felt it too. But there was more. Some unexplainable kinetic force surged through them both. It felt like a magnet. He felt it pull him forward. Lazer started walking. He couldn't think. He could only release to this warm energy course that called him to her. It had happened a little the first moment they saw each other across the crowded transport station the day he landed. But there were so many people and so much excitement and chaos. But this time the air was clear and it, whatever it was, was happening again. In that moment, everyone and everything around them disappeared. She started to walk to him until a very large varsity player stepped between them and broke the flow. Lazer moved faster and then over the loud speaker he heard his name.

"Cole Lazerman," the coach called out. "Please come to the players' box."

12

HANDS OF POWER

DUCANE COVAX PACED like a caged animal. He shook with rage, furious, trapped, a prisoner in his own domain, held captive by his own creation. Pi stood nearby, sorting through the piles of scattered micro disks and broken furniture that had once been Covax's private research lab. The room had been ransacked.

"He can't do this to me," he hissed to himself and slammed what remained of his intercom. "Five! Respond, you worthless piece of . . ."

Before he could finish his tirade, the door slid open. A very different Five entered the room. He was still the metallic biodroid that stood taller than most men, but the smooth particles that formed his head were reconfiguring, first into a mouth and now into what could only be described as a human face—the merest holographic suggestion of eyes, nose, and mouth. Two gray eyes blinked awkwardly at Covax.

"How dare you override my . . ." Covax ignored the anomaly.

"I need my army," Five interrupted. The ghostly lips, formed by the shifting particles, moved out of sync with the words.

"No!" Covax barked.

"No?" Five said.

Covax watched the floating features on Five's holographic face as they blinked back with an awkward, crooked expression of what looked like surprise. Then Covax saw a flash of anger. Five was struggling to control the strange array of new emotions that percolated beneath his holographic face. It was easy to see that the connection between feeling and emotional expression was challenging at best.

"I won't allow you to reprogram my peacekeepers into your butchers. Now give me your vitality bands," Covax commanded.

Five raised his metal fingers and projected a pulse of energy that slammed into Covax. This time, it was as if a thousand volts of electricity stabbed into his body. Covax went into a grand mal seizure; every muscle in his body cramped and twitched in full spasm. The voltage racked his body for a full ten seconds before Five released him and Covax crashed to the floor.

"No."

Again Five's face reflected only a hint of emotion, an expression of humor at Covax's frail defiance. "The mutants have already joined us, and many of the clones believe I will succeed. They come each day by the hundreds to join our forces."

"You can defeat the Atlantians, but it will take an army of biodroids to crush the politia," Covax spoke with confidence, using what strength he had to drag himself up from the floor.

"With or without you, I will succeed," Five said, with cool arrogance. It hung just beneath the calm and confident tone with which he spoke, but it was there as clearly as if he had shouted in Covax's face.

"Not . . . without an army," Covax fought the residual waves of pain. He pulled himself up onto what had been the corner of his research table.

The particles of Five's face shifted, swirling like desert sand caught in a tiny sirocco. They formed and shaped themselves into a mouth, an eye, a nose, flickering in and out like a cheap holographic projection with bad reception.

"I have begun to decode the data our biodroids discovered from the first Gnorb. It holds more than you humans could have ever imagined. Even without the genetic lock, it is eager to give me its knowledge." Five's half-formed eyes looked at Covax. There was a long pause before he added, "I will make a trade. Join me, Dr. Covax, and I will give you Atlantia on a platter with all its land, power, and wealth, in exchange for the binary codes."

Covax blinked. Who was this being to think that it could give him anything? He considered the arrogance and asked: "And the humans? Will this perfect new world of yours have humans?"

"If we are accepted and left in peace. I have no quarrel with you or them." Five smiled awkwardly, evading the ultimate answer.

A disembodied voice echoed in Covax's mind. *There will be no humans if the biodroids win.* It was as real a possibility to Covax as if it had already occurred. He knew this to be true because Five was part of him. Five's DNA, unlike the rest of the Series IV, was his DNA, and it carried all the dark thoughts Covax had suppressed for years. His anger at his betrayal, the cruelty of his exile, his hatred for what had been stolen from him—dignity, fame, and adoration. These were his blackest thoughts and, somehow, when he gave Five his DNA, they had been transferred from the recesses of his mind into Five's. It was true he had wished for the death of all humanity—a wish made in tears during his lonely exile. It was his own anger that echoed back to him beneath Five's words.

13

HISTORY OF THE WORLD

LAZER CONTACTED HIS MOTHER as often as he could without making her crazy. But it wasn't the calls that got to her; it was his constant inquiry about what was going on in Atlantia. Had there been more attacks? Had the underground militia begun to form? Who was helming it? Where were they stationed? Detra had not been forthcoming with any information because there wasn't much to give. Everything was quiet on the surface and, Universal God willing, it would stay that way. Detra shared only that life in Atlantia trudged on with little or nothing out of the ordinary to report. So Lazer counted the days and tried to act as if being at Tosadae had a purpose.

Classes were in high gear and Lazer was carrying a full load. Each day he would tell himself to focus, that it would make the months pass more quickly until his preliminary passage rites. The final Rite of Passage wouldn't be for three years, but primary was in six months and that at least would get him certified. Certified was what he had promised his mother. He begged time to go by faster. But nothing except his fantasies about Elana Blue could sway his thought away from Atlantia and all the pain and promise it held, and Elana was unattainable. He completed mountains of homework. His only other escape was sleep, which he fell into each night when exhaustion overtook him. But even that gave no respite from the nightmares. The attack on the mines played over and over in his tormented sleep with a hundred different scenarios, all ending in disaster. He asked himself again and again, *What could I have done differently?* He never came up with an answer that erased his guilt. His conscious mind knew the past was unchangeable, but his unconscious mind did not. Relentlessly, the nightmares persisted.

Time crept by and Lazer fell into the monotony of daily life. His teachers were interesting and he enjoyed learning, especially battle techniques and basic splicing, but there was still one class that hadn't started: Masta Lia Poe's Visionistic Arts. Only a select few, the *crème de la crème*, were even considered, and *never* a first-year cadet. Lazer didn't know why he had been chosen, and until today—the first day of class—he really didn't care. Still, the stories of the great Masta Poe had intrigued him and he was excited by the idea of all that he could learn from her.

His Monday/Wednesday/Friday first period class was with Kyla: "The Age of Light, History of a Brave New World." An ancient professor named Markus Rothstein, with his shock of silver hair and still classically handsome features, taught it. He looked to Lazer as though he had personally lived through the global transition and had been ready for his new body implant for at least a decade. Professor Rothstein had watery eyes and multiple allergies, so sneezes and symphonic nose blowing usually accompanied lectures.

In the first few weeks of class, they had gone over the basics. Dr. Rothstein had done a dramatic show-and-tell, using an immersive holo-projection that played out in graphic detail, to show how a few years before the Mayan calendar ended, on a crisp, clear winter day in December, the planet Earth was quietly caught and pulled into the gravitational forces of true galactic alignment. Earth's orbit did not change,

but the world shifted off its axis so slightly that no one realized the sub-
tlety of the change, except Mother Nature. Slowly, methodically, the
planet began its seventeen-year transformation. The first degree of shift
brought relentless rainstorms and hurricanes. The next two-degree twist
wrenched the tectonic plates, cracked the spine of three continents, and
hammered the planet into global chaos.

"Over the next ten years," Rothstein had said, pointing to the
images as they unfolded, "an enormous land mass was belched up
from the ocean floor, a leviathan-sized territory that divided the North
Atlantic Sea into narrow watery straits. The displaced water formed
tsunamis, which rose up like an army of giant hands and slammed
against the jagged shores of Europe and Africa, as well as both South
and North America. Mountainous lands emerged and divided what
was once Central America from what remained of the United States.
Africa split in two. Asia and Europe fissured, splitting into seven separate regions."

Lazer's favorite lectures covered the chapters that told how vast
portions of South America were liquefied and vanished, while massive sections of the remaining lands, whose intricate root systems still
anchored the Amazonian rain forest, were sucked down whole to the
bottom of the sea. Ten years into global shifts, not far off the coast
of Japan's North Pacific Sea, a continent once thought to be only an
ancient Asian myth, called Mu, erupted from the sea. Like its sister
provinces that had risen in the Atlantic, Mu became part of this changing world. Both territories had been inhabited eons before by Earth's
first inhabitants, the Celians. Located on each of the newly risen continents, buried in silt and coral formations, explorers found fantastic
pristine cities made from unknown metals and filled with a collection
of marvelous mysteries waiting to be solved. Twenty-three years later,
true north was located at the center of what had been Nova Scotia.
The equator no longer ran through the Congo, Indonesia, and northern
Brazil. Antarctica laboriously drifted inside what had been the Tropic of

Cancer, melting into great fertile regions, while cities like New York and most of northern Europe froze into icy wonderlands.

The computer-generated graphics and eight-point surround sound system made the presentations into heart-stopping events. Rothstein showed them geologically how, over the course of those life-changing years, the planet cracked, jerked, and rumbled as it must have when, in the Paleozoic Era, Gondwana, then Pangaea split and redefined the first ancient supercontinents. But it was the Great Quakes that caused the recent continental shifts of this ever-changing planet, which redefined the modern world at the speed of a galactic breath. He took their imaginations on a journey of what must have been a horrendous time when continuous upheavals, pounding quakes, and unnatural storms caused by the shifting lands, waters, wind, and weather patterns terrified the humans and animals that were clever or lucky enough to survive. Swollen rivers and oceans swallowed whole shorelines and erased cities. And then, when the planets completed their galactic passing, Earth fell silent. One by one, the remnants of mankind crawled from their hiding places, desperate to rebuild their lives.

"It was in those dark years that the surviving billion or so members of the population overcame the terror and destruction that had forever changed the world and, for the first time in history, unified under a common good: the survival of humanity," Rothstein had said, with tears in his eyes.

The students were assigned reports. Kyla had given an amazingly intelligent report of how people toiled together to find the remnants of global businesses and technology and used the corporate networks and infrastructures to bind into a global people. From the depths of that unfathomable darkness and despair, humanity joined together, conquered all, and stepped into the Age of Light.

"Time began again in the Age of Light," the professor interrupted Kyla's report and reminded them that it wasn't until 48 A.Q. when history began to be recorded again.

Kyla continued, explaining how pockets of humanity pulled themselves up from the chaos and used what remained of the old to create brilliant new and innovative technologies. Six executives from the global corporate conglomerates met to discuss how to use their infrastructure to save themselves and, ultimately, mankind. They represented the most vital needs—food, clothing, transportation, communication, finance, and energy. (Rothstein's early work in finance had defined many of the global monetary laws that were still in use.) These global giants understood that if they didn't act quickly, civilization would fall into the abyss of a dark and apocalyptic end. In this time of greatest need, the corporations created an alliance and used their global infrastructure and product resources to link the world together through internal communication networks of their world offices. The corporate leaders and the Svalbard Global Seed Bank began reseeding the planet with non-genetically modified seeds free of any toxic herbicides for a better life. Those companies were shut down if they still existed at all. The seeds were of such diversity that they fed, clothed, and cared for anyone who would work to help rebuild civilization. Everything was plant based: food, clothing, and fuel

As Lazer listened to Kyla, he had found it almost unfeasible how, within a few short years, hospitals, homes, schools, and businesses had sprung up around the world and the corporate leaders of the "Big Six" became the voice of a unified world. When individual governments tried to step in and take over, the people of Earth unanimously said *no*. The Big Six installed a triumvirate ruling body and empowered them in the name of one Universal God to create the laws that would define a new society. The Triumvirate gathered the best elements from a variety of governments that bound them to righteousness and a belief in shared knowledge, and went on to establish a consciousness based on global equality and the world's collective humanity. Together they rebuilt the world, tapping into the farthest reaches of imagination, technology, and scientific ability.

Lazer's report had been on the unification of global resources and the physical changes that had allowed civilization to take enormous leaps forward. Humanity doubled the speed of technological and scientific discoveries. One hundred years previous, humanity had, in the blink of a cosmic eye, brought the world from the Industrial Age into the Information Age, creating in a few decades what had not been achieved in the millennia that preceded them. Inspired by past successes, mankind conceived a new future and celebrated a new kind of genius. No one could ignore the results of the genetic manipulation that had been explored in legal and illegal hot spots all around the globe. Over the years before and after the Great Quakes, a wide and fascinating variety of new species had been born that would forever be a part of Earth's new future.

"And we welcome them and revere them for their great contributions," Rothstein said.

Kyla and a few other splicers and clones that spotted the class had sat up a little straighter and prouder.

"So," the professor concluded after Lazer's report, "while mankind filled the brave new world with hope and peace and searched the boundaries of knowledge, technology, and nature, science created and enhanced plant and animal life forms, all in the name of a better world—a world where hunger and war did not exist. The ultimate goal was to exist in unified peace."

"That didn't exactly happen. Did it, sir?" Lazer interjected.

Rothstein liked Lazer. He liked his passion for learning.

"Not exactly," he smiled and blew his nose, which made the class laugh. "For nearly one hundred years, all went according to plan. The few wars and minor altercations around the globe that erupted were immediately suppressed, thanks to the politia. I congratulate all of you who are here for that reason," Rothstein said, giving the honored V salute.

This time it was Lazer and the other cadets who had sat taller in their seats.

Near the end of the fourth week, Kyla had asked Professor Rothstein about the prophecy film that had been found decaying in some film archives in the lower regions of Covax City. Rothstein promised to bring a copy he had procured to the next class—today's.

The class was packed full, for many students had heard about this mysterious cult film, but few had seen this celluloid movie that had been made just after the turn of the twenty-first century, called "Days of Future Past." It foretold of Earth's shift, the reorganization of the world's land masses, and the death of billions. It also told of man's most ingenious and unique creation: ten-foot tall, silly-looking robots that an Einstein-type scientist with bug eyes and a crooked nose had created. The robots rose up with plans to destroy the humans, who, of course, fought back. As the armies of men and the armies of the robots faced each other for the defining battle, a single soldier was sent out from both sides. The humans sent a boy into battle; the robots sent their biggest and fiercest warrior. Like David and Goliath, they prepared to fight to the death. The little movie abruptly stopped and Professor Rothstein told the class that the ending was lost.

Lazer and Kyla looked at each other.

"We probably lost. That's why they destroyed the ending," Kyla said with a smile.

"It was a bad movie and nobody cared what happened to the creepy, ugly people," Lazer whispered back, making her laugh.

"This was our tomorrow," Professor Rothstein said, with his ancient voice quivering. It was his favorite phrase and he said it at the end of every class. Then he snorted, blew his nose, and assigned three chapters to read, which he downloaded to everyone's wristsponder before he dismissed the class with a final blow of his nose.

Lazer and Kyla met Cashton for lunch in JR Kelly Hall, named after one of the leading founders and great biomass alternative fuel pioneers of the twenty-first century. Kelly Hall fed the majority of students on campus. Each student, through an almost instantaneous process, had their exact nutritional needs and dietary requirements deciphered and were served the appropriate meal. The hall was a vast cavernous space drenched in the warmth and glow of natural light. The sun's rays fell from the circular windows that lined the great arched ceiling and criss-crossed the hall; as the sun crossed the sky, long beams of light moved across the floor like spotlights. The hall always smelled of fresh bread and cookies, but the machines that dispensed the school's meal plan carried little that resembled anything that had once been alive. Lack of flavor was a sore spot that the new administration had vowed to correct. There were other restaurants around the Tosadae campus with better tasting food, but for fast, cheap, and nutritious meals, Kelly Hall was the place to go.

Over lunch, Lazer, Cashton, and Kyla compared notes, talked politics, and dissed whichever teacher was giving them the most grief. Lazer's wristsponder vibrated. He was late for the one class he was actually excited about. He jumped to his feet, stuffed his face with the last of his lunch, grabbed his pack, and raced out the door. Kyla and Cashton wished him luck, both of them wishing they were joining him. *Maybe next year.*

15

SERENDIPITY

LAZER RAN ACROSS CAMPUS, weaving through the slower students with the grace of a downhill skier. He did his best to remember the shortest route to the one special class that started later in the semester than the rest. This was the class he had been waiting for and he was sure it would be his most exciting: Masta Lia Poe's Visionistic Arts. That fact that he'd gotten in was a perplexing miracle. The fact that he was late would be inexcusable, and now, to make matters worse, he was lost. Lazer slowed down and looked around at the unfamiliar buildings of the west campus. These were the upper-class buildings and he was a first-year student.

Still walking, he called up the global positioning systems that were part of every wristsponder and commanded the directions.

"Directions from here to the VA complex, Tosadae, Mu, Earth," he said.

A series of holographic lines lifted from his wrist and projected in front, to the side, and behind him taking the shape of a three-dimensional sphere with Lazer standing at the center. Within seconds, a map formed before his eyes calculating the precise coordinates and showing him a detailed layout of the west campus. Lazer watched as red lines reached forward guiding him down a series of twisting pathways. He looked out to the farthest point and saw the path that would take him across the commons and directly to the Visionistic Arts and Powers Building. Excited by his newfound information, he neglected to turn off the holograph and he took off running. Lazer was in a full stride and completely focused as he followed the complicated visuals that blocked portions of his view leaving him all but blind to anything beyond the projected images of his map. With a crack, he body slammed hard into someone. He felt the smack of the collision and instinctively reached to grab whatever or whoever was moving downward with him through space. Lazer could feel the other body press warm and firm against his own. The momentum of the fall thrust out of control by the forward motion. Something made Lazer reach out and encircle the person with his arms to protect them from being hurt. He could sense the ground getting closer and in the last moment, twisted them both around to make sure he hit the ground first and she fell on top of him. His last thought being his body would break the other person's fall. They crashed hard and tumbled over the ground. The impact scattered their possessions every which way. They came to rest on the grass that was softer than the concrete that bit into his back. He felt the person fall on top of him and then everything stopped. Mortified, Lazer opened his clenched eyes to find that his face was inches away from the most enticing pair of feminine eyes he'd ever seen in his life. His breath mingled with hers as reality rushed in. This was no ordinary student he'd accidently tackled, it was Elana Blue! Lazer panicked and jumped to his feet with the speed of a gazelle evading a lion, but without the grace.

"I'm so sorry. Are you okay?" he offered her a hand.

After looking at the tear in her tunic, she took his hand and let him pull her up. He lost his grip and she fell again. He offered his hand again.

"It helps to look where you're going," Elana said, though this time she ignored his hand and stood up on her owe.

"Yes. I mean, no. I mean . . . I'm so sorry," he finally managed to say.

"You said that."

"Right. Yes. Are you okay?" Lazer asked as he gathered her belongings from the ground.

"You said that too," she said and took the items from his hands.

Lazer stared at her with absolute awe, fighting the barrage of emotions that pummeled him—sad, wonderful, horrible, incredible—all ending in embarrassment.

"I don't suppose we could start over?" Lazer pleaded.

She looked him up and down. Despite his awkwardness, he *was* cute and he was the infamous boy hero. She knew the story of how he'd rescued the transport and saved a thousand students. She knew the story as well as every student on campus and most people in the world. His name and likeness, however, had been withheld from the press, but his bravery was still the buzz. She'd seen him at zoccair practice as well a few times but this connection had taken her into his aura. She knew if she could have read his aura, she could read his thoughts. There was something else, something strangely familiar about him that she couldn't place. She'd felt it from the first time she saw him at the transport and each time at the zoccair field. She chalked it up to a new face around campus, and let it go.

"You could pretend I didn't bump into you," he said.

"I don't think so," she said as she turned and walked away. "Unless time travel is one of your abilities." She glanced back and gave him only the slightest flash of a smile.

That smile was all he needed. Lazer loped after her, falling into her stride. "Have we met before?" He flashed his most charming smile.

Elana Blue didn't answer. His voice had a familiar ring to it. *Yes,* she thought, *we've met before, but where?* She said nothing and kept walking. Elana prayed he wasn't somebody who knew her from the few times she was allowed out on Atlantia. She had been privately tutored her whole life to protect her from the press and the negative side of her father's reputation. Covax had even changed her official name for school from Covax to Blue to ensure her anonymity.

"Fair enough. Anything I say will just bury me deeper. Right? So, if you could just tell me where . . ." He had forgotten where he was going. He checked the wristsponder, "Masta Lia Poe's Visionistic Arts class is?"

Elana Blue stopped, eyeing him as if he actually existed. "How did you get into Masta Poe's class?"

Gotcha, he thought. Lazer shrugged. "Is that a yes? Or are you planning to let me arrive so late I make a complete fool of myself with everyone else?"

"You'll do that fine on your own," she said.

Elana Blue liked him. She'd liked him from the moment she saw him at the transport station. The memory pulled at her again. A hazy fog of something, but no matter how hard she tried, it wouldn't reveal itself.

"Follow me. We're both going to be late if we don't hurry."

They walked in silence around the circle path that led to the Visionistic Arts and Powers Building. As they walked, Lazer stole clandestine glances at this vision who'd been haunting him for weeks; her lashes, her lips, her skin, the curve of her shoulder, the way the sun shimmered in her hair. He was captivated. He wanted to speak, say something nice and smart, but nothing coherent came into his mind to translate into words.

He looked up at the Visionistic Arts and Powers Building. It was truly the crown jewel of Tosadae, with its towering, elliptical panels that curved, twisted, and folded open like a flower offering itself to the new day. The panels turned to catch the rays of the Sun as the Earth moved and gave power, heat, and light to the building. The Visionistic Arts and

Powers Building was a gift from the Celians who'd left it behind long before the dinosaurs walked the planet Earth.

"So, how did *you* get into Visionistic Arts?" she asked. Her words were more emphatic than mere curiosity.

"What?" Lazer asked.

"You're a freshman, aren't you?" she asked.

"So are you," he said with a shrug as they reached the building. "How did *you* get in?" Lazer neared for the door.

Elana Blue looked at him with those magical blue eyes and raised her hand pointing toward the door. Using a pulse of magnetic energy, she sent a wave that he could see emanating from her fingers like heat thermals. The waves reached out and the metal door hinged open on its own. "I was invited."

Lazer was stunned.

"Don't make me hold it forever. Go in." She tilted her head as tresses of flaxen hair slipped across her cheek.

Lazer entered. "Impressive."

"Yeah," she said playfully.

They moved quickly across the entrance.

"I can't do any tricks," Lazer said, then instantly regretted the words that still hung in the air.

"It's not a trick; it's a power," she replied. "If you're here, Masta Poe knows you're capable."

"Then she knows more than I do about me. Her syllabus did say all humans are capable," Lazer replied.

"Genetically yes. Only the ones who aren't too lazy or afraid to do the needed work. It's all about remembering your powers," Elana said.

They entered the foyer and more so than the exterior, the title of Visionistic Arts and Powers Building suited its alien design, with long spiraling corridors that flowed to the various classrooms. Each room had large elliptical doorways built into the walls of the corridor off a system of bending hallways that somehow always lead logically to the center most lecture hall. No matter which way you turned all the hallways ended at the central auditorium. It was impossible to get lost. Lazer thought the design was awe-inspiring.

He glanced down and saw the floor was made of a transparent substance that had been built over a tributary of the Silent River. The main river ran peacefully by Tosadae and this lovely little tributary allowed a variety of aquatic creatures to swim and crawl beneath the students' feet.

Lazer walked beside Elana, still stealing glances whenever he could as they made their way up the entry isles. Whenever she caught him staring, he pretended to look at the messages and notices emitting from the walls. The ever-changing notices were written in various shades of colored lights that told of special concerts, events, exhibits, and lectures to be held in the VAP auditorium over the next few months. Lazer did his best to look deeply interested in the information, but he found himself enamored by her. He was captivated by the scent that drifted in Elana Blue's wake. She smelled of the sea and a spice that seemed both familiar and exotic at once. He liked the way the colorful hues from the refracted message lights reflected off her skin and hair.

They reached the main lecture hall. Again, with the slightest, graceful motion she gestured and the door swung open to her command. It held for Lazer.

"Better hurry. You don't want to be late for your first day," she said over her shoulder as she rushed past Lazer to grab a seat.

Lazer watched her go. His heart pounded inside his chest with the patter of thick summer rain. He smiled and released an unintentional, audible sigh and a thin girl giggled understanding the object of his motivation. Embarrassed, he looked away and only then fully noticed where he was. Lazer stood at the second center tier of the lecture arena. It was a theater in the round, with a thousand seats that rose in graceful tiers to the top. Above, a dome crowned the top of the arena. Encircling the dome, a ring of multicolored, oddly shaped windows that looked like faceted jewels. Lazer watched as the sunlight spilled through and painted the floor in precise, geometrical shapes made of rainbow colors. Without thinking, a mathematical formula filled his mind. It had been designed to represent a variable; a numerical calculation of the projected geometric shapes. His eyes drifted to the center of the arena; a large naked stage anchored the room. The vast room was almost empty and on the large stage sat about thirty students speaking quietly among themselves. They, Lazer guessed, were the select few who qualified to sit at the literal feet of the brilliant prophetess, Masta Poe. Lazer was sure it had to be a fluke of scheduling that had brought him here. He and two hundred additional students filled the first few rows. *Why the need for such a huge arena for so few students?* he thought.

Lazer made his way down the stairs and sat next to Elana Blue. He couldn't help himself. He liked being near her. He liked her scent, the way her skin glowed a warm blushing pink, and how her lips pouted when she went into deep thought. He was smitten. He gathered his courage, took a breath, and just as he was about to speak, the entire room of students stood and began to applaud. Lazer, caught by the surprise of the moment, jumped to his feet not having a clue as to why other than that Masta Lia Poe must have entered the room. It was just that he hadn't seen her actually enter, she was simply there.

Masta Poe stood center stage and all eyes were on here. Lazer studied her. Masta Lia Poe was a high-bred splicer, more human that her genetics revealed, born into the treacherous, underground labyrinths of the Fissure Forests some twenty years after the Great Quakes. Many of the early clones and splicers had been illegally created in those labs and killed before the world could see the freak experiments scientists were creating, but Masta Poe was the daughter of one of the rarest and most wondrous anomalies—Tinga.

MASTA LIA POE'S MOTHER was the first successful splicer and the model for all future generations. Her name was Tinga. She was created in vitro and born in a controlled environment made of countless, hermetically sealed rooms deep under a secret lab somewhere beneath the great expanse of Los Angeles, California. Tinga had been created in a Petri dish, half-human and half-gibbon monkey, and was birthed from an artificial womb as an albino with blinding white skin, silver hair, and pale, purple eyes. When she was only seven months old, her creators discovered some of Tinga's amazing abilities—kinetics, telepathy, the manifestation of complete objects from thin air, and a few paranormal talents that insured she would be kept alive. She was a highly intelligent, living specimen fated to be probed, prodded, and studied. Tinga spent her early childhood in a glass cubical with a few objects and no people to comfort her. She was constantly tested by the scientists who created her. They came and saw her day and night looking at her as nothing more than a very special, glorified white rat. Then, at the age of seven, even though completely sequestered from the world, she calmly prophesied the first tectonic upheavals, floods, and storms that began to escalate in the first three decades of the twenty-first century, building and culminating into the last and most devastating of what would become known as the Great Quakes.

Only one person believed her warnings—a handsome young scientist named Doctor Dean Lee Chopin. Because of his wisdom and relentless tenacity, at least a portion of South America survived its decent to the bottom of the sea. To the very second, she accurately predicted the pull of Earth off its axis caused by the cataclysmic forces that changed the world as humans knew it. But the violent eruptions, in all their terror, turned out to be the key that set her free. The day of the greatest of the quakes, the eruption lasted thirty-seven minutes. It was felt on every continent and changed the face of Earth. Tinga closed her eyes and quietly meditated as her building was sucked below the surface. Those who did not know what she knew panicked, and many died of sheer terror and stupidity as the dirt around and below her entire building was swallowed whole, sinking straight down into a muddy abyss. The balance and narrow, linear structure of the building, thirty stories high and thirty stories below ground, is what saved them. As the ground vibrated faster and faster, it liquidated the dirt turning it to quicksand and the weight of the building dragged them straight down like a free-fall roller coaster plummeting under until they reached bedrock and slammed to a stop. They were buried alive, but they were alive. The lab that held Tinga and the others of her kind were designed to be totally self-sufficient in case of infection and the Plexiglas rooms protected their inhabitants. The final jolt when they hit rock bottom broke the locks on almost every splicer's door. After years of imprisonment Tinga was miraculously free. Free to spend, with those who'd survived, the rest of her life living in the twisting labyrinths of tunnels, caves, and caverns of the newly formed underground world.

There was a fight Lazer remembered reading about in high school. Splicers against the surviving humans who refused to admit life as they knew it was changed forever. In the end, all would come together. The humans needed the splicers for their telekinetic powers and the splicers needed the humans for their technology. So that banded them together. Once they got out of the building, they discovered underground root forests, rivers with strange fish, and vast lakes. They lived in caves, illuminated by glowing algae and warmed by thermal pools. They hunted for food and water in the dark surrounding forests of living tree roots and ate the strange, exotic vegetation that thrived on the artificial lights and plants left by the scientists.

Tinga was their leader. She was not alone. She spent the first twenty years of her youth caring and being cared for by her human teacher and friend, Dean Lee Chopin, a brilliant physicist and a passionate philosopher. She had saved his life that fateful day, protecting him from the splicers who had been freed by the quake and wanted all humans destroyed for the pain they had inflicted. Tinga had convinced them of Chopin's goodness and they had granted him life on the condition she and Chopin live apart from the others.

They found a series of small caves at the edge of the root forest and made their home there. They cut the biogenetically engineered vegetation that grew uncontrolled over the destroyed labs, warmed by the constant glow of the halogen grow lights that spilled from the wreckage. She learned quickly which plants had been enhanced by the humans and were deadly, and which were rich in vitamins and minerals. Numerous plants, which had been meticulously bioengineered to grow without sunlight, covered the dark cave walls; vines and roots hung like primitive, living stalactites. Blooming phosphorescent nubs illuminated the blackness every six hours with their eerie shades of lavender, red, and pale green. Thanks to the miracles of science, Tinga grew healthy and happy, focusing on the strange and fascinating joys that filled her new life.

Tinga and Chopin found water and grew food and herbs for medicine. She cared for his wounds and nursed his aging body. In return, the great philosopher and physicist taught her everything he knew. He became her mentor and she his greatest love. Together they explored her amazing gifts of telepathy and manifestation, creating the foundation for what would become the Visionistic Arts. For thirty years, Tinga Poe and Dean Chopin lived together in their dim, dank caves with their love for one another as the only warmth to comfort them.

Chopin died and Tinga Poe was left with the one gift she had begged for: a child. Tinga gave birth to a beautiful baby girl and named her Masta Lia Poe. Masta resembled her mother in almost every way, right down to her lavender eyes and silvery skin. But she also had many of her father's human features, like his height, his hairless face, and long silken hair, which flowed down her back like white fringe. Masta Poe's Visionistic powers surpassed even Tinga's. They lived beneath the phosphorescent moss and spoke to the splicer creatures that ventured out from the deeper regions of the Fissure Forests. Splicers, both wondrous and bizarre, came to gather edible vegetation from the old labs, which had all but vanished beneath the thick undergrowth. Tinga taught Masta Poe how to use her Visionistic powers to manipulate matter, alter time, and read the auras of plants, animals, splicers, and humans. Masta, in turn, taught the children of the surviving splicers what she could of her gifts. The population grew with each passing year. Masta eventually brought her mother back into the splicer community and encouraged her to share her knowledge of herbs and medicines. There, for decades, they lived in peace and happiness beneath the black earth and far from the eyes of men, until the sound of machines grew too loud to ignore. On Masta's birth celebration day, a human construction crew began excavating a site directly above them that would become the world headquarters of Sangelino for the unified planet.

Most of the splicers ran away in fear, but Masta Poe stood her ground. She was ready to meet the humans she had only read about in e-books and seen on ancient DVDs stored inside ancient computers. Construction workers drilled through her cave's ceiling and the first human faces Masta had ever seen stared at her, backlit by the blinding glare of their lights. Rock and soil rained down from above. In her panic, Tinga ignored the avalanche of rocks and, thinking only of Masta's safety, rushed to save her daughter. They struggled toward each other, their hands reaching through the blinding clouds of dust that suffocated them. With only inches between them, time slowed, and every minute detail of their final moments together played out around them. Then, in a hush of silence, everything turned into inky blackness. The next time Masta Poe opened her eyes, she was inside a beautiful hospital room of lavender and white, bathed in a warm, hazy glow that hurt her eyes and made her skin tingle. It would take weeks to open her eyes without squinting in pain, but on that day, for the first time in her life, Masta Poe saw the light of the sun.

Year after year, Masta returned to the excavation site and visited the cold, sterile camps that had been built for the splicers who chose to live on the surface. She searched for but never found her mother. Tinga, who had previously survived the caged cruelty of the humans, had given her life so that her daughter could live in the sun. Masta Poe was grateful for her mother's sacrifice, but witnessed firsthand the hatred, both subtle and overt, humans had for splicers. Her mother's stories of her days in captivity rang sadly true. Masta, though more human than Tinga, was still a splicer. Every day that she drew a breath in the upland world, she felt the sting of intolerance. It was not until the humans discovered Masta's powers that their disdain turned to reverence, for she freely offered to teach them the forgotten secrets of her Visionistic Arts. Only then did they begin to respect and honor her.

In the black years that culminated in the Splicer Fiasco of 93 A.Q., during which so many splicers died at the hands of fearful and intolerant humans, Masta Poe remained courageous. Respect for her grew because of her exceptional powers—powers that came to her as naturally as breathing. Her wondrous abilities to transcend dimensions and manipulate matter, Masta Lia Poe believed, resulted solely from combining human genetics with her mother's primitive genome. This complex mixture heightened her ability to use the deep cosmic memory that flowed in her human brain and connected her to powerful energy sources. The knowledge of these powers is what Tinga had taught her daughter and what she, in turn, would teach her students.

These amazing abilities, she told the young, eager faces that sat before her, were theirs by right of birth, gifted to all humankind, but forgotten and then lost to most of their kind for millennia. Over the centuries, there had been those few who, on their own, had discovered their inner gifts. Great humans like Jesus Christ, Mohammed, Krishna, Moses, Buddha, Leonardo da Vinci, Nostradamus, Albert Einstein, Nikola Tesla, Martin Luther King Jr., and Edgar Cayce, to name a few, had understood and shared their gifts with the world. Others, because of the same exceptional light that they shone out into a dark ignorant world, were persecuted, crucified, tortured, or murdered in the name of some primitive fear or religious dogma designed to control the body, but not to enlighten the spirituality that lived in every soul.

Masta Poe's teachings would return her students to their greatest powers—their very own humanity. The work she did with her students was intense and focused. Only the most dedicated and willing to trust completely could open their souls to the universe, and remember. The simple act of entering into a state of bliss reopened the human mind to these amazing powers that she called the Visionistic Arts.

16

MASTA POE

"IF I TOLD YOU I could show you a way to convert thought into vibration, vibration into energy, and energy into matter, would you want to know how?" Masta Poe said.

Masta Poe shimmered onstage as her voice echoed in from a distant place far offstage. She, in actual physical form, stepped from the lower aisles that led in from the wings and crossed to the illusion she had created. The illusion faded and disappeared.

"What is an illusion and what is real?" she spoke in a deep, husky voice. "Inside the power of the mind, there is no difference, only perception."

Bo Rambo slipped in with one of the other zoccair players, an Asian man named Carel Bell. They used the diversion of Masta Poe's entrance to grab seats next to Elana Blue, hoping their entrance would go unnoticed. It did not.

"If you are late for my class again, Cadets Rambo and Bell, you will find the doors no longer open for you."

Bo and Carel shuffled in their seats. They should have known that nothing went unnoticed by Masta Poe.

"To those of you who have been with me before," she continued, "I pray you come in light. To you newbies, welcome to the Visionistic Arts. Over the next few years, you will learn the primary powers of the human mind. Powers like . . ." Masta Poe pointed to a skinny girl with long, sinewy arms and spider-like features.

The girl returned a high-pitched, rapid-fire response, "Levitation, shielding, telekinesis, pyrokinesis, matter and energy manifestation, mental and physical telepathy, astral projection, teleportation, aura detection, dream shadowing . . ."

"Excellent. Thank you, Lalice. Welcome back," Masta Poe said cutting her off. "We'll let them learn the rest on their own. The 'rest' is a list of powers already in your genetic knowing, deep in your subconscious mind ready to be released, and the 'more' are up to you for they exist in your imaginings. And, by the way your 'What if?' test will be in six weeks."

Masta Poe smiled and gave a nod that made the spidery-limbed girl beam with pride. "Those are only a few of the multitude of powers humans have forgotten over the millennia. Today begins your journey to reclaim them, for they have always been with you, waiting patiently in the recesses of every atom in your body simply to be remembered. For a select few of you, who will reach the ultimate state of BAI; I am honored to be in your presence."

The state of BAI stood for Bliss And I and represented the individual embodiment of the oneness with the universe achieved through a state of pure emotional bliss.

Masta Poe explained how the class worked. There would be labs, research, and practical application. First theory, then application with each other, then defensive training against a variety of creatures and splicers to perfect their survival skills, and finally, the infinite possibilities to manifest into reality whatever the mind could imagine.

Half listening, Lazer's attention was still fixed on Elana Blue. He leaned toward her and was just about to whisper when a voice filled his head. *So, Cadet Lazerman, you have arrived.* Lazer sat straight up in his seat. It sounded as though the voice was all around him. His eyes widened and he looked at the faces of the other students. Hadn't they heard the strange disembodied voice?

If you were paying attention, Lazer, you would know who I am. Lazer looked straight into Masta Poe's lavender eyes. *Welcome to Visionistic Arts. You and I have much to speak about, and you have a great deal of work ahead if you are to be ready for the dangerous path on which you have been chosen to embark.*

Lazer could see Masta Poe's mouth moving, but the words in his head were not the words she spoke. She was across the room, and yet the sound of her voice seemed to whisper into his ears. Lazer looked at Elana Blue. Her attention was on Masta Poe.

Okay, this is too strange, Lazer thought.

Only if you judge it to be so, Masta Poe thought back to him. She was reading his mind.

I . . . I don't understand. Lazer shook his head as if waking from a dream.

This is the first step to your 'knowing,' Lazer. I need to see what you hold in your mind that you do not yet comprehend. Close your eyes and give the visions to me. This time, I will guide you.

Lazer watched Masta Poe as a look of puzzlement filled her face. She tipped the angle of her head and looked at him oddly. Her mouth still moved as she talked to the rest of the class about homework, study groups, and tests.

You have the soul of a hero but, sadly, I see no light in the emotions that guide your path, only a shroud of darkness. Her look shifted from one of questioning to one of concern. *A great darkness surrounds you that you alone must conquer. Look, Lazer, here is the door to what is coming.*

Suddenly, it felt as if some part of her split from the form that held the stage, crossed to him like a great rushing wind, and passed directly through him. *Lazer, take my hand.* Lazer gasped. A rush of terror jolted through his body. "No!" Lazer blurted out loud.

The entire class turned.

For one brief moment, he saw their faces before he stiffened as if a shock of electricity had ripped through his body. His eyes rolled back into his head, his mind screamed out with pain, yet nothing hurt. In a flash of light, he was transported and found himself racing alone down a tunnel-shaped corridor, surrounded by violent winds that slapped his face and ripped at his clothes. The vision whirled around him, as if he were in the eye of a hurricane. He saw a thousand pictures that flashed by in rapid succession, spiraling at light speed, and rushing past in a blur of color. Suddenly one image stopped, peeled itself free, expanded, and hung before him. *Was this his future?* Lazer saw himself—taller, older, and stronger—manning the controls of a fighter. A hail of shattered particles pelted the windshield that arced above him. Hundreds of FX-80 fighters buzzed the sky in aerial combat. He recognized the basic model, but these were different, newer. The fuselage of one of the ships changed from chrome to blue-and-gray camouflage and vanished into the clouds before his eyes. A woman's face inside the next ship screamed out to him, then exploded into flames.

A second image devoured the first, and Lazer saw himself hanging from a cliff. A huge archeop, a wild ten-foot splicer, half-condor/half-Komodo dragon with enormous leathery wings, dove at him, its beak ready to tear into him. A loud whoosh and the next image materialized as a silent shadow. He stood at the edge of a dimly lit hallway. He was alone and confused, with only the howling of wind to fill his ears. Just ahead, he could see a large protius, part-lion/part-bear/part-porcupine, crouched, waiting to pounce. Behind the protius, a man stepped from the shadows into the light. Just before his face was revealed, Lazer was swept into another group of images. He stood in a great void, and across from him stood a young woman with thick, honey blond hair. Her back was turned. Her hair blew in the torrent of wind that whipped at them. The girl turned to face him. In her hand was a weapon that dripped a black liquid. She stared at him with sad and frightened turquoise eyes. Just as she called out to him, he was whisked away.

More images rushed by with the intensity of a train at light speed—frantic flickering images that melted into ribbons of light, strobing and flashing until everything dissolved around him. Lazer stood in the middle of a massive battle. He looked down to see he was standing on sparkling purple sand. In his hand, he held the Orbis Gnorb. The immense field of purple sand was ringed by thick vegetation so bizarre and alien he knew he had to have been transported to another world. He spun around and the blur of images once again encircled him. When he stopped, he was in the middle of a great war: tens of thousands of beings—humans, creatures, droids—battled in every direction above him. Lazer was a witness—an invisible voyeur observing the carnage. A series of brilliant explosions ripped into the landscape, each blast building into a chaotic frenzy, faster and more intense, until everything climaxed in a blinding flash of pure white light. Lazer shielded his eyes and, in an instant, everything went black.

In the classroom, Lazer's body jumped and jolted. He gasped, fainted, and crumpled onto the ground with a thud.

Masta Poe showed no emotion. She looked at Lazer. *You are safe for now, Cole Lazerman. Sleep.* She looked at Rambo and spoke, "It seems Cadet Lazerman won't be joining us for the rest of class. Cadet Rambo, Cadet Bell, if you would please take him to my chambers."

With a gentle hand motion, she levitated Lazer's body four feet above the ground. For the first time since his father's death, Lazer slept in a state of tranquil peace.

17

PRISONER

COVAX WATCHED the horrors of what was already unfolding from his prison tower. His mind spun searching for a solution; how to get away? How to warn the Triumvirate? How to protect his daughter?

"Five wants an answer," Pi's soft voice broke the hollow silence of the room and pulled Covax from his thoughts. Pi entered and the two Black Guard sentries closed the door behind him. "Five needs the codes and he's losing patience, Dr. Covax. Please."

"It can rot in eternity for all I care," Covax said. He hissed out the words, each one vehement with the frustration and anger that had been building since his incarceration. Covax did not turn. "It has no power over me and it knows I'm not afraid to die."

Five was still a thing as far as he was concerned. As one final insult, Covax refused to give the machine a gender.

"My fate hangs as precariously as yours, Doctor," was Pi's only response. "I beg you."

"No, Pi. It will destroy everything I've built," Covax whispered more to himself than to Pi.

Covax heard the door open. Still he did not turn.

"This is not about the past, Covax. It is about the future. You failed to realize your own dreams long before my actions," Five said as he entered.

This time Covax turned. His stomach turned at the site that presented itself. He could not ignore Five's ever-emerging facial features that appeared: a veil-like haze of particles that formed above his mask, dark narrow eyes, aquiline nose, a thin mouth, and the illusion of white close cut hair that could be seen and easily changed at will. Covax noticed the features seemed denser, more refined as they lay set against the pale, grayish-white skin. Covax studied his creation, but said nothing. Today it had an illusion of hands over its mechanical claws.

Behind Five stood a young mutant named Massi. Covax didn't recognize the pale scarecrow of a man, perhaps in his mid-twenties, with copper cotton-like hair and huge protruding eyes. Covax studied him, thinking only that the boy reminded him of a lanky, ugly, albino frog with copper wire for hair. He must have been part splicer, but sometimes the genetics were so subtle it was hard to tell. Covax didn't care or want to guess. He wanted to get out.

"The satellite feed has been set in place?" Five asked the youth.

"In two locations. We can monitor most of his movements through the school's security," Massi explained.

"And Masta Poe?" Five asked.

"As far as we can tell, she suspects nothing," Massi responded.

"You are to keep constant vigilance on him and his friends," Five said, speaking in an almost fatherly tone.

"Yes sir," Massi answered.

"You must find a way to destroy him.'

"He's well guarded but I'm looking, sir," Massi said.

"Good. Then I want to know the moment he leaves Tosadae Academy. Do not fail me, Massi," Five said.

Massi nodded. Covax watched as the boy almost bowed, and then hurried from the room.

Five too watched after the youth. Covax could read by his expression the biodroid was feeling a kind of pleasure given by his enthusiasm. Five looked to Pi.

"Did he tell you the codes?" Five said.

"He did not, sir," Pi said.

"Traitor," Covax added.

Five nodded instructing Pi to leave. Covax watched as he followed Massi and, unlike the overly zealous and demeaning reverent Massi, Pi left without ceremony. He did glance quickly back to Covax. The fear in his eyes said more than enough. Five turned his focus on Covax and began to speak.

"How curious. You think I disobeyed you?" Five asked with a casual lilt.

"I won't play a game of semantics with you, Five. You know exactly what you did when you overrode my protocols, governors, and security programs to reach sentience. Yes, I would call it disobedience. What would you call it?"

"Think of it as fulfillment. You once told me that the next time the Corporate Alliance rejected your proposals to represent Atlantia, you would unleash your Black Guard against them and conquer their petty world. So, in fact, I am doing exactly what you desired," Five said, His partially transparent eyes blinked awkwardly.

"That's not what I said," Covax explained.

"It's what you wanted to say," Five said.

"Do you honestly believe you can crush the entire world Collective?" Covax asked in disbelief.

"You did."

"You are *not me*," Covax was emphatic.

"Was I not engineered from your DNA? Was it not you who programmed my memory bands with all the greatest knowledge of humanity? Was it not you who personally taught me the art of war as we played our countless games of chess, held philosophical conversations and grand debates? Miyamoto Musashi, Zang Yu, and Niccolo Machiavelli were my teachers through you. Were they not masters of war and domination? Great strategists who came to me through you," Five said.

Covax watched as Five stopped and turned his gaze out the window to look at the city and pondered his own brilliant hypothesis. The biodroid stood silent for a long, arrogant moment.

"But yes, you are right, I am not you. I am far superior to you."

Covax didn't flinch. "I see," Covax said. "And once you have destroyed Atlantia, then what?"

"We will hack and capture the Vybernet, control all communication and transmissions, and take access to every machine that exists. There will be a brief, tactical, but lethal war fought with an army of biodroids against the humans, clones, mutants, and splicers who defy me. A war the likes of which the world has never seen. Once my biodroids hack in and take control of all machines, I will set my warriors, biodroids, machines, and those carbon-based beings smart enough to understand the fate of humanity and willing to join me in this fight, and we will destroy and erase this insipid race you call humanity. And, with or without your help, Dr. Covax, I will crush human genetics from existence and send mankind where it belongs . . . into extinction."

"You need us," Covax said. His voice held an icy challenge.

"Do I? Either way, it has begun." Five waved his hand above the controls to Covax's holoscreen, and called out, "Channel code 9041. I will activate the internal information feed for the facility monitors for you to observe the birth of my new world order."

The images on the holoscreen were from biodroid design labs at Temple Mountain. On them Covax could see the main biodroid production assembly lines. He had designed them as a vast open assembly line, a robotic factory filled with hanging racks of biodroid bodies, but where he had been producing one hundred in a month, Five had expanded production to thousands a week. Covax looked at one hundred thousand Black Guard in the making. Covax felt the sweat of fear on his skin. He felt cold and clammy but he still felt in control.

"Impressive, but you and I both know they're useless shells without the binary programming codes you don't possess," Covax said. He was suddenly calmer. He knew he held, locked in his mind, the keys to the more powerful hand. He knew it and so did Five.

"Don't test my patience, Ducane." Five's facial features faded shifting into a swirl of swirling molecules. When they dissipated, they left only the cold, blank steel of the biodroid mask stripped by two green lines.

"In this, too, you will fail. Understand, you have built mechanical slaves to run your world, to serve your needs, and provide the comfort and security you love, but when you lose control of them, you will be reduced to a weak pile of water and carbon and then you will be gone."

Five turned and headed to the door.

"Open!" the biodroid shouted with an edge of impatience.

Covax stared after him watching the large double doors swing open and once again close, sealing him into his prison tower. He exhaled, releasing the breath he had been unknowingly holding. A strange relief and feeling of victory, momentary as it was, washed over him. He still held one of the most important keys to Five's victory locked in his mind; the binary bio-codes that would program and launch his army and build his nation of sentient biodroids to replace humanity. Covax understood what Five didn't. There was still hope of defeating this monster he had created. Covax knew that until Five could program the bio strands, he couldn't build his species. Until he could override the security controls that protected the cable, Vybernet, and wireless satellite information feeds, Five couldn't control the vast array of machines that man had allowed to become the engines upon which human society ran. Five could not reprogram the machine to turn against and destroy all humanity from Atlantia. And most important, until he killed the boy, Cole Lazerman, he couldn't bond with and link himself to the four Gnorbs. If the Gnorb theories were correct, this boy, who had somehow begun the Gnorb bonding process, could unleash the powers of the four Gnorbs and open the pathways to the portals of travel and knowledge we call the universe. Covax's eidetic memory began to recall the pages he has seen from the Gnorb files. They were filled with information gathered by teams of scientists who analyzed the four Gnorbs desperate to understand their meaning and purpose. They shared with each other and with the great minds with high I.Q.'s what they had learned and, if they were correct, Cole Lazerman, by connecting with the first Gnorb, had begun the process. If he could connect with all four, he could access what some believed to be the powers inherent in lost knowledge of the universe. Theoretically, he could, by connecting these knowledge orbs left by Earth's first inhabitants through his mind and body, understand and control the forces of gravity, space, and time. If he could master all, he could manifest a new destiny for humanity. *If,* Covax thought.

18

THE VIRTUE OF PATIENCE

A WEEK HAD PASSED since the embarrassing fainting incident in class and Lazer retained little or no memory of the onslaught of images he had seen. People asked him if he was well and, for the life of him, he could not even remember passing out in class or being taken to Masta Poe's office. What he did remember was that he awoke in his dorm room the next morning, feeling as though he'd had the best sleep of his life. But on the third night, *dreams* began to fill his sleep. Pieces of the vision were scattered in each dream. Slowly, elements, faces, places began to reconstruct themselves. The images were frightening and wondrous, but left him feeling anxious and confused. He wanted to understand. Snippets and slivers of the vision, coupled with the stories people from the class that day had recounted, began to make sense, but the reasons eluded him. Finally, frustrated beyond words, and after a good talking to from Kyla, Lazer gathered his courage and went to see Masta Poe.

The door to Masta Poe's office hung open, which meant an invitation to anyone curious or courageous enough to enter. Lazer wasn't feeling courageous, but he was curious as hell to know what had happened that first day in class. He stepped in from the artificial light that filled the hallway and scanned the small, cluttered room. Almost every available inch was bursting with books and artifacts that reflected her remarkable life. High-def light paintings filled even the smallest space on her walls with digital art from the likes of Picasso, da Vinci, Rembrandt, Michelangelo, Michael Parks, and Georgia O'Keeffe. The images appeared and disappeared, periodically morphing from one into another, while soft soothing music played in the background.

Masta Poe's science lab was at the far corner of her office. She stood among racks of test tubes and beakers that boiled, bubbled, and dripped with various chemicals that changed textures and colors as they congealed or interacted with one another. Exotic plants and pungent herbs grew inside spheres of glass, living prisoners in their own perfect microenvironments.

Lazer hung back near the doorway. "I . . . missed the end of your class," he said. The door closed on its own, forcing him inside.

"The basics of telekinetic theory as a form of kinematics—moving mass via mental projection. We touched on spontaneous combustion and the mind's ability to control molecules for the alchemy of antimatter to matter transformation, manipulation, and reconstruction. And we discussed one of my favorites: energy shielding." She turned to peek at him over her shoulder, letting several strands of her snow-white hair fall across her face. Lazer thought she looked like an innocent child. "Shielding's a must for your battle skills," Masta Poe said. There was the slightest hint of a mischievous smile that flashed across her face and hung in her voice.

"I'd like to know all of those," Lazer said, feeling suddenly braver.

"I'm sure you would. The truth is, you already do. All humans do. You must simply remember these knowings and the limitless powers they carry," she said as she walked over to him. Masta Poe picked up and offered him a small vial. "Drink."

Lazer studied the goo in the vial. It was thick and a disgusting brownish-green. He eyed her and then the drink suspiciously, then drank wanting to stop but unable once he tipped it to his lips. It tingled like little firecrackers on his tongue, popping an array of tastes; first sweet, then sour, and then warm as it ran down his throat and into his stomach.

"Whoa! That's cosmic! What's in this? I feel great!" he said as he felt a rush of energy and clarity. His entire body tingled.

"Poobamba. A vitality elixir. My own blend," she said and smiled. "Next semester, if you have the courage to stay, you will learn the powers of plants and herbs. The earth gives us everything we need. If we would learn, we would never have to eat another animal again."

Courage to stay, a curious choice of idioms.

"Every remedy and healing medicine you humans could ever need has been provided to you by the plants of this Earth. You just have to know where to look." Masta Poe smiled, pleased with herself. "Come back tomorrow and we will begin," she said as she turned to walk away.

"But I . . ."

". . . will come back tomorrow," she ended the sentence for him. "Go in light," Masta Poe added, obviously ending their conversation.

"I . . . don't understand." Lazer stepped closer.

"That means, may your next evolution be into the light of wisdom, and may you be at one with the powers of the universe."

Lazer was dumbfounded. His feet refused to move. He wanted to ask her a thousand questions. He wanted to know about the visions. He had to. "But Masta Poe, I . . ."

". . . will come back tomorrow," she cut him short again. "I can only guide you to *some* of the answers you seek, Cole Lazerman, and only when you are ready, which," she emphasized, "you are not. The rest, like your powers and how to find your BAI, you will remember in good time."

Behind him the door swung open. He had been dismissed. The answers he sought would not come today.

19

WINDS OF CHANGE

ALEECE PILOTED EAGLE ONE, a Harrier FRS.MK 30 hover-craft used by the Triumvirate leaders. It had been a while since she had been able to leave Sangelino or simply take time to fly. She had missed the pleasure of the subtle controls of a stratospheric transport, the feeling of soaring in free flight as it cut through the lavender velvet sky.

Commander Fielding entered the cockpit and offered her a cup of her favorite ginger and honey tea. She nodded for him to set it down; she wasn't ready to turn on the autopilot. Fielding slipped into the copilot seat. She was a great leader. She alone had gotten the Collective to send a politia advance investigation team into Atlantia, suppressing Mangalan's emergency motion and lowering the defense dome alert to that of ready status only. The politia were ordered to install the dome, but not launch it until a full investigation and review of the report took place.

"Is Commander Bailer ready to take his controls back?" she asked.

"Soon enough. Besides, you look as though you're having too much fun."

"It shows, does it?" Aleece laughed.

"How much longer?"

"We've just entered Atlantian air space, so my ETA would be at about 1800."

"The advance has not been able to locate Dr. Covax," Fielding told her.

"I want to meet with our team tomorrow."

"It's all been arranged. Oh." He punched up a communiqué. "V-mail from your office. It must have come in when we crossed into Atlantia's satellite band."

The young aide from Aleece's office appeared in the hologram projection that floated between them. "Triumvirate Avery, I was able to locate the hypothesis we spoke about. It referred to the probable effects of conjoining the four Gnorbs at a single location as a single source of power. Ma'am, it was written five years ago by Triumvirate Baz Mangalan," she said his name with an uncomfortable edge. "I've attached a copy. Please tell us who else should see this."

The aide's face faded from her holoscreen just as something caught Aleece's eye. What she saw refused to register for a moment. She wanted it to be a mirage, an aberration, but it wasn't. A sortie of eight Shadehawks was heading straight for them. "We've got company," she said calmly.

Fielding saw the Shadehawks fall into attack formation. He activated the intercom. "Bailer, Code Blue. Get your ass up here!"

Multiple faces of the escort sortie that flanked Eagle One appeared on the heads-up screen, replacing the Triumvirate seal.

"Y'all getting this visual?" Eagle Two's commander asked.

"Are their comms open?" Aleece asked, hoping the Shadehawks were friendly.

"Negative," Eagle Two responded.

"Shields up. Arm your weapons," Fielding ordered.

Each of the fighter escorts reported in. They were armed and ready.

"Who's where?" Fielding asked as he brought all defense systems online.

"Bates and Warner on your flank. I'm on point, and Shift and Timmer have got your wings," Eagle Two reported.

"Copy that," Fielding responded. "I suggest we take evasive action, Madam Triumvirate."

"Can we outrun them?" Aleece asked Fielding. His look said everything. "Then I should give you back your controls." She reached for her restraints release just as Bailer burst through the door.

The first blast slammed into them. It took out Eagle Four. A ball of flames sent a concussion wave into Eagle One. The cockpit tipped, throwing Bailer to the floor. He cracked his head against the wall and was thrown to the floor. He was out cold.

"Eagle Two. Do you copy?" Aleece shouted.

"We lost Eagle Four!" Eagle Two's pilot shouted.

"Let's get the hell out of here!" Aleece ordered.

"Call it!" Fielding released the controls, throwing his hands up in the air. This was on Aleece.

"Get ready to break on my command. Lotus break. In three . . . two . . . one!"

They broke into a lotus pattern, flowing out in all directions. The Shadehawks scattered, splitting two-on-one. Aleece pulled straight back on the stick, sending the craft into a half loop. It rolled, then banked left. She headed back for the shoreline. Another blast! They took a hit. Hard. The fuselage shuddered. Smoke filled the cabin.

Outside, three more FX-80s were blasted from the sky. Eagle Two took on the two Shadehawks that trailed him. He dropped, reversed throttle, and fired. He blasted out the lead Shadehawk, pulled back around, and got two more. Two Shadehawks dove on him. He looked out and saw the smoking fuselage of Eagle One. It was falling from the sky with a trail of orange smoke. It was the last image the young pilot saw before he was obliterated.

Eagle One's survival pod ejected and the parachute blossomed into a nylon pyramid. A second parachute followed with Fielding at its controls. The pod drifted to Earth as Eagle One crashed into the Atlantian hills and exploded into a ball of orange and emerald flames a hundred meters away.

The remaining Shadehawks stopped in midair and hovered a moment, then drifted down to see what treasures they had captured.

20

LESSON ONE

LAZER AND MASTA POE stood together on the stage of the empty lecture hall. They had been there for the better part of the afternoon and Lazer was tired and irritated by their lack of progress.

"Try again," she said in a patient tone. She asked him to close his eyes and focus on the gentle rhythms of his heart, as it beat strong and steady inside his chest. Lazer had the heart of an athlete, slow and even.

It was obvious he wasn't going anywhere anytime soon. His only choice was to commit to her once and for all. There, in the open silence, Lazer forgot about all the things that were bothering him and let go, exhaling a long sigh. Finally, he had submitted to the moment. For the first time he wasn't in the past, remembering the sad events of his life, or daydreaming of the future, imagining how he would destroy the Black Guard; he was simply present in the here and now. Lazer began to hear his heart; he breathed in a gentle rhythm, listening as it ebbed and flowed and mingled with the subtle, ambient sounds of the room—the hissing of the ventilation system, Masta Poe's breathing, the brush of her cloak as she stepped away from him. Then, he heard his name. The voice did not come from spoken words, but from someplace deep inside his mind.

"Good," Masta Poe told him. "Stay focused on your heartbeat and open your eyes."

"Now, move as I move," she gently commanded. She opened her hands and brought them gracefully together at the wrists. Stretching open her fingers, she cupped them into an ellipse. Lazer mirrored her actions and waited.

"What do you feel?" she asked softly.

"Nothing," he whispered back, with a hint of facetiousness.

"Then we will do it again," she said, just as patiently as the other dozen or so times. "Breathe. Now, start over and stay inside yourself."

Nothing happened. Lazer was exhausted. He broke his stance and clenched his fists, a petulant child about to have a tantrum. "We've been at this for hours. Just tell me, what is it I'm supposed to feel?"

"If I tell, you will not remember." She wanted to will him to understand, but his defenses were up—a thick, impenetrable black wall wrought with anger. His emotions were negative and his mind was a jumble.

Finally, she gave in. "This is about what is easiest and most pleasurable, Lazer. Think of energy as pure vibration. Now, imagine the energy into undulating waves—sine waves—see them as part of a pure, pulsating electromagnetic spectrum, spinning with such velocity that they can, upon your command, become sound or heat. They can turn into light and exist and, upon your will, shift through the power of imagination, between gross matter and the ethos of antimatter to become whatever you allow your mind to see each, be it energy or a single atom. You give it power by making it, through your mental thoughts, reality. You are capable of re-creating anything inside the energetic forces that exist beyond your imaginings until the moment you imagine them into being. Across the energy inside your thoughts a multiverse of parallel dimensions wait for you to create them into being. See them, Lazer, feel them, taste them, know them for they are you and you are them. Transcend through your mind and manifest the thoughts into energy, the energy into waves, the waves into particles, and the particles into physical matter, and manifest reality. Go."

Lazer stared at him. His mind struggled, desperate to understand the connection between thought, energy, and matter.

"How?" Lazer was overwhelmed by the concept. "We exist in four dimensions, including time. That's it. Where do you expect me to go? I don't understand."

"*You* do. You've done it. Accept the knowings and be at one with the universe. With this power, you can go anywhere, do anything. Once you allow yourself to imagine it through precise thought, you will attain the level of master and the doors will open in your mind. Step into bliss and get out of the universe's way. Stop trying to look through your physical eyes. We don't exist in four dimensions; we exist in limitless dimensions. So far, you have chosen not to see beyond the teachings on the handers who control your thoughts through fear. Use your thoughts and explore your imagination," Masta Poe said.

She began to circle him as she spoke. Lazer watched as she raised her hands, and with a gesture, manifested various objects—an apple, a knife, a wristsponder appeared from thin air—solid, physical, real—appearing from out of nowhere. They appeared in her hand and as she opened her fingers, she set them gently afloat in midair.

"Remember the knowings of your soul."

"How can I remember what I haven't learned?" Lazer said, the frustration building inside him. He sighed in utter exasperation.

"How can I teach you what you already know?" she smiled. "The Visionistic Arts are a collective knowledge that exists inside the core of everything, from the universe to the smallest atomic particles. They are in your body as in everything that exists. Inside," she said as she touched his chest, "you have a projectable state of mind that will give you infinite possibilities, if you ask it. These are the gifts that humans have always held, but have lost the will to call upon because they were told to. It is the right of every human being on this planet to levitate, shield, read auras, manifest, project their vision into the future, communicate with plants and animals, and call into existence their smallest or greatest desires creating them into reality through the will and bidding. You must have faith in your powers."

"My father said that but I didn't understand him either," Lazer said.

"Right now, if you chose to do so, you could go negative or . . .'"

"Go negative?" Lazer interrupted.

Masta Poe touched an object that she had been levitating. It vanished. Yet Lazer could see that the faintest trace of its form still existed beneath her fingers.

"To go negative, to become invisible, to shift your quarks from a positive state to a negative state. If you can imagine it and believe with your entire being, then it must be," she patiently explained. "The Eastern spiritualists practiced various forms of the Visionistic Arts long before my mother and I wrote them down. Many people have done acts, miracles, and great feats of bravery without realizing it. Sometimes they act out of a state of fear when faced with grave danger, and it is seen to others watching as an act of great bravery. Talk to men who have survived great trials, even battles. It is believed they used acts of some kind of transmutation or invisibility and walked unscathed through arrows and bullets, because they believed they could not be seen or harmed. Because they believed, because of their faith in the universe of imagining, they became invincible. This is one of the infinite powers of the mind, Lazer. These are the gifts you humans have forgotten over the millennia. You have lost your higher self. You wanted only to survive the dangers of the night and the trials of the day, but surviving is not the true art of living. It is the lowest of all existences."

Masta Poe stared at him. Lazer felt as if she were looking though him.

"You still let anger and hatred of an unchangeable past control your emotions. These are what block you," she said.

Lazer's face was a blank. He felt naked and vulnerable. Exposed to a truth he couldn't deny.

Forget what you have learned and remember what you know, Masta Poe sent as thoughts into his mind. "Imagine and believe it to be. To shift dimensions and create a better life, you must manipulate your vibrations from a state of bliss. From there you can create your thoughts into matter, explore space and time, and become the best version of yourself. Hear me, Lazer. Thoughts are the essence of antimatter, and from thought, need, or desire, matter is made real. Imagine what you want and manifest it into being. Do it, Lazer, or you will forget and fall into the abyss of hate and ignorance," she said.

Lazer studied her as she, once again, held her hands together in a cup.

Masta Poe extended her arms away from her body. She focused her thoughts, and commanded energy to form inside her hands. At the center, a point of visible light appeared. She's created inside that negative space a ball of glowing, energetic heat particles that swirled and spun. Lazer watched as the spinning ball gained momentum. As it twirled, it collected each newly created, energetic particle together, and growing in size, the energy particles fused together as one. Masta Poe separated her hands and stretched the floating ball of energy into an elliptical. Lazer watched, amazed, as the curved membrane expanded and formed itself into a flat force field that shimmered before her. It was a shield. Lazer could feel and see the clear, pristine, barrier of energy suspended before her body and face. It emanated from her hands, invisible but perceptible.

"Touch me," she commanded.

Lazer reached forward. His hand bumped into the force field, stopped by the edge of an invisible and impenetrable bubble of energy that suddenly completely encircled her.

"No physical weapon can penetrate, if your mind is strong enough." Masta Poe nodded for Lazer to do as she had just done.

Lazer copied the position of her hands and her physical stance.

"Focus everything into the space inside your hands and visualize the energy that exists outside you. Draw it in and let it pass through every cell of your being. Now, imagine what it will look like when you form the force field, then will it to pass through your hands as infinitesimal particles flowing in from the universe and out through your pores. This is the same kinetic energy you use when you maneuver through the dark and send your inner self outside of you."

Again, Lazer closed his eyes. He imagined the vast energetic fields that drifted through the air around him gathering closer and passing inside though his skin. He felt the energy tingle inside of him as it connected and gathered in every cell that made up his being. He felt himself bursting with a powerful energy. It felt warm and thick. He willed the particles to form into waves and channeled them out through every pore. Lazer's eyes were closed, but he could see the force building as he focused his thoughts into a single point inside his hands. He smiled as he felt an odd tingle buzzing between his hands. It felt like a small insect trapped, growing in size and pushing against his hands to get out.

Masta Poe smiled. He could tell by her expression she knew exactly what had happened.

"Good. You have found the first door to your BAI, your connection to the universe." She saw the particles that had begun to spin in his hands. "Reach deeper, Lazer. Reach out to the universe and into your core. See the energy as pure antimatter, a force that your mind has the power to convert into anything you *will* it to be. Now, re-create it into a solid, tangible object. Define every detail and manifest it into existence."

The tingling energy in his hands grew and expanded as he opened his arms.

"Now open your eyes," she whispered.

Lazer opened his eyes and what he saw made him give a small gasp of surprise. Lazer saw it—pure living energy swirling between his hands. He stretched the spinning ball of energy. He expanded it. It clung and pulled like a gooey, crystal liquid bubble that shimmered as he opened his arms so wide that the circle engulfed him and stretched around his body. He could see as it fluctuated and expanded, regrouped, and fluctuated again. It was inconsistent, moving, alive, and wavering, but amazingly solid. It felt powerful. He felt powerful.

Masta Poe pushed on his shield. It gently bowed but kept her outside its form. Lazer beamed. He was ecstatic. He held pure energy in his hands and commanded it. It was energy that he had summoned with a single thought and imagined into physical mass.

"I did it!" Lazer blurted with the boastful pride of a four-year-old who had just tied his own shoe. He felt the joy of bliss.

Masta Poe smiled playfully and vanished, reappearing almost instantaneously across the room. She focused on an object that floated before her—a crystal apple she had earlier manifested. In a single blurred motion, she plucked the apple from the air and hurled it at Lazer's head.

Everything after that happened too fast and at the same time went into a kind of slow motion; Lazer flinched, his concentration shattered, and the shield evaporated into a haze of shimmering particles that scattered and then vanished, leaving him completely exposed. The apple, a second from smashing into his face, froze in mid-flight, one sliver of a millimeter from slamming into his nose.

In the same instant, Masta Poe appeared in front of him and plucked the suspended apple from the air. "Faith. You did not trust your BAI. You let the fear of what was supposed to have happened block your abilities. For one brief second, you did not trust your powers!" she stated.

"I tried," Lazer blurted, in an attempt to cover his embarrassment. He felt Masta Poe's disappointment in him.

"Tried? Try to sit, or stand, or walk; the act of trying is impossible. By hiding behind the word *try*, you limit the scope of what you believe. Never use it again. Be certain the shield will hold, and the apple will be stopped. You must trust first yourself and then what you create. A famous man named Henry Ford said, "Whether you think you can or you think you can't, you're right."

"I don't understand," Lazer said. He was suddenly even more frustrated than before.

"Then it is so," she said, as she shook her head sadly. "That is why you thought you could not call back the ship's shield; it wasn't the ship's shield—it was yours but you chose not believe in yourself."

"That energy was mechanical! It failed because the shield on the transport was drained of its own power," Lazer defended his actions.

"The ship was out of power; your mind was not."

"You expect me to believe I could have shielded the entire transport with my mind?"

"I know you did. I have no expectations, and you will believe what you want. My purpose is to show you the power of possibility. What you do with it is your decision."

Lazer suddenly realized she knew all about the attack on the transport. "I . . . never told anyone except Commander Hague."

"You wear your guilt of that day just as you wear the guilt of your father's death. Pain, sadness, hatred, revenge—those are the shadows that cover your soul and stifle all that the universe desires to give you."

"Are you saying I could have saved my father?!"

"I am saying you have always had the power to do anything you could imagine. We are taught at an early age to believe we are limited. We are taught not to imagine the impossible. So, most people don't understand they CAN do anything they imagine. The knowing is as basic and factual as the color of your eyes or the air you breathe. If you accept reality as an inalterable fact, you can never change it or yourself. You were guilty in that you had not obeyed your father, and you were fearful for your own life that day. How could you have saved anyone with those emotions smothering you?" Masta Poe said.

Her words pierced him as did the look in her eyes. Once again her gaze penetrated him, passing through him like an icy wind. He felt as though she could see straight into his soul, his heart, his mind, exposing all the secrets he wished so desperately to keep buried there.

Lazer wanted to speak, to deny the facts. He opened his mouth, but Masta Poe stopped him.

"Have faith, believe, and do it, Lazer. When you are ready to see the whole truth of who you are, send me word. You alone must find your BAI and hold it. Until then, I can do no more. Go in light," Masta Poe said. He knew from her look she had concluded her lesson. Without another word, she vanished into thin air, leaving Lazer alone to ponder his choices—to live in a state of anger and revenge or embrace his bliss and evolve.

21

THE DECISION TO DOME

NO ONE ON ATLANTIA or in Sangelino knew Aleece's crash had been digitally scrambled by the Black Guard to look like an accident. Even as an accident, it was obvious events on Atlantia had escalated. Dante was told a massive search and rescue was underway and that Aleece's final request, as her plane went down, was for Dante not to come. She asked that he be installed as her alternate.

The disappearance of Aleece Avery and the immediate demand to launch the dome had become the key subjects of debate between the World Corporate Council and the Triumvirate. Without Aleece's voice of reason, the argument to seal off whatever rebellious action might be building inside its airspace by doming Atlantia for the safety and protection of the world was one-sided, and Mangalan was winning. The Triumvirate expected a vote of unanimous approval to come within a matter of hours. Dante paced, worried about the safety of his wife, and felt helpless to stop the inevitable outcome of the vote until he was instated as alternate. It was decided, for matters of security, to withhold the information from the general Collective about the potential dangers of a biodroid rebellion and the decision to dome Atlantia. They focused the press on Aleece's tragic crash and hung everything else in a cleverly constructed information blackout until more was known about Aleece's whereabouts.

The voices of power in the unified world now sat inside Blane Fahan's office. The top World Corporate Council members and a few select members of the politia brass argued about the fate of Atlantia. They had been arguing most of the night. Holograms floated above the huge conference table, showing constantly changing information about the latest happenings in various hot spots around the world. Their concerns focused primarily on the safety of the world.

"A decision on Atlantia must be made today," Mangalan commanded.

Mangalan and Fahan were the two remaining Triumvirate leaders and they both knew the final decision would be theirs.

Dante Labov was there as a loving husband, desperate for news of his missing wife. If she wasn't found by tomorrow, he would be sworn in as her alternate. By then, the vote would be cast. All he could do was listen. He stood by the large tinted window and watched the morning sun break over the cliffs east of Sangelino. It had been seventeen hours since Aleece's disappearance and there had been no further word. He was worried about his wife, but tried to focus his thoughts on the dire matters at hand. The entire night he had only heard bits and pieces of the debate as the leaders shared statistics, the probability of escalating danger, and if they invaded, acceptable losses.

"There are no acceptable losses!" Blane shouted, pounding his fists on the table.

Finally, Dante agreed with someone.

"It's genocide to seal them in," Dante said calmly.

"You are not being objective, Dr. Labov," Mangalan replied.

"Triumvirate Mangalan is right," an elderly corporate commander replied. "We have no choice but to dome Atlantia until we understand who is in control. We have to prevent the Black Guard from getting out and building a following anywhere else."

"Isn't it obvious from these hot spots erupting across the continent that the Black Guard rebellion has already begun?" Mangalan pointed at the plumes of smoke billowing from several tiny dots along the Atlantian coast. The image was projected on their screens from the satellite relay.

"I know I have no voice as of yet in this matter, but we need to send in a division with weapons and make our presence in Atlantia known to the Black Guard and to the Collective," Dante interjected.

Fahan and Mangalan exchanged a look that was not lost on Dante. They were about to change the focus of the problem.

"We can't invade Atlantia because of an accident—even one as critical as the possible loss of a world leader. Give the search-and-rescue teams a chance to find her," Fahan said to Dante, with the patronizing tone of a father to an irrational child.

"We are all concerned about the fate of Triumvirate Avery, but we must be realistic. We don't even know if she's alive," Mangalan said without emotion.

"She's alive," Dante snapped back.

"If anyone could have survived the crash, I'm sure . . .," Blane Fahan started.

"However, until we have proof, I move we approve ordering Atlantia domed and all traffic in and out of Atlantia monitored," Mangalan interrupted. "We all agree, the biggest issue is that we must quash these rebels immediately and contain their leaders."

"With a dome in place, we can monitor all communications out and in, sir. If they are holding her hostage, doming will force their hand," the older commander said to Dante.

They were beginning to agree. Everyone was fearful for his or her own safety.

"This is unjust!" Dante shouted.

"We have no other choice," Mangalan countered.

"Triumvirate Mangalan is right. It is our only option," Blane Fahan said in a soft acquiescent voice. He was tired. He knew what they were doing was for the protection of the world, but his instincts left him tingling with the horrific feeling he was condemning the Atlantians to their deaths.

"No, I won't concede. Sending in forces is an option," Dante shouted over the still murmuring crowd.

"Not that you have a vote in this, Dr. Labov, but know we will send in forces. However, it will take time. We need corporate approval," Mangalan added, trying to quell Dante. Ultimately, he hoped Dante would become a powerful ally once he stepped into Aleece's seat.

"That will take months! And who wants to be held responsible for the slaughter of more Atlantians while we hide under policy?" Dante's voice boomed across the room. There was an embarrassed hush. They all knew he was right, but the safety of their families had to be considered. Their hands were tied. Within twenty hours of Aleece's crash, in a private session, the motion was brought to the floor, voted on, passed, and the order to dome Atlantia was approved *without* informing the Collective. Mangalan, as a precautionary measure, previously had ordered stanchions put in place just in case they were needed for the dome. It took months of preparation, but Mangalan had felt it was better to act and apologize later than not to be prepared in an emergency.

What they didn't know was that on the other side of the world, as the sun melted into the western shores of Atlantia, the original Politia Investigative Task Force—the PITF—stood ready to send in a preliminary report that held information vital to Atlantia's situation. The task force had uncovered intelligence that a biodroid named Five had taken over Covax's labs and factories. There were unsubstantiated reports of an attack the summer before, where witnesses, who could not be found, had seen and attempted to destroy a huge cache of weapons and the nanobands that were being created to drive an enormous biodroid army that was supposedly being constructed inside the facilities at Temple

Mountain. Covax could not be reached to confirm or deny, and the secondary investigation revealed nothing to substantiate the accusations. These preliminary findings were to be delivered to the newly appointed head of the Security Committee Task Force, Baz Mangalan, and the Triumvirate in Sangelino from the temporary PITF security office at the Atland City Airfield.

Just as the PITF started to send their report on a secured Vybernet channel, an emergency message came through about the downed craft that held Triumvirate Aleece Avery. They did not know that moments after Eagle One entered Atlantian airspace, the dome controls had been captured by the Black Guard. After the attack and subsequent crash of Avery's craft, the Black Guard had launched an isoluminescent miasma—a dense digital haze that refracted all visual observations from satellite surveillance. Across the isotropic haze, they played a loop of satellite visuals in which everything on Atlantia looked in order and the crash of Eagle One looked like an accident. It was a brilliant ploy—a subtle movie that played on a cloud of reflective light, designed to keep what was really happening on Atlantia shrouded from the world's view.

By sundown, the Black Guard had taken control of Atland City. Just before the dome went into lockdown, Five sent out a secret communiqué to his global forces—cells of followers who would take to the streets in cities around the world and rally a small coalition of clones, mutants, and splicers to fight against humans. Small uprisings were meticulously scheduled to erupt in cities everywhere. The trouble would be enough to keep the corporate politia busy and give Five the time he needed to build his army and prepare for the coming invasion.

The politia headquarters on Atland Field was taken, along with their controls to the dome locks. The core members of the Politia Investigative Task Force were killed, or eluded capture by the grace of the Universal God.

As the commanding officer on watch in Sangelino prepared to download the file that had been sent by the PITF, she was the first to notice that information was not being received. She tried to communicate back and hit the wall of white noise caused by the dome lockout. All communications from Atlantia and the investigating politia team inside had been severed. The young commander's heart jumped into her throat. She could only assume the inevitability of what the shimmering hiss that played on her holoscreen meant.

After a long, still moment, she communicated in to tell her superiors that Atlantia had been domed.

22

A REASON TO BELIEVE

AT TOSADAE, Lazer attended his classes with a new resolve. He stood on the mock battlefield with General Donald Petersen, an expert in military strategy who had served in England's Special Forces Division M6 prior to the Great Quakes. He had cloned his body and had his brain transplanted into it; his new body was now about fifty-five, his mind nearly two hundred. Petersen called the class to attention using 3-D, full-circle holographic images. He walked them through the greatest historical battles of all time and analyzed, point by point, every detail of the attacks from a variety of angles.

Today's battle was a reenactment of Africanus Cipio against Hannibal—second-century Romans against the last of the Carthaginians. The toy-sized hologram had the class at the center of the attack. Petersen input a code to enlarge the visual to life size and launched the attack sequence. Lazer looked into the holographic face of a warrior; his eyes were wild, bulging with bloodthirsty anger, and in his hairy fists he held a mallet and an ax. The fact that the image of the falling ax wasn't real didn't take away the rush of terror that quickened his heart when it passed through him. Lazer felt suddenly grateful for modern weaponry. Petersen then touched a series of sensor pads on the small handheld control and the holographic projections shrank, providing the class with an aerial, God-like view. Again Petersen launched the sequence, letting the battle play out at their feet. Lazer watched carefully, noting the intricacies of the battle's strategy as it unfolded. He wasn't sure why, but as he watched, the center flank rose up from beneath the ground, having hidden until the Romans marched into battle. The Romans were surrounded with Carthaginians at their back and front. Then Hannibal ordered the advance of his right and left flanks and the Romans were surrounded and destroyed. It was brilliant.

His other classes and electives kept him more than busy. Lazer would see Elana Blue every Tuesday and Thursday in flight simulator and Monday, Wednesday, and Friday in primary genetics, which was taught by a mutant named Hawkins. Nyrani Hawkins fit her name. She had a hawk's face, with piercing gold eyes set on either side of her head, which protruded slightly forward. She could see 260 degrees in her peripheral vision. The hard beak she had for a nose hung over her upper lip and made her speech stilted and awkward. Her wings—fleshy mounds of a double hunchback—had been severed by her parents to save her, leaving only the nubs to protrude through her clothes. Her hollow bones prevented her from venturing out when the wind was high. But she was a good teacher who cared deeply about her students. Nyrani Hawkins was personally invested in making sure every one of her scholars understood the responsibility that came with any act of genetic creation. Primary genetics was Kyla's best class. She had also bonded personally with Hawkins, volunteering for every extra credit project that came across the light board.

Other than the flight simulator sessions, primary genetics was also the only class Lazer, Kyla, Cashton, and Elana Blue took together. In class, they worked with a variety of DNA strands via computerized microscopes and simulated Petri dishes. Sometimes they worked in tandem to build genetic integration formulas and match basic DNA patterns to learn cross-genetic applications.

Lazer and Cashton had somehow ended up together on today's experiment—the blind leading the blind. He typed in the data and Cashton calculated the solutions. The computer began the creation sequence. Using the sim program, the computer reconstituted their work in perfect virtual replication and produced a deformed ball of teeth and a puff of hair with two bulging eyes that teetered precariously on a set of crab legs. The creature blinked back at them. Its life expectancy calculated out to about three days, which was the time they were required to care for it until its pathetic virtual death.

While Kyla waited for her own calculations to be reconstituted, she laughed at the mess her friends had assembled. But, as Cashton had often said, he was an inventor and mechanical engineer, not a geneticist. He had proved his case when he melted the doors off one of the Arts and Powers labs while testing a small device that combined terahertz, or t-rays, with lasers designed to project light through solid objects. The act sent the three of them into a week's detention. Far too many of his inventions had been equally disastrous, and a hundred times more deadly than the hideous little creature that he and Lazer had just created. Finally Kyla's creature was reconstituted, and it was equally as frightening. It would survive a week. Cashton wrinkled his nose at her.

Elana Blue's was perfect. Her simulation program, if she wished, would convert to a living set of cells that could be grown in an artificial womb and born in a few months to live a relatively normal life. Hawkins applauded her as the shining example of creative responsibility.

Kyla was annoyed by the praise Hawkins had heaped on Elana Blue. It was bad enough that Lazer doted on her. Kyla refused to admit it, but in her heart she knew she was jealous.

Every now and then, Elana Blue would smile at Lazer and he always smiled back, far too eagerly for Cashton, who insisted Lazer at least pretend to be a little more ice. But Lazer's heart melted every time he got even the slightest bit of attention from her. They hadn't exchanged many words since their unfortunate first meeting, but their physical attraction to each other was obvious, especially to Bo, who somehow always managed to appear just as Lazer was getting the courage to speak to her.

Days passed and the humdrum of routine seemed to make the clocks move slower, no matter how Lazer tried to fill his time and guide his thoughts away from his daydreams. Eventually, they always came back to Elana.

Lazer and Kyla were returning from Allopathic studies, which combined basic homeopathy with diagnostics. It was a prerequisite to the psychic healing techniques first introduced by Edgar Cayce in the early twentieth century and then brought to new heights by the healers and splicers that taught at Tosadae.

Cashton rushed up from behind them with wild, excited eyes. "I got an old feed from my E-3 that looks like it had been there for a while."

"You said you weren't gonna spy on her," Kyla reprimanded.

"That's not important. Donna's farming co-op was attacked," he blurted out, breathless from the run.

"That's near where Evvy use to live," Kyla added. She still missed her friend.

Cashton's face was filled with concern that went deeper than he wanted to show. But Cashton was terrible at hiding his feelings, especially from Lazer and Kyla.

"Close to Vacary?" Lazer's mind filled with horrible thoughts about his mother being so close to danger.

"No, she lives in Eastern Atlantia," Cashton shook his head.

"It's on Atlantia, and that's close enough."

"I don't know about you, but I haven't been able to get through to my mom for a couple of days," Kyla pondered.

"Yeah, me either," Cashton agreed.

"Neither have I, now that I think about it. Something's not right. I've got to get out of here and get home!" Lazer glowered.

"After our Rite of Passage!" Kyla reminded them.

Lazer was trying to get onto the Vybernet through his wristsponder. A wall of white noise hovered before him.

"Look, it's probably some kind of system glitch from Mu," Cashton said. "Same thing happened last month during security check when they discovered somebody had hacked into the campus video system."

"What if it's not a glitch?" Lazer's voice was racked with concern.

"Whatever it is, it can't be serious or we would have heard about it over the news feeds. Besides, you promised your mom and we agreed to wait," Kyla reminded him, more emphatic than before. "At least complete your level-one passage or you'll be digging ditches the rest of your life. That was the deal. Remember?"

"Yeah, yeah, yeah, I know," Lazer huffed.

"Kyla, let me know what you find out. I gotta bounce," Cashton said, as he gave the V salute. "I'm first up in flight simulator today and Elana's on my wing. So, if you challenge us, you *will* be particle dust."

As Cashton bounded off, blabbering about Elana's exemplary skills as a pilot and how she could be on his wing in or out of the sky, Kyla did a quick read of Lazer's aura. He was furious and worried. It was obvious his emotions were not about the all-too-perfect Elana Blue; he was angry about what was happening and worried about his mother. They were all worried about home, but what could they do?

Kyla wanted to throw her arms around him and take away his pain. She wanted to tell him everything would be all right. But most of all, she wanted to touch his face and look into his eyes, to whisper that he was more than just her best friend. She wanted to shout to the stratosphere that she had always been in love with him. But the words hung in her mouth, dry and bitter as cotton balls soaked in vinegar. Kyla was too terrified to speak the words, afraid it would ruin a lifelong friendship and make her lose the one thing her heart wanted most—for Lazer to love her back.

Kyla glanced at Lazer again and watched as his aura changed from the fiery red to a curiously cool cerulean blue. She followed Lazer's gaze and flinched when the source of Lazer's emotional change came into view. He was looking at Elana Blue. The dry bitter taste that hung in Kyla's mouth turned sour and her stomach twisted into a giant knot. She watched Lazer melt into a helpless puppy, eager for a scrap of attention, until she couldn't take another moment. With a growl, Kyla turned on her heels, flipped her ponytail in Lazer's face, which whacked him in the head, and marched away in a huff.

Lazer looked briefly after Kyla, perplexed by her sudden change, then turned back to take one last look at Elana Blue. She smiled at him. His heart fluttered in his chest like a small caged bird desperate to be free. *Now or never*, he thought, and took two steps forward. He would walk her to simulator class. They would talk. He would somehow find the courage to ask her out. His feet moved him forward, as if by their own volition, and new courage filled his veins. In spite of the fears that pulled at his mind, it was happening. He was going to do it. Suddenly Bo Rambo appeared from nowhere, stepped in, and blocked Elana from Lazer's view. Bo uttered a few words and, like an eagle swooping in for the kill, scooped her off as he gallantly offered to walk her to the simulators. Elana hesitated, glanced all too briefly at Lazer, and sighed. Frustrated by the intrusion, but held by some obvious obligation, she accepted Bo's invitation, and in a heartbeat, they were gone. Lazer, crest-fallen, could only watch.

2 3

HOME

THE VACARY MINING SETTLEMENT where Lazer had spent his childhood was going through the motions of another day. Kids played as their parents went to work, at least those who had found jobs after the mines were destroyed. The rest went out each day hoping to find work in the surrounding areas. They prayed the fires would stop burning and the mines would be rebuilt, but so far their prayers had gone unanswered. Some families had moved away, but most had neither the finances nor opportunity and had stayed, helping one another however they could. Detra had willed herself the courage to go back to the temple research and study facility. The Gnorb was gone, but there was still a smattering of data that had been recovered from the backup strands left to analyze. So she worked a few days a week as a fundraiser for Orbis. It gave her something to do. It kept her mind off her loneliness and the memories out of her head, but today was Saturday and as a distraction she busied herself by reorganizing the kitchen pantry, again.

Like a massive wave crashing on shore, the peaceful silence of suburban life was suddenly shattered, replaced by the low rumble of the Black Guard's peacekeeper hover tanks. They were coming closer with every breath. Those who were curious enough to open their doors were the lucky ones. They died instantly from the spray of DT pellets that ripped them apart. The more cautious peeked from their windows and watched in horror. They were being invaded.

The hover tanks reached the center of Imagine Lane and lowered to the ground, clattering like metal monsters as they went through their mechanical transformation. Like the gaping jaws of a giant shark, the bay doors hinged opened, exposing the Black Guard, clones, and mutant forces that had been strapped into the inner walls of the transport. The clones and mutants sat uniformly dressed in armor similar enough to the biodroids to make their allegiance obvious. Some of the faces peering out of helmets were human, some were not, but all were there to carry out their orders.

The platoon disembarked from the transport and moved out, splitting off into every direction. They crashed through the front doors of the houses, grabbed everyone they found, and dragged them into the streets. They murdered those who resisted or ran.

It happened so fast no one could think. Detra ran out of the pantry to find her house being ransacked. Before she could protest, she found herself struggling in the arms of two mutants. One of them spoke to her, his voice both fierce and kind. "Don't fight. At least for now they'll let you live," he whispered. Detra stopped, chilled by the fear she felt under his words. She looked into the huge sad eyes framed by pointed ears and a long, horse-like face. It was obvious he didn't want this responsibility, but for some reason he had chosen sides and would see it through. Detra jerked her arm away from the other mutant.

"You're no better than they are," she scolded him, her face suddenly more angry than frightened.

"At least they don't hate us just because we're not like them. That's for humans to do," the other mutant said. There was sadness in the mutant's words, and Detra could not argue that prejudice and bigotry had been directed at the mutants, clones, and splicers over the past century. *Somehow mankind always found someone to hate*, she thought.

They shoved Detra onto the street just as her neighbor, an older man, rushed out of his house. He carried an AK-47 rifle, part of some collector's memorabilia from the turn of the century. It was old, but it worked and he had decided to fight back. He fired, taking out several of the clones and a few mutants. Using the distraction, people scattered and ran into the foothills. It looked as though the tide might turn, as some of the men and women pried weapons from the hands of their fallen enemy and they, too, began to fight back. The rally was short-lived. The tanks opened fire, killing Detra's neighbor and destroying his home in one fiery blast. Those who had armed themselves dropped their weapons, but it was too late. The Black Guard opened fire, murdering them where they stood. Detra felt tears rolling down her cheeks as she was dragged into the town's center. Detra closed her eyes.

24

ARMY OF DROIDS

COVAX CALLED TEMPLE MOUNTAIN his little campus, but since the unsolved attack over the summer, the massive, underground facility had been under high security. Five, Dr. Muller, and his first assistant, Dr. Jean Larousse, walked observantly along the catwalks that overlooked the main assembly line. Five wore his human face. The delicate particles sifted and reformed, becoming more defined with each passing day, allowing him to better articulate each expression and the subtle emotions that percolated beneath. The expression of the moment was irritation.

"There is a problem with the Series IV." Muller shifted uncomfortably, but his words were informed and precise. Although human, he had worked hard to emulate the cold perfection he admired in biodroids like Five. Muller had been in point position for quality assurance since Five's coup. He enjoyed no longer having to answer to Covax's ego. But with power came the responsibility to reconstruct Covax's programming codes. He was nervous about the lack of progress in decoding the complicated software, though he refused to let it show.

"Problem?" Five asked.

"All the Series IV have . . . a corruption," Muller said in a muted voice. "A . . . kind of . . . corruption."

"Corruption?" Five turned to listen.

"Infection might be a better term," Muller corrected himself. "It seems the Series IV are dying."

Five tilted his head, trying to grasp the notion that a biodroid could die. "What a preposterous concept. We were not born; therefore, it is not possible to die. It's basic logic, Dr. Muller."

"Shutting down. Dissipating. Disintegrating. We have not been able to isolate the cause or trace its origin, but we know something is manifesting in the Series IV biodroids and collapsing their molecular bonds," Larousse stuttered. He was a pig-faced man with narrow eyes who perspired copiously when nervous. "Perhaps seeing is better than explaining."

They reached the south laboratory and opened the door. Inside were several biodroid carcasses, motionless, at various stages of decay. They resembled 3-D versions of Salvador Dali's surrealistic paintings. Portions of their molecular structure had begun to fade, leaving gaping chunks of missing matter.

"Covax knew of this?" Five demanded, peering through one of the biodroids.

"He had seen the bacteria bonds collapsing several months ago, but the particle disintegration was miniscule then. Dr. Covax attributed it to weak protein strands. That's why he held back the programming sessions until he could stabilize or replace the strands." Beads of sweat dripped down the folds of Larousse's neck.

"Why have I not been affected? Why have my Series III Guards not been affected?"

"After the attack, all the newer Series IV were given T-cell strands," Dr. Muller added.

"Change the rest out," Five insisted.

"That will take time we don't have," Muller responded.

"How long will it take?" Five said clipping each word with a staccato rhythm.

"Six months to grow the DNA strands, three to replace them with human and viral protein bands, and then several days to program them with the chemical codes necessary to attract the metal ions needed to bathe them in cobalt oxide and gold solutions. After that, we can charge the polymer strips of the electrodes, or we can't activate the brain matter," Muller answered.

"We have been able to slow the disintegration," Dr. Larousse added.

"I don't want it slowed. I want it eradicated!"

"We're doing everything we can. As long as the Series IV remain inactive . . ."

"I am in a war to take Atlantia. I need an army and enough of my kind to settle the lands I conquer!" Five yelled. "Isolate the strands. Create an antibody. Inoculate all the protein rods. Find out what is causing this decay!" He turned to Larousse. "Prepare the Series III for battle." Five turned on Muller. He stuck a metal finger in the doctor's face. "Isolate whatever is doing this and destroy it or you will join Dr. Covax." Five's rage mingled with a new emotion, fear.

"We've already flushed every protein band. It's impossible without Dr. Covax's help," Dr. Muller blurted, irritated that Five would not accept his solution.

"Impossible?" Five hissed. The particles shifted across his face and flashed a brief, deadly warning. His eyes narrowed and his nostrils flared. Then, in a blur of motion, Five raised his hand and shot out a haze of molecules that slammed into Muller's body. The molecules burrowed into his flesh, ate through his skin, and burned into him as if he were made of paper. Muller arched into a spasm and shrieked in agony. His body temperature accelerated, then he spontaneously combusted into a ball of flames. He felt a spasm, lost his balance, and fell over the rail, plummeting to his death five stories below. Time slowed as all eyes watched with horror as what remained of Muller as he hit the ground. First, the sharp clatter of bones, then, gracefully drifting behind, a snow of sparkling embers, which had only a moment before been a living, breathing man. The embers floated down and settled into a pile of gray ash.

Five turned to Larousse. "Bring Brochenbourough and Hudson in from Atland City. Put all efforts into isolating what is causing the decay. I need an army!"

"What about the codes?" Larousse was sickened by Muller's death.

"I'll get the codes."

"We need Covax's help," Larousse begged.

"No," Five said, his voice far too calm for the carnage he had just caused. The particles that formed his mouth twitched. "Covax must never know of this. Bring him to me," he ordered.

25

GNORBS

THE WEATHER ON TOSADAE was changing. The warm, sunny days had become shorter and cooler, and the morning fog that was usually gone by nine clung to the tops of buildings and looming hills until well past noon. A chill wind blew in from the north each day promptly at four and taunted the leaves to change from shades of hunter green to deep rusty reds, pumpkin orange, and shimmering gold. It was late fall and the icy clamp of winter was not far behind.

Lazer's first Rite of Passage seemed an eternity away. He struggled to stay focused on second-quarter finals, hoping the workload of endless studies and practice sessions would distract him. He felt he was ready, but the list of challenges that defined his first passage was unnerving. It was only a first-level exhibition, fiercely monitored and supervised to prevent almost every possible danger. Passing it was enough to qualify him for marriage, housing, and a few basic jobs. As far as he was concerned, that was enough to satisfy his promise to his mother. He would pass, then call his mother and go home. *Finally*.

There was one more thing he had to do before he left Tosadae—talk with Masta Poe. He had been avoiding her classes and knew if he didn't make amends for his absence, he would never be allowed to complete his studies under her tutelage. And if he did not come back, he needed closure. Lazer sent her a message and Masta Poe responded, telling Lazer to meet her outside the library promptly at 4:30, and not to be late.

As he crossed the circular courtyard, he stared at the cone-shaped spires of the Tosadae Library. They blocked the sun and painted long narrow shadows over the grass and striped the buildings on the other side. Inside, the towers held a vast array of data, all neatly organized and recorded onto amino acid strands that represented the entire, collective works of man as he had evolved throughout history. It also held the infamous Celian Gnorb, one of three Gnorbs that still remained in human hands. The security around the Gnorb had always been profound, but since the theft of the Orbis Gnorb on Atlantia, protective measures had been tightened even further.

Masta Poe was waiting for him. She stood near the curved eaves of the library, the afternoon wind playfully whipping at her burgundy cloak and tousling her mane of silvery white hair. Her large eyes peered from behind pale green tinted glasses, which to Lazer seemed humorously old-fashioned and made her face seem older than it was. Lazer had almost reached her when she turned and entered the library, saying nothing. Dutifully, he followed. She passed the security sensors and walked to the central spires. There was a brief exchange of words between her and the guard that ended before Lazer caught up with her. The security guard nodded and walked away. Lazer's eyes widened as he realized what she was about to do.

"I'm not allowed in with the Gnorb," he whispered to her.

"I know."

The guard returned and handed her an imprint tray. Masta Poe instructed Lazer to stick his fingers in the gooey gray substance, which captured both his fingerprints and his DNA. With a few strokes of the touch pad, the guard handed Lazer a one-hour security pass.

Masta Poe and Lazer crossed through the arched entry and stepped onto an automated walkway that traversed the central structure. They swiped their pass cards at the first door and a series of security devices read and identified them via ocular scan, fingerprints, and DNA. Finally cleared, the massive decorated doors slid apart, making a great sucking sound when they opened and a thundering clang when they reverberated shut. The moment Lazer stepped into the central chamber, his mouth dropped. The room appeared to expand in all directions. It gave the feeling of motion, though nothing moved. It was as if one were floating in the middle of the beautiful azure sky and drifting up into a perfectly sunny, cloudless day, no matter what was going on outside. It was an optical illusion, designed to keep anyone who shouldn't be there confused and disoriented.

Masta Poe nudged him forward a few feet and the strange illusion faded. Another section of the spire opened. The core chamber was tapered and slender, and at its heart a cylindrical staircase spiraled upward, seemingly into infinity. *Another illusion*, Lazer thought. The staircase was bathed in a multitude of colors that flooded in through the jewel-colored glass that adorned the top of the cone. The glass caught the light of the sun as it traversed the sky, scattering it in every direction. The painted light that was projected through the geometric shards of glass spilled into patterns that splattered across the walls and floor and changed by the hour, creating a series of complex, mathematical puzzles. At the central point of the structure floated the Celian Gnorb.

Masta Poe began to ascend the staircase. Lazer hesitated, as the unwelcoming eyes of researchers, guards, and a dozen security beams traced his every move.

"You are with me. Come." Masta Poe, of course, felt his trepidation. Her voice was calming, and he obediently followed her lead.

Lazer stared at the Gnorb. His eyes transfixed on it and a wash of memories flooded his mind.

"I . . . I remember something . . .," Lazer stuttered. "I saw the Orbis Gnorb twice . . . twice and . . ."

As if in a trance, he told Masta Poe about an incident that had happened when he was about six. His mother had arranged for his class to take a tour of the temples. He, along with his classmates, were granted special permission to see the Orbis Gnorb. Once inside, the students had been invited to get a closer look at the spherical orb with its opalescent hues and swirling mystery. They passed in small groups, standing about a foot away from the sealed chamber that held it. It was beautiful, Lazer remembered, and it seemed to call to him with such feeling that he stopped and turned to face it. As Lazer and seven other children leaned in closer to gaze into the smoky haze and watch the tiny, firefly-like eruptions that appeared and faded gracefully inside, Lazer felt compelled to reach out his hand. He wanted to touch it, to feel the energy that radiated out to him from the Gnorb. Before the adults could intervene, the Gnorb changed colors and brightened to a blinding blaze of light. A high-pitched whine screeched out with ear-crushing tones that affected everyone in the room except Lazer and the other children who stood with him. They were mesmerized by what was happening inside the Gnorb.

In the midst of the chaos, Lazer and the other children felt safe and calm. The brilliant light that sent everyone else cowering to the floor soothed his eyes. The piercing sound that forced the others to cover their ears played like celestial music, singing to him in words he couldn't understand; yet in his soul he knew the meaning. Only Lazer and the other children with him were captivated by the bliss of the event. Their young faces beamed with pleasure, while everyone around them stumbled along the walls, protecting their eyes and ears. Lazer's mother reached into the haze of blinding light and grabbed Lazer, pulling him away. Instantly the glaring light subsided and allowed the rest of the staff members to snatch the other children to safety. They were immediately whisked from the room.

Detra was the only one who witnessed the truth. She knew it was at the very instant when Lazer separated from the Gnorb that its glaring, boisterous turbulence subsided and it fell back into its gentle lull, except for one difference—the pure white color had deepened to a silver ever so slightly and, from that day on, had remained. Detra had seen the way Lazer and the Gnorb connected to each other. Detra never told anyone else what she had seen, although she had asked Lazer what he remembered. That day the temple changed its visitors' policy. No one outside the core research team was ever allowed to get close to the Gnorb again.

Lazer told Masta Poe that, until this moment, his mind would become a blank whenever he had tried to talk to anyone about the details of that day. What he saw and heard that day was indescribable, yet the images stayed in his memory as clearly as if they had happened only a moment ago. He and the other children knew only that they had shared a common experience, but no words about the event had ever passed between them. "You're the first person I have ever been able to tell." He stared at her with a look of astonishment.

"Perhaps the nearness of the Celian Gnorb unlocked your memory." She smiled. "And the second time?"

"It saved my life," he said. Lazer hesitated. He had sworn to Kyla and Cashton never to tell, and Evvy had taken the secret with her to her grave. Lazer changed the subject. "How many have been stolen?"

"Two. The blue Orbis Gnorb in Atlantia and, yesterday, the one with crimson hues was stolen from Panazia."

Lazer knew that there were four, and that each Gnorb had a subtle shade of color that distinguished it; silvery white, golden yellow, sapphire blue, ruby red. This Gnorb was a soft, almost imperceptible sapphire blue.

Nearing the step, Masta Poe cupped her hands a few inches from the Gnorb. It began to glow and hum. Lazer was captivated by its beauty.

"Do you know what they do?" Lazer asked.

"On that, you know more than I. It has spoken to you, twice. We believe their creators came and left long before man evolved. They took with them the secrets to their wisdom, with the exception of these Gnorbs—doors to something we have yet to unlock." Masta Poe opened her hands, allowing the Gnorb to float between them.

The old memories filled Lazer's head with out-of-focus images like shadows in a dream. His eyes glazed over as the Celian Gnorb drifted closer and drew him in. Masta Poe watched.

"What do you see?"

"The Gnorbs are not doors, they are . . . a key," he mumbled, suddenly monotone.

"What kind of key?"

"To keep out . . . to keep out the . . ." Lazer stopped and shook his head, trying to shake the strange fog that had suddenly engulfed his mind. He looked at her, his eyes filled with a dark fear even he didn't understand.

"Keep out the what?"

"I don't know," Lazer backed away, as he fought to return from the waking dream that pulled at him.

"Why are you afraid?"

"I . . . I'm not afraid." Lazer's defenses rushed back into place.

"You fear for your mother?"

"Atlantia's at war."

"And what will your worrying do?"

"I can't help caring about what happens."

"To care is a gift of love; to worry is to deny the powers both you and the object of your concern have. Believe in your heart that you have already vanquished your enemy and that your mother is safe, and it is so. Worry equals fear and fear blocks your core. Without your core, you and your mother are lost."

"I will take care of my mother," he said with an arrogance that raised one of Masta Poe's white eyebrows.

"Yet you still refuse to claim your BAI, and that's what makes you weak and keeps your visions in darkness." She reached out for the Gnorb, willing it back to him.

"Look inside, Cole Lazerman. What do you see?" Masta Poe insisted.

Lazer hesitated. He didn't want to look. He wanted to leave, to run away and forget everything. Yet something inside of him had to know. He stepped forward again, his heart pounding, his mouth dry. He peered down into the swirls of haze, letting the sparkling lights reflect in his eyes. But unlike his first encounter with the Orbis Gnorb, there was no brilliant glare, no siren's song.

"Open your soul to it as you did when you were young. Do as you did when you allowed the Gnorb to guide you from danger at Temple Mountain. Look deeper, Lazer," she whispered.

Again, Lazer's eyes glazed over.

"I see . . . a great fog . . . explosions and fire . . . death . . . so much death. It's too dark . . ." Frustration choked him.

"Trust the *knowing* to guide you through the darkness. Create the vision of what will be and see it."

Her words challenged him. Lazer stared deeper into the Gnorb. The haze swirled faster. Sparks of light began to flash. The swirling mass formed a series of 3-D images—battles, creatures, places, buildings, faces, people he knew and people he'd never seen. The last image congealed into a man. He resembled Lazer, but he was older, much older. The image was hazy and unclear, except for his eyes. Lazer saw in them a murderous hatred that raged with the force of an uncontrollable wildfire.

Lazer's father appeared behind the image of the man with burning eyes. His father called out, but each time the man tried to turn, a swirling shadow fell across his face and pulled the man's focus forward. Then his father faded and Lazer's mother, Elana Blue, Kyla, and Cashton appeared and screamed out to him. Their open mouths made no sound. It was as if they were trapped behind a glass partition, their voices silenced by its presence. Behind them a sea of people rose up and chanted words he could not hear. Still the man with the blazing eyes did not turn, his gaze was fixed on the unspoken terror that swirled before him. He raised a weapon. It was strange, awkward, and otherworldly. He looked at Lazer, aimed, and fired, obliterating the vision in a blanket of white.

Lazer stumbled backward, startled, breathless, snapping out of the trance that had taken him into its vision. The image inside the Gnorb faded, turning once again into the lush blue mist and sparkling with tiny explosions of fantastic colors that popped and vanished inside the soft haze. He fought his way back from the confusion and looked at Masta Poe.

"Why do you stop?"

"Why do you care?"

Masta Poe was manipulating his emotions. *But why?* He studied her face for the answer. If she wanted a confrontation, he was ready for it. Suddenly, only anger filled his mind. It was cold, hard, real, and familiar. He felt safe in its ugliness.

"I can't protect you . . .," she began.

"You're asking me to see results of things before they happen?"

"I am telling you to imagine your future. Only you can bring your desires to reality, Lazer, and knowing what is coming will give you time to make the best choices." Her tone was calm, yet filled with compassion and hope. She wanted him to understand the wisdom behind the emotional walls that blocked him. She wanted him to enter the door he refused to pass through.

Lazer heard her words, but stood motionless, blind to the truth that felt so close.

"You can't will something into being!" he blurted. "I can't will my father back to life, or be home, or destroy the Black Guard!"

"If that is what you believe, then it is so. You alone are the angel of your destiny. You alone are its demon."

Lazer turned to face Masta Poe. "No!" he whispered, still panting from the fear that filled him. "That was not my future." He pointed at the Gnorb.

"I told you the day we met, you held in your soul a great calling," she stated.

"My only calling is to avenge my father!" His voice echoed through the vast chamber.

"And what of *your* visions?"

"I'm not that man!"

"Lie not to yourself, for if you do not conquer your fears of the future and master your destiny, your powers will abandon you. You must face your calling or you will be useless to all. Abandon the anger and stand in the light, or death will claim you and all you love."

Lazer fought back tears. He was being suffocated by truths he could not face. He backed away from Masta Poe.

"No. Anger is my greatest power! It gives me the strength to get up and fight my way through every day. If my powers fail me, I will pick up a weapon—a stick, a rock, I'll fight with my bare hands—and fight until every biodroid is vaporized. That's my destiny!" Lazer backed away. He turned and ran across the platform, down the stairs, and out of the Gnorb chamber.

Masta Poe looked after him and then back at the Gnorb.

"He has the stardust of two Gnorbs in his veins," she said to the now quiet ball that floated beside her. "He is more powerful than I thought. But still, he is not ready to believe, and my time is running out."

26

MORE TIME

OVER THE NEXT FEW WEEKS, Lazer attended classes in body only. He listened to the lecture series on the Mutant Wars. It had been a favorite part of history for him in high school because each night he would come home and discuss the various strategies and battles with his father, who had fought in them with heroes like Aleece Avery. The war claimed more than ten thousand mutant, splicer, and human lives, but in the end freedom was won. In the final thirty-six hours, at the battle of Pelipon, Pouwin's generals surrendered and the war was over. Lazer's father had been there. Lazer imagined with each passage and horrific image the class was shown what it must have been like for Rand in those final hours. Lazer gained an even greater respect for his father and, by the end of the lecture series, his determination to fight for Atlantia had reached a new resolve.

Lazer's mind was preoccupied, however, with fighting the inner voices that badgered him each day to go home. Every night, unable to sleep, he would slip from his dorm and race through the black night, sneaking into the flight simulator. There, alone with the demons that haunted him, he would run battle program after battle program. Images of day or night skies would appear around him in the 3-D holographic projections that completely encircled the cockpit. Lazer would fly into the most dangerous and complicated attack sequences and battle against every kind of enemy ship imaginable—always the lone warrior with a single adversary, fighting to the death.

Far too many nights the complicated programs would defeat him. The unknown adversary would blow his fighter into vapor wash, or send him spiraling into a mountain, or the desert, or the sea. Each night Lazer would slam his fists against the control panel and tremble alone in the darkness. He was frustrated and angry that his emotions could so easily overwhelm him and, in the end, he could not deny that he was his own greatest enemy. Furious at himself, he would restart a new program and try again. Time and again, Lazer would lose each battle until, exhausted, he would drag himself home and fall into bed.

Masta Poe often watched Lazer, unnoticed from the observation chamber above. She couldn't help him. She knew, above all, that Lazer would have to take this journey alone. When Lazer left, Masta Poe would turn to look at another of her students who fought in the simulators, perfecting the skills of a great fighter pilot—Elana Blue. She had her own collection of tortured demons, filled with anger and disappointment that shadowed her like a black cloud. Her demons were betrayal and abandonment—the pain of a motherless child's desire to feel important and needed.

27

UNIVERSAL GOD

THE ENTIRE STUDENT BODY sat, danced, stood, or lay under the lush trees that grew beneath a small proton perpetual climate dome as they read and sang the collective works of praise, celebrating life under the love of Earth's One Universal God. *The Book of Spiritual Oneness* had been created from the commonalities found among all religions and was dedicated to the unity of man, his place in nature, the universe, and his immortal soul. After the Great Quakes, mankind longed for unity among Earth's survivors—those who had been separated by the newly divided continents and those who had crawled out from the fallen cities and devastated towns. They looked for the word of a single God in everything that was done to save man. Together they rejected anyone who sought leadership based on fear or any kind of dogma that lessened the value of one human being over another—be they man or woman, black, yellow, red, brown, or white. Mankind had finally accepted that all humanity stood as equals. Splicers, clones, and even zomers were welcome, though full equality under the law was a different story for them.

Lazer and Elana Blue sat on opposite sides of the field from each other and listened to a choir sing an old standard by John Lennon called *Imagine*—a beautiful ballad that had been written over a century ago and played in honor of a great dream that had been realized by a united world. Another set of eyes watched their exchange of glances and shy smiles. Bo Rambo saw the glances that passed between Lazer and Elana and he, now more than ever, wanted her flirtation to belong only to him. Bo was Lazer's archenemy on the zoccair field and in the flight school, and now a new arena of contention came into focus. Lazer knew that Bo was the villain who thwarted his every attempt at happiness, the foe who had deemed it his personal mission to block the only two pleasures Tosadae held for him: zoccair and Elana Blue. Bo was handsome, talented, relatively smart, an amazing pilot, and competitively athletic, but Lazer had heard that Bo was to Elana Blue only a 'friend.' So Lazer did his best to ignore Bo's burning stares and gazed happily upon Elana Blue. Again the hulking shadow stepped in to block him as Lazer attempted to make his way across the field after the end of the service.

"I'll see you on the practice field," Bo said threateningly, before grabbing Elana Blue by the arm and pulling her away. "We need to talk," Bo insisted in a hushed voice. She looked at him and then at Lazer. She knew she had to confront Bo once and for all.

They walked out of the dome and into the chill as they crossed the circle. "You've been avoiding me like the plague. What's up?" Bo finally had Elana alone.

"I'm not avoiding you, Bo. I told you, I can't go out with you anymore."

"Why?" He was almost pouting.

"We've been over this," Elana spoke with a tone filled with both frustration and sadness. "I want to get married, Bo, have children. The laws against humans and clones are definitive. You know that."

Bo was crestfallen, but knew she was right. He was a clone and the procreation laws when it came to clones were final. They had been put in place in 95 A.Q. after the Splicer Fiasco. The deaths of so many humans had decimated Earth's population. First the Great Quakes killed more than half the planet, and then tens of thousands died in the jaws of the splicers. The human race had to be protected. In the cloning process, the reproductive genes somehow switched off, which made it impossible for clones, male or female, to have children. Because clones couldn't have children, marriage between clones and humans had been strictly forbidden. Some humans, whose love had been strong, had defied the laws and married their clone lovers, but their unions were not sanctioned, which meant they would not receive corporate benefits like housing, education, and most top-level jobs.

"We could still be together. I've heard about these settlements," Bo begged.

She looked at him. Bo's pain washed over Elana like a turbulent storm. She felt his sadness press against her heart. Bo was a strong young man, but in her hands he was butter melting in the summer sun. His pleading eyes defied the champion he had become. He didn't care; Bo wanted her. "Please, Elana, don't throw away what we have."

Stopping in the shadow of a massive tree whose limbs stood as bare and naked as Bo felt, she looked into his eyes. "We don't have anything, Bo. That's what you've never accepted. We dated in high school and it was fun, but I didn't love you then and I don't love you now."

"It's because I'm a clone," he said sadly.

"I told you how I felt before I even knew you were a clone."

"Then being a clone doesn't matter?"

"Not to our friendship. Please understand. If I loved you, it wouldn't stop me from defying the system to be with you, but I don't. Not like that."

"How do you know, Elana? Give us time."

"I know that love will touch my heart and fill me up with so much passion I'll explode just hearing the sound of his voice. Being away from him for even a moment will be like living without the sun to warm me.

I want to breathe his air and share his dreams. When I find him, I'll be happy and safe, and we'll build our lives together, have children, and make each other complete. Don't ask me to settle for less, Bo. I won't."

"I could be all that, Elana." Bo touched her face.

"You will be, for someone else," she said as gently as she could.

"For you, Elana. Give us time."

"If that were true, I would have known the first time my lips touched yours. I believe when you meet your soul mate, you know without a doubt that love is forever. I'll know from that first kiss. It isn't you; it just isn't. I'm sorry, Bo."

There was nothing more Elana could say to ease the pain he was feeling. He loved her. It was real and strong and good, and if she could have settled for less than the passion she knew in her heart was possible, she would have given herself over to him—but, she couldn't. She turned and walked away.

Bo stared after her, his chest tightening with hurt and anger. His ego did not want to accept the finality of her words. He blamed the rejection on the fact that he was a clone and stormed away across the circle and into the stadium to prepare for the varsity game.

He reached the tunnel and turned, crashing into Lazer and slamming him into the stadium gate. Bo stopped for one brief second. He was blind with emotion, but he saw all too clearly the single face that brought clarity to his defeat. Bo shoved Lazer again and was gone.

Kyla and Cashton walked from the locker rooms, valiant gladiators ready to do battle, until they saw Bo shove Lazer.

"What was that about?" Cashton's eyes locked on Bo.

"You got me," Lazer said, picking up his gear.

"If looks could kill, you'd already be a rotting corpse," Kyla nodded toward Bo, who joined his gang of upperclassmen.

"Something tells me they are not about to play fair," Cashton added.

"You better stop taunting him, Laze," Kyla said.

"I'm not doing anything." Lazer adjusted his shoulders to take the tension out of them just as Elana Blue appeared in the stands. Again Kyla watched as Lazer's energy melted. Kyla rolled her eyes in disgust.

"Yeah, right. You'll sabotage us if you don't stop focusing on her," Kyla said, nodding at Elana.

They entered the zoccair arena to the sound of cheers. It was varsity versus junior varsity today—a slaughter at best. The antigravity field activated before Lazer could respond. The goals launched, rising and falling at opposite ends of the field. The two teams engaged their palm pads, the familiar orange ball spun up into midair, and the call resounded: "Game on, Tosadae! *Bacco!*"

28

ATLAND CITY

THERE WAS A GRAY HAZE over the city that smelled of burnt skin, hair, and death. The streets were empty except for the occasional peacekeepers and hovercrafts that drifted overhead in the early morning light. A squad of clones and mutants armed with DT phasers patrolled the streets, looking for any humans who had not been killed or captured, or who had not taken shelter inside the elaborate sewers and caves that crisscrossed beneath the city.

Aleece survived the crash, but in their descent, the chute of her escape pod caught in some trees and she was captured. Fielding drifted north and, she hoped, escaped. She was held in a barren outpost and questioned for what seemed like weeks. Although starved and brutalized, she wouldn't tell them anything, so she was transferred to the main sports stadium in the center of Atland City. There, with a host of other POWs, she awaited her fate. The first night, alone and hungry, Aleece worried about her life, her family, and the horrors she could not relay back to the Triumvirate. Frightened and exhausted, she finally fell asleep.

Aleece awoke filthy and sore, but still alive. She struggled to her feet and gathered her strength, checking the cuts and scars that marked her arms and legs. Slowly, she let her eyes drift across this somber place that held her captive within its walls. All around her were the signs of war. Women with filthy faces clutched their frightened children, as they huddled by piles of glowing, tangerine-colored embers, desperate for a moment of stolen warmth. Aleece gasped, taking in a soft, involuntary breath. A rush of fear engulfed her. She wanted her husband and daughter. She wanted to be at home by a roaring fire, laughing and talking with her family and friends. But devastation and hopelessness stared at her like an ugly face, peeking from the shadows of a cold, harsh reality. She was a prisoner. Aleece's heart sank and she pitied herself, sick at the thought she was lost to all she loved. There, in a swell of emotional despair, she felt the pull of despondency dragging her into its abyss. *No!* Aleece thought. It was a soft distant voice cried from deep inside her being. With that moment of denial, a roar of courage flooded her. It was the same voice, amplified a thousand times and it came from her heart. It called to her, demanding that she not give in to the darkness. She was a leader, a trained officer of the Politia Forces, a mother with a child that needed her and a husband that loved her and she loved him. She needed a plan. Her thoughts organized and in a split second jumped to Fielding. Was he alive? Maybe he had survived. Was he a prisoner here, as well? She searched the arena, but Fielding was nowhere in sight. The men and women must have been separated.

Aleece walked, taking in every detail of her prison. Before her lay row upon row of wounded women and children, human carnage left alive for the moment by a heartless foe. Her eyes scanned the dimensions of the fifty-eight-foot-high walls of her prison. The fingers of panic clutched her throat until it started to close. *Stay focused*, she thought to herself, repeating it again and again like a mantra. She studied the chain-link fence, capped by razor wire that looped along the lower rows of seats, encasing the center road of Atland City's raceway arena. The weeping and agonizing moans of her fellow captives reverberated off the massive corporate billboards that ringed the arena. They had come to Atlantia to advertise and sell, but the corporations weren't willing to take the Atlantians on as constituents. She couldn't blame the corporate leaders entirely. They had given their power over to the Collective and the Triumvirate long ago, but they still had a voice, and on the subject of Atlantia they had been far too silent.

The women had managed to organize what supplies they had to help the sick and dispose of the dead. They had organized themselves in sections. The wounded in the center lay under poorly constructed tents. Children and older men and women, no longer able to fight, gathered against a north wall. The dead lay in piles at the south end. Life moved on. Aleece listened as a young woman read to a group of five- and six-year-olds, trying to keep their minds off the horror of their circumstances. She smiled, remembering the many times she had read to Riana. She needed to stay in the present, figure out where she was and how to get out. She studied the exits and towers, determined to find a way.

Aleece stopped a woman who was carrying a sack of powdered supplements. "What can I do to help?" she asked.

"I don't know. What *can* you do to help?" The woman was gruff, but beneath her edgy voice there was an honest warmth. She eyed Aleece, sizing her up. Aleece could tell by the exhaustion in the woman's face that she had been there for a while.

"I'm a doctor," Aleece said.

"Surgeon?" The woman's face lit up.

"Used to be."

"Used to be still counts. Follow me. The name's Maya," the woman commented with a polite nod.

"Aleece."

"Were you on the health staff of the Atland City Care Facility?"

"Sangelino. I came to Atlantia on . . . on personal business."

"You got family on Atlantia?"

"I don't know," Aleece answered with an expression of sadness that would deflect any further questions. Maya nodded. She understood the pain of loss, of not knowing the fate of those you love. Maya told her she had lost her entire family, her husband, her sons, and her parents. Aleece didn't have to say another word.

They stopped at a makeshift tent just as someone rushed inside carrying a young girl who had been shot in the leg. Through the opening, Aleece could see tables, beds, and a few supplies. They had only the bare minimum needed to sustain life and deaden pain, but it would do for now.

"It ain't Sangelino's All Health, but they managed to keep *me* alive," Maya said. She pulled back a flap on her tunic and revealed a blood-soaked bandage.

"You're bleeding again."

Aleece moved to check her bandage. Maya stopped her.

"I'll be fine. That little girl needs you more."

Aleece nodded, entered the tent, and became a doctor again.

29

ELANA BLUE

LAZER DRAGGED his battered body up the dormitory steps, still wearing his soiled Tosadae zoccair uniform. Neither he nor his team had fared well at today's game. He walked past a group of students who all but sneered at him, turning their faces away and adding to his newly acquired pariah status—his punishment for losing the last point of the varsity game and costing the underclassmen their junior varsity championship title.

Elana Blue saw the exchange and excused herself from a group of girls who were talking about the embarrassing defeat the junior varsity had taken. She headed over to Lazer at the top of the stairs and smiled. Her heart went out to him. He had played as best he could today, but Bo had been on a mission to destroy Lazer's confidence, and the mission had been accomplished.

"Hey, you played a good game today. Really." She smiled again, catching up and falling into his stride.

For the first time her incredible smile didn't break the somber cloud of defeat that surrounded him. "Too bad Bo Rambo thinks I'm the alien enemy of his life."

"He's threatened."

"Threatened? Yeah, right."

"Veritas!" she said, bubbling with a small, almost beatific smile. "You're good. Even beyond good." She looked around to see who was within earshot. "Coach Darius is talking about making you lead striker on varsity next year," she whispered into his ear.

"What? A sophomore?"

Elana Blue shushed him, looked around again, and gestured that this was top secret information. "Swear you won't tell anyone I told you."

"Swear. Look at me. I'm in particle surge!" He had goose bumps. He cracked his wonderful smile. True or not, it was the nicest thing she could have said.

"It's true. At least as long as you keep playing the way you played today. That setup and slam was digital. Bo's last move was a total cheat and I can't believe the referee missed the call."

"Thanks. I owe you one for that."

"Yeah? I'll remember that the next time we meet," she said with a conspiratorial wink.

Her voice, the words, the shadow that fell across her face suddenly brought a wash of memories flooding back from the day he was rescued at Shooting Falls. Lazer's mouth fell open. It all made sense. He had met her before. "It was you!"

Elana Blue looked at him, but couldn't respond. She had no idea what he was referring to. "Atlantia—the Wedge—Shooting Falls. You were in the Wedge with . . . with Ducane Covax!"

Now it was Elana Blue who finished putting the pieces together. "The boy on the Zakki," she said. "You were that jerk." Lazer felt a rush of the same wild anger that had almost cost him his life. He remembered the fury that racked his body when he saw his sworn enemy at the controls of the Wedge. That inhuman, heartless species who murdered his father and who, in a moment when he had begged for death, had saved his life.

He looked at Elana Blue and realized it had not been some mindless biodroid that had saved him, but this angel from a dream who now stood before him. She had given the order that had saved him. Yes, he had been vicious and ungrateful, but with cause. And now he had to tell her why.

"I . . . I had just lost my father in the Vacary Mines attack. The sight of your Black Guard . . ." His words caught in his throat.

Elana was at once empathetic to his pain. His memories were filled with sadness, and Elana Blue experienced every torturous stab. His pain was hers and it seared into her flesh with such torrential emotion that her eyes welled with tears for him.

"But Ducane Covax . . .," he asked, desperate to understand.

" . . . is my father. We decided to drop my last name so I could just be normal." She fought to control her own anger. The pull of his sadness bound her to him.

Lazer nodded, understanding the pressures she must have been raised under as the only daughter of Ducane Covax.

"I'm . . . sorry about your father." Her words tumbled out with such a depth of honest sincerity that they touched Lazer's heart.

Lazer nodded gratefully. She understood. They stared into each other's eyes. Something began that defied time and logic. Now it was his turn. "I . . . never got to thank you for saving my life." He froze, "So . . . I . . . I have to go," Lazer turned and limped away.

Elana felt the turmoil that churned inside of him. She liked him, but the history of who she was and the death of his father was a curtain between them. Her whole life she'd had to deal with what her father's work had unleashed, and once again it was about to deny her something she wanted.

30

TAKING CHANCES

OVER THE NEXT FEW MONTHS, Lazer and Elana passed
each other on the grounds of Tosadae. They stole glances of each other
across lecture halls and classrooms. They battled each other on the simulators and in the forum labs with Masta Poe but, no matter how hard
he tried, it seemed Lazer couldn't avoid looking into her face and catching the depth of her amazing eyes. The truth was he didn't want to avoid
her. He wanted to talk to her. Kyla told him it was his natural instincts
warning him to keep away. Cashton said if he didn't at least talk to her,
she'd haunt him for the rest of his life.

"If you ask her, you have a fifty-fifty chance of getting a yes. If you
don't, you got nothin'," Cashton told him. It was a line from a movie
based on one of his other favorite shows on the Old TV Vybernet feed—
Quantum Leap. Cashton loved the show, the characters, the adventures,
and the fact you could travel through time, step into other people's lives,
and make a difference. He was sure they had used Einstein's theory:
time and space were limited, so two bodies couldn't occupy the same

place at the same time. He also liked the particle acceleration/deceleration theory they used as their means of time travel, so much so that he had begun working on his own time travel device based on the principle.

Meanwhile, Lazer struggled with how to get around the memory of the attacks. He imagined the battles that were being fought every day on Atlantia because of Ducane Covax and his monstrous Black Guard. He wanted to blame Elana Blue for being Covax's daughter, but it wasn't her fault, so why punish her and ultimately himself? He'd find out soon enough how far the apple fell from the tree. *How totally corny,* Lazer thought. It must have been a line from *The Beaver,* another of Cashton's favorite shows, but it fit.

Lazer had made up his mind to tell Elana how he felt about everything—the attacks, his father's death, the day at the falls, and her father. He was a man on a mission. He moved in long purposeful strides across the campus, passing the sculpture garden and the floating fountain that gurgled serenely at its center. His eyes darted from the holomaze of changing lights to the geometric menagerie as he looked for a glimpse of her. He checked the student bio behavioral bar because he'd heard a new collection of mood-enhancing art was on show for those students who needed to alter their dispositions, or just escape for a few hours from the workload that came with life at Tosadae. Elana Blue was nowhere to be found. Lazer's heart felt heavy, burdened by the weight of what he so desperately wanted to say to her. Although he'd rehearsed it a thousand times, the words mulled around his head in a jumbled mess. His chest was tight and he found himself taking long, deep breaths that seemed to end in frustrated sighs. Just as the noon bell began to chime, she appeared, turning the corner right in front of him. Their eyes connected and she smiled, walking toward him. In the next instant, she stood face to face with him.

They stared at each other smiling like two Cheshire cats. No one else was anywhere around. She stood silently looking at him with those eyes that could melt an iceberg. Without thinking, Lazer reached out and gently touched her hand. A jolt of energy buzzed through his fingers and raced through his entire body and into his head, making him almost dizzy and taking away every concern and fear. Lazer was mesmerized. It was happening again, this incredible feeling that defied time and logic.

"I . . . never . . . finished thanking you for saving my life," Lazer said softly.

The world around them melted away. She was part of everything good he thought had been lost to him. He knew her every thought, wish, desire, every fiber of her being as well as he knew the deepest secrets of his very own soul. Unable to stop himself, Lazer leaned forward and kissed her. It was an action as familiar to him as if he had done it a million times before. A kiss so gentle, so natural, that she couldn't help but kiss him back. Her lips were sweet and soft, and for those few precious seconds, life slowed, swirling into a warm haze that cocooned them in its magic. The world stopped, perfect and complete. Their lips parted, but their eyes held each other in a trance.

"Wow. You're welcome," she replied, breathless from the kiss.

"I've wanted to do that since the first day I saw you on the zoccair field," he whispered.

Before she could respond, a group of students, returning from the game, converged on them. Lazer and Elana smiled and stepped to one side, letting the building's arched shadows shelter them. Lazer wanted to say something brilliant and clever, but he was at a loss for words. Dazed, Lazer nodded, turned, and started to walk away.

"Wait!" Elana Blue followed after him.

He stopped and spun to face her. Elana was just as surprised as Lazer by her forward behavior. She struggled for something to say, suddenly as awkward and as vulnerable as Lazer had just been the moment before. She looked at him, her eyes as innocent and lost as he felt. Lazer melted. She was as open as a book with blank pages, eager to be filled with life. *Ask her*, he thought. *Now!* Lazer gathered his courage, filling his lungs with a great gasp of air. He knew this would be his only chance.

"Elana, look, I know I've been a total dweeb, but could we . . . I mean . . . would you want to . . ."

"Yes!" she blurted, excitedly.

"Yes?" Lazer was unsure if she knew what she was agreeing to.

"You were going to ask me to the Spring Jam."

"Yeah, I was," he muttered, his confusion swirling in a hint of suspicion. "You read auras?"

"I read boys. Seven-thirty? I'll be wearing your favorite color . . . cobalt blue." Lazer didn't question how she could have possibly known his favorite color, but it pleased him beyond words that she did. She was glowing. Her smile turned from coy to seductive and Lazer felt a warm tingling that raced from his head to his toes and made his head spin. He wanted desperately to kiss her again. But Elana beat him to it and brought her lips to his. This kiss was even better than the first. It was the kiss she had been waiting for her entire life. She knew in that moment that he was The One. His was the soul that matched hers. They parted, their eyes still staring into each other's.

"Until the dance . . .," she said before heading off to her dorm room.

As soon as she was out of sight, Lazer lost it. He let out a whoop of joy that echoed across the commons and then raced in the opposite direction, never allowing his feet to touch the ground. He had a date with Elana Blue.

31

DOMED

FINALLY THE POLITIA DECIDED to admit that Atlantia had been domed. The ANN Vybernet news reported that it had been sealed under a proton bubble with both the politia and the Atlantian leaders' joint approval. But it was a lie. Neither the politia nor the Atlantians had launched the dome, nor did they have control of it. The Collective only knew of a few incidents that had happened months before, and in retrospect they seemed like terrible anomalies that couldn't possibly happen again. The news of the doming had everyone talking as they waited for the politia's investigation team to submit their reports. But in the end, everyone seemed to agree doming was the appropriate option. At least for the moment, the world would be safe. Those select few who knew the truth realized that hell could be raging in all directions inside Atlantia. Until he could get more facts, Baz Mangalan unilaterally decided not to let Dante, Fahan, the Collective, or Corporate know that the Black Guard and not the politia controlled the dome. It could set off a worldwide panic.

Behind closed doors inside Sangelino, conspiracy theories raged.

There was an unsubstantiated suspicion that Aleece's crash had been digitally scrambled by the Black Guard to look like an accident. Somehow the Black Guard had hacked into the satellite feeds and reconfigured all the visual and audio information coming out of Atlantia to look like and say whatever they wanted. But how? For all intents and purposes, things on Atlantia appeared completely under control. It wasn't until a few sporadic and very frantic personal messages began to leak through their digital scrambling program a few weeks later that anyone suspected they had been misled by perfectly done propaganda. The bits of information that slipped through their encryption programs as partially unscrambled cries for help were put into the hands of the Politia Intelligence. What they could decipher was sketchy at best, but it was all they had to go on, at least for now.

Dante had heard but not seen the unencrypted V-mails. He was only a substitute for his wife and had limited access and limited powers. Everyone knew the people of Atlantia didn't want war, but the few unencrypted wristsponder calls and V-mails for help were being buried in a quagmire of political confusion. In the end, the Atlantians were victims of war crimes that could not be substantiated.

On Atlantia, Five and his biodroids had been more than ready. The Black Guard's isoluminescent miasma continued to play its CGI movies of normal life on the dense, digital haze, hiding the horrible events that were happening across the territory from satellite surveillance. Everything on Atlantia looked in order. With the inadvertent assistance of Baz Mangalan, the world had been blinded to what was happening on Atlantia by Five's genius.

32

BLISS

IT WAS FRIDAY and Lazer was in his favorite class: hand-to-hand battle techniques inside the Arts and Powers battle forum. The course was required for the politia's leadership positions, but he knew it would also serve his ultimate mission back on Atlantia. The arena's design looked like an ancient coliseum. Today it was filled with young gladiators, ready to face death in the name of Caesar. The battle forum was one of the few buildings that had been constructed by the politia to house weapons and creatures—a primitive necessity not required by the original inhabitants of Tosadae, but mandatory for the humans who followed them as lords of Earth. Along the bottom ring were transparent force-field cages that held some of the most violent splicer creatures in captivity. Most of them had survived for years in the fissures and tunnels of post-quake Earth: prometheii, archeops, bilyons, krakans, tigots, pythozebs, and a nest of very nasty scarabites, just to name a few. They had been captured from around the world and brought to Tosadae to be studied and utilized in battle training. But creature theory class was on

Tuesday; today was hand-to-hand combat. The creatures watched from their cages. Some paced, agitated by the students and their aggressive energy. Others ignored the lessons, knowing at least today the work was human to human.

Elana exchanged sweet, surreptitious smiles with Lazer as Masta Poe explained how to block a weapons attack from a battle wand. Elana hated hand to hand almost as much as she hated creature conflict study, which would be next year's challenge. Just being in the same room with the creatures made Elana uncomfortable—a fact everyone knew but no one knew why. There were rumors about almost being eaten by a splicer when she was little, but she had been far too young to have been around for the Splicer Fiasco, and the new laws made all access to splicer pets illegal. No one but Lazer knew her father had been the creator of the splicer pet phenomenon and that he continued to experiment with genetic crossbreeding and high-level cloning. Lazer's anger at Elana's father simmered under everything in his life. No matter how hard he tried, he couldn't release it completely. But he wasn't about to let his feelings for Elana be hindered by a fact she had nothing to do with and which he couldn't change . . . at least not right at this moment.

The students, wearing protective padding made of a lightweight gelatinous substance that was covered in a spongy flexible concrete, were placed around the room facing their partners. An electronic gong rang out every three minutes, and the students would bow to each other, change partners, and fight the next person. It was a combination of street fighting, taekwondo, and battle wand against basic Visionistic Arts. Each counter weapon posture was steeped in the mastery of Masta Poe's teaching. Somehow she oversaw everyone at the same time, appearing at the right place at the right moment, mentoring each student, adjusting their moves, and pointing out their strengths and weaknesses.

The gong sounded and Lazer bowed to his latest opponent—a girl almost as tall and strong as he. He took the chi stance and faced her with his bare hands. She swung her battle wand and he blocked it with two small but well-placed shields. Lazer was focused and accurate with every move, until he happened to look up and see Bo Rambo partnered with Elana. Bo, along with a few of the upper-class students, had volunteered to assist Masta Poe. Lazer watched as Bo smiled at Elana Blue. Bo, who held the wand, was wonderfully gentle with her. He was calm, determined, and obviously vying to win her back from Lazer.

Lazer smelled it. He was too far away from them to hear their conversation, but Bo's body posture was blatant. He was hitting on Elana, hard. Lazer glared at him, trying his best to will his machismo across the room. He took a sharp blow to the head with one of the training wands, punishment for not paying attention. He hadn't noticed that it was Bo's best friend, Carel Bell, who was facing off with him for the round. Lazer pulled his attention back to Carel to save his neck, but still glanced occasionally at what was happening with Elana and Bo.

"I want to take you to the spring formal." Bo was as charming as possible.

"I have a date." Elana stayed aloof as ever.

Bo glared at Lazer. "Please tell me it's not the outback cowboy from Atlantia."

"It's really none of your business, Bo. It's not you and that's all you need to know." She whacked him just as the gong sounded.

Masta Poe was called out of the arena. In the instant after her exit, Lazer was across the room, unleashing a flurry of kicks and hits with his battle wand that dropped Bo to the floor. A stunned Bo found himself in a heap. His surprise turned to fury when he saw who was behind the attack. Bo rolled, arched back, and leapt to his feet. He took three lightning fast strides and jumped into Lazer's chest with a flying kick. Lazer ducked and spun into a roundhouse; he kicked Bo backward with such force that Bo bounced off the wall and fell face first into the dirt. Lazer's eyes were wild; all he knew was he had to defend Elana. Again Bo jumped to his feet and charged Lazer like a linebacker.

Lazer dropped his battle wand and jutted his hands out in front of him; without thinking, he summoned a ball of sparkling energy between his hands, then with a shove, shot it at Bo. Bo saw the bolt, dove, rolled, and dropped his battle wand. Jutting his hands forward, he, too, formed and shot an energy bolt into Lazer's chest. Direct hit! The ball of energy struck Lazer with such force it pounded him into the wall twenty feet away. Lazer, winded and sore, crumbled into a heap on the floor. Gasping for air, he struggled to his feet. Bo attacked again, this time turning his palms upward. He lifted them, levitating Lazer off the ground, and with a violent swinging gesture, tossed him like a rag doll against a wooden column. The force hurled Lazer into the worn wood, splintering it into a shower of pulp and dust.

Lazer landed flat and looked at Elana Blue. Her heart was with him and the terror in her eyes told him he had to win for both their sakes. With a graceful roll, Lazer pushed himself back onto his feet. He ignored the pain that throbbed through every inch of his body and, using a single burst of energy, he jumped six feet into the air, narrowly avoiding the next blast of fiery white light that shot from Bo's hands. Lazer landed like a cat and let his rage overtake his logic. In rapid retaliation, he hurled a silver stream of curling wind with such speed and force it caught Bo off guard. The swirling funnel hammered into Bo, bored into his chest, knocked him over, and slammed him onto the ground. Bo went ballistic. He defied gravity and flipped to his feet into a fighter's stance. He formed an icy, black energy ball with enough power to kill. It swirled, building between his hands. Just as he was about to shoot it, Masta Poe's voice exploded across the room.

"Stop!" she shouted as she appeared in front of Bo. Masta Poe immobilized him and stepped in to shield Lazer from the death ball. "Use your anger one more time like that and you will be expelled from my studies!" she told Bo, as her outstretched hand focused on the death ball.

Bo was rigid. Masta Poe released her hold on him, forcing him to drop the energy ball that still swirled in his hands. The particles hung for a moment more, then dissipated and floated away in a shimmering swirl of ashen snow.

"Enough," Masta Poe said to the entire class. "You are all dismissed. Go in light."

Bo glared at Lazer, said nothing, bowed, and walked away.

Elana crossed to Lazer with a look of concern.

"Are you okay?" she asked, brushing the dirt from his sleeve.

"I'm fine. What about you?" He was more concerned about her than himself.

Masta Poe looked at Elana and nodded for her to go. It was obvious she wanted to talk to Lazer alone.

"I'll wait for you by the dispensary." Elana crossed to the door.

A few of the students worked a little longer on style and stance while the rest dispersed. Some mumbled to each other about the rivalry between Bo and Lazer. Many commented that they had never seen Masta Poe lose her temper. The room emptied. People were grateful to get away from the negative energy that still hung in the air as thick as a spring fog. The last to leave was Elana, who stopped near the door to give Bo an icy glare. Finally, she turned and exited with a group of students.

Alone, Masta Poe turned her attention to Lazer. "Where was your focus?" she asked Lazer. "He could have severely wounded you."

"I'm fine," Lazer said, as he gathered his things.

"Has your spirit left us already?" Masta Poe asked.

"What?" Lazer was surprised that Masta Poe could read his thoughts with such clarity. She was right, his thoughts were of home, and his heart was already there. He ached to know what was really happening on Atlantia—the dome had caused a communication malfunction for a week. There had been a complete live feed, V-mail, and wristsponder blackout. After it was repaired, the few V-mails he had received seemed stilted and strange. On the surface, they said everything was fine, but between the lines it was obvious something was terribly wrong.

"You wish to go home to defeat the Black Guard?" she asked.

Lazer stared at her.

"You think you are ready?"

Lazer knew there was always an extra meaning beneath her words. Again he said nothing.

"If you think you are ready, then go. If you do not have the courage to learn all that I have to teach you, do not waste my time, Cole Lazerman." Masta Poe turned away.

Lazer felt a rush of panic surge through him. He needed her as a mentor, as an ally, as a friend. She was always in the strange distorted visions that haunted him. He knew she was an important part of his future, but he didn't understand why.

Flustered, he stepped in her way. "I admit it. I can't control the arts yet."

"You believe you can control the universe? You are further away from the light than I thought. The goal is to release into your BAI, trust, and let the universe exist as one with you."

"I have learned cloaking and levitation and I can create energy balls and shields to protect . . .," Lazer babbled at her, desperate to say the right things.

"Those are tricks, not powers. And without the universe to empower them, they are as shallow as the heart that wields them. With only that to guide you, *you will fail*." Masta Poe's words were cold and direct.

"I won't fail. I'll do whatever it takes to destroy the Guard! And . . . and I'll do it with or without your help!" Lazer shouted in her face before he turned to walk away.

"What was the vision you saw that first day in my class?" she called after him.

Lazer stopped and turned. It was as if she had commanded him to face her and his body had obeyed. Masta Poe stood motionless, waiting for his response. It was not her powers that compelled him, but the core of his soul that told him he must know the meaning of the images that haunted him constantly. His mind held answers, but she alone had the key to understanding them. "I don't know. Was it my future?" he demanded.

Masta Poe shrugged. "You tell me."

"Was it or wasn't it? I have to know!" Lazer was trembling.

"You do. All the answers you need are inside you right now."

"Then why aren't I sure?"

"Ask yourself, Lazer, not me. Look how you tremble, not with anticipation and the wonder of what will come, but with the frustration of what you cannot control. Don't you see? Your emotions are clouded by anger, and your heart is still blinded by hatred. You live in its blackness. It coats your soul with tar, and that blackness leaves you powerless," Masta Poe spoke with compassion.

"They murdered my father," he said defensively.

"A reality you cannot change."

"I can't change the past, but I will change the future. I will destroy the Black Guard and anyone who stands with them."

"It is will and purpose that define the depths of your powers. It is the truth and nobility of that purpose that define the man. Look to your purpose, Lazer." Masta Poe manifested a miniature Black Guard that floated above her hand. As Lazer glared at it, Masta Poe willed it into a life-sized version.

Lazer's reaction was instantaneous: hatred coursed through his veins.

"Fight him," Masta Poe commanded.

Lazer raised his hands, summoning an energy ball and hurling it into the Black Guard. The Guard easily blocked and diverted the blast. His metallic hands transformed into phasers—a succinct series of smooth metal tubes, shifting and sliding with rapid precision, pushing and pulling into narrow slots until the barrel and trigger formed with such speed that the action was a blur of motion. The next instant he fired a barrage of DT pellets. Lazer shielded.

"Master your emotions so that they do not master you," Masta Poe instructed. "If you want to defeat him, will it with a pure, clear mind. Don't defeat your foe, defeat all that he represents."

The pellets pounded Lazer's shield. It glowed with the heat from the hits and began to thin. Lazer's arms trembled under the pounding forces. Beads of sweat crowned his brow.

"You fight from revenge. When will you understand that revenge is not a hero's calling?"

The Guard switched to a cannon blaster and leveled his aim. Lazer panicked as the last of his shield dissipated. He wasn't strong enough. The shield evaporated, leaving him exposed. Masta Poe extended her hand and dissolved the Black Guard illusion.

"I protected you this time. You must find a way to release the anger that binds you and the revenge that drives you."

Lazer shook all over. His hands stung. "Revenge *is* my calling!" Lazer shouted at her.

She shook her head, looked at the ground, and released a long, deep sigh. "In the end, it will be love that will be your greatest test. The next battle you will face alone. Go in light, Cole Lazerman," Masta Poe said before she vanished into thin air.

Lazer was alone, abandoned by the mentor he was depending on. There was still so much to learn. In two days, he would leave for his Rite of Passage and then, with or without his mother's permission, he would find a way to get home.

"You can't stop me!" he shouted after Masta Poe. She was gone. His words echoed against the empty stadium and melted into the walls until only silence hung in their place.

"Why do you taunt her?" Elana's voice filled the void.

"She taunts me," Lazer snapped at Elana, turning away from her to hide the fury that filled his eyes.

Before he could speak again her arms were around him, her hands pressing into his chest, her face against his back. Elana sensed the anger that emanated from his body like heat rising from searing hot pavement in summer. It caught in his throat and held his breath captive. It stopped his heart and made his blood pound until his face flushed a deep burgundy. His vengeful emotions were strangling all goodness from his heart. The intensity of his fury frightened her, yet she also felt his pain of loss and sadness. She focused only on the goodness that had originally drawn her to his side. Elana held him still tighter.

Calmed by her touch, Lazer turned to her, wanting to find respite in her loving arms. Her touch soothed his tremors of rage. He fought to regain balance and open his heart to her. Lazer surrendered to her; his lips grazed her silken strands of ice gold hair and his nose inhaled her fresh, spring rain scent. Lazer's anger began to ebb, along with the sorrow that threatened to destroy him. He melted into her, letting her touch strengthen him. He was grateful for her love and the feeling of safety he found in her arms. *How could a simple touch give so much peace?*

"She only wants what's best for you," Elana whispered.

Lazer pulled back to look at her. His hand lay against her velvet smooth cheek. He did not want to speak. He only wanted to lose himself in her eyes and forget the troubles that plagued his mind.

Elana rose up on her toes, brought her face level with his, and inhaled his warm, musky scent; sweat still glistened on his skin. Her eyes never leaving his, she pressed her lips softly against his mouth. The world faded away.

Lazer slipped his arms around her back and lifted her from the ground. He kissed her, giving back everything good she had shared with him. The sweet tingle from her lips radiated through him. His face blushed and his skin quivered with delight. She seemed weightless in his arms, as light as warm air swirling up into the heavens before a storm. Lazer felt as though even Earth's gravity could not hold him; he was as light as air as long as he remained in her embrace. Slowly, in the hazy afternoon light encircling them, they drifted, savoring a single kiss. The pure sensation of first love, not yet explored, filled each of them with the excitement of anticipation.

Time held still until the kiss subsided. Their lips parted. Elana opened her eyes. At first she saw only strong shades of beautiful blues and golds and pure silver in Lazer's aura. Not until she looked deeply into his adoring eyes did she catch a glimpse of something out of place reflected in the blackness of his pupil.

The images of windows and sunlight reflected in his eyes didn't make sense to Elana. Lazer kissed her again, but this time Elana didn't close her eyes. She tilted her head and focused on what appeared to be windows floating in the air next to them. Elana blinked, but nothing changed. Without breaking their kiss, she pressed her foot into what should have been soft black dirt. Her toe pointed. Her eyes darted down. They were floating, gracefully hovering just above the ring of windows that elegantly capped the forum arena, forty-two feet above the floor. Elana gasped as she gently broke his kiss.

"Don't move," she whispered softly. Her eyes demanded his gaze stay locked on her alone.

"I don't want to," he replied with a smile. Closing his eyes, he kissed her again.

They rose higher.

"Lazer," she said, a tinge of fear creeping into her voice.

Easily fifty-five feet off the ground, Elana realized this miraculous feat was somehow caused by Lazer. Intuitively she knew if she panicked, he could lose control and they would fall, most likely to their death.

"Keep your eyes closed and listen to me," Elana said.

"Only if you'll kiss me again."

"Keep your eyes closed. Please," she begged.

Lazer smiled but kept his eyes closed.

Elana kissed him gently and they drifted up another few inches. Her heart was starting to race. "Lazer, I want you to . . . imagine walking with me."

Lazer's eyes opened, confused by her request. "Imagine?"

"Eyes closed. Promise!" she blurted out, while trying her best to remain calm.

He closed his eyes and laughed. "I would walk with you to the moon, Elana Blue."

She held onto him and snuggled into his side, supported by the waves of kinetic energy generated by Lazer. Elana tried not to look down. She swallowed, but her throat was being blocked by her increasing fear. *Remain calm*, she told herself. She had to figure out how to break Lazer's fantasy without killing them in the process. "I want you to imagine that . . . we are in my father's house."

"I've never seen your father's house."

"I know. I'll describe it and you'll walk with me. You have to imagine it and take physical steps exactly where I tell you."

"Oooookay," Lazer replied with a tone of playful curiosity.

She kissed him again, "We're standing on the second floor, right at the top of the stairs."

"What are we doing on the second floor?" He kissed her back.

"I . . . was showing you my room."

Lazer smiled slightly, blushing. "Your father lets you invite boys up to your room?"

"I'm grown and it's you, and only today," she replied, holding his neck. "I want you to pick me up."

Lazer obediently gathered her into his arms, dutifully keeping his eyes shut.

"Now, slowly, step by step, take me down the stairs before we get in trouble."

Lazer laughed and stepped down the invisible stairway.

He stopped, his brow furrowing. "Is it a straight or curved stairway?" Lazer asked.

"Curved. Circular," she replied, guiding him. "There are tapestries hanging on the walls; old ones with red and gold threads on a black background, dragons and tigers preparing to fight. Don't stop until I say so," she said, looking at the ground still four stories below her. With each imaginary step, they moved closer inch by inch to the ground. *It's working.* They were descending.

"And what's so special about today?" Lazer teased.

"What?" Elana replied.

"What's so special about today that your father thinks it's all right to let me come up to your room?"

"Uh, because you are the first boy I've ever cared enough about to bring home."

Lazer opened his eyes to look at her, thrilled by the thought that he was as important to her as she was to him. In that instant, Lazer realized their predicament. His concentration broken, they dropped like rocks before Lazer could react. Elana attempted to levitate them both but she didn't have enough strength to hold them. They slowed only for a moment. But that moment provided Lazer enough time to create a force field beneath them to catch them in its invisible net at the last possible second. The force field stretched like a piece of thin elastic, breaking their fall, then instantly vanishing. They landed face first on the ground. Wide-eyed terror registered as thoughts of what could have been raced through their minds.

"What just happened?" Elana said breathlessly.

"We didn't die!" Lazer said.

Then, with a shared look of grateful amazement, they exploded into laughter. It was a laughter fueled by relief. They laughed so hard tears streaked their dirt-covered faces, which made them laugh even harder. Still tangled in each other's arms, sides aching, they eventually caught their breath and smiled at each other.

"I like you," Elana said.

"I like you too," Lazer replied, as he helped her stand up. "I guess you'll have to be careful how you kiss me from now on."

"Never."

Lazer gathered their things and took her hand. Lost in each other's gaze, they walked toward the exit.

"Would I really be the first boy to make it to the second floor?"

"You would if we had a second floor," she smiled.

33

THE FINAL BLOW

THE COMMON ROOM in Lazer's dorm was always a hub of activity. Plush purple chairs surrounded a large circular hearth that burned constantly during the colder months. Floating luminescent balls gave off a cool light that was perfect for study.

To the far left was the holoscreen that usually played a variety of escapist entertainment. Today, however, it played special news reports that provided only a splattering of information that had leaked out of Atlantia.

Kyla and Cashton, along with a cluster of other students, stood around it, hungry to hear some news from home. Lazer entered, still glowing from his encounter with Elana. The warmth faded quickly as he read the panicked look on their faces. He knew from their expressions that the news wasn't good.

"The Triumvirate's lost control of the dome," Cashton whispered to Lazer and Kyla. "They reported it tonight, but it's been out of their control for months. They think all the V-mail that has been coming out has been scrambled and reconfigured to say only positive things."

"My parents' letters have been so weird. What about yours?" Kyla asked.

Lazer and Cashton both nodded their heads in agreement. Lazer pulled Cashton away from the other students. Kyla followed.

"Can't you access the camera in that doll you gave what's-her-name?" Lazer asked, desperate for some news.

"Cashton, you said you couldn't get any transmissions," Kyla blurted.

"I can't."

"Check it again?" Lazer pleaded.

"I am worried about my mom," Kyla admitted.

"We need to know what's going on. Whether or not you do, I'm going home," Lazer said as he walked away from them and headed toward his room.

"I'll check again, but I'm sure any new feeds will be blocked along with everything else," Cashton reminded him.

"How do you plan to get yourself into the dome?" Kyla stopped him.

"I'll find a way."

"What about our passage?" Cashton asked

"Hang the passage." Lazer turned to storm off.

Kyla and Cashton were on his tail.

"What about the promise you made your mother? If you don't complete your Rite of Passage, you can't even buy a ticket back to Atlantia," Kyla said. "And if you do manage to get back, you can't get a decent job, get married, own property, or fly. You can't fly, Lazer. You *have* to do your passage. We *all* do," she added, trying to be the voice of logic, even though she wanted to go home too.

"Look, passage is only a few weeks away," Cashton said.

"I don't care," Lazer responded.

"Kyla's right. We don't have a choice. We do our passage and head home together. Deal?" Cashton asked.

Lazer paused, considered the reality, and gave a reluctant nod. They each gave the V salute.

"We use the next two weeks to get everything in place," Lazer added.

"Ice with me. At least we don't have to worry about the Spring Jam wasting our time," Kyla said.

"That takes your Elana Blue fantasy date to the jam from slim to not gonna happen, Ace," Cashton ribbed Lazer.

"Actually, she kind of asked me," Lazer said without thinking. He thought nothing of the fact that Kyla was standing next to him.

"Whoa, whoa, whoa. Reality check. In what lifetime?" Cashton challenged.

"After the varsity game. Actually, we've been kind of seeing each other. I didn't say anything because I thought she might change her mind and then when she kissed me, I . . . well, talk about walkin' on air."

Kyla could see, feel, and taste his aura. He was telling the truth. Her heart raced like a hummingbird beating its fragile wings against death's door. Her worst fear flashed before her eyes: she was losing Lazer to Elana Blue. The pain of that loss sucked the air from her lungs and took with it every hope and dream she'd held since she was six years old. Her vision of their lives together was burning to ashes.

"Stellar!" Cashton slapped Lazer's back, thrilled for his friend.

Neither of them realized that Kyla's heart had just shattered. The room faded around her. Their voices blurred into a shrill, cacophonous screech that rang senselessly in her ears. The walls closed in, and great swirling shadows weaved into an ever-shrinking circle, until all that existed was Lazer's face in the center. She had to get out before she fainted. Without a word, leaving Lazer to tell Cashton the details of how he had captured the elusive Elana Blue, Kyla silently retreated.

Lazer shared every intimate detail of his incredible first encounter with an eager Cashton. Two of his dreams would manifest soon: Elana Blue in his arms again, and the right to go home to Atlantia and fight the Black Guard after his passage—everything else was irrelevant.

34

TWO WOMEN

ALEECE AVERY'S SKILLS as a healer and surgeon were in almost constant demand. Her apron was splattered with dirt and blood and represented not only her hard work, but also their lack of supplies.

"Why don't you change into these?" a voice said, offering her a clean surgical apron and lab jacket.

They weren't white, but they were cleaner than the ones she had on.

"My name's Detra Lazerman. I have a son at Tosadae," she said proudly.

"I have a daughter in Sangelino," Aleece responded.

"At least they're not here."

The moment Aleece saw a flash of recognition on Detra's face, she placed her fingers on Detra's lips.

"They don't know I'm here," Aleece whispered.

"What about the politia? Are they coming soon?"

"I don't know."

"I need to get word to my son. I have to let him know I'm alive."

Detra's eyes welled with tears. "He'll try to come if he doesn't hear from me."

"He can't get back in through the dome. The Black Guard has control," Aleece told her.

"What about your daughter and husband? Do they know you're alive?" Detra asked.

"I hope so," Aleece said, knowing that the only thing she could give this woman was hope. Aleece looked down and read Detra's holographic ID tag. "You'll see your son and I will see my daughter, Detra Lazerman. The politia will annihilate the biodroids and all who've joined them." Aleece gave her bravest smile and squeezed Detra's hand. "*Know* that your son is safe in Tosadae. *Know* that you are alive and will see him again."

Two guards were approaching. The women went their separate ways: Detra to her laundry and Aleece to the bed of her next patient. One of the guards stopped Aleece.

"Come," he commanded. Their huge forms bracketed Aleece. Detra watched helplessly as Aleece was led away.

Back in Sangelino, Riana sat in her room. She refused to go to school, and what little she ate would hardly sustain a bird. She felt her mother's suffering, so she knew without question that she was alive. Sometimes when she slept she could see glimpses of the place where Aleece was being held captive. She told her father and then wept in his arms at the sadness that surrounded her mother every moment of every day. Riana felt helpless. She was young and powerless. Her father—the only other person who was important to her—was doing everything he could, but the Corporate leaders and rest of the Triumvirate were against him.

"You have to eat," Dante said as he entered her room. He looked at the tray of untouched food and sat down next to his daughter.

"She's so afraid," Riana told him.

"Your mother is an incredible person. She has an inner strength that goes beyond the physical. But if she feels she is straining you, it might weaken her. She needs to feel that you believe in her, Riana."

"I do!" Riana said.

"Then let her feel your strength." Dante took his daughter's hands into his own. They looked so small and frail, yet he knew she held a greater strength than he could ever possess. "You are her touchstone, Riana. When you are well, she is invincible. The connection between you two will tell her what you're feeling. Give her your strength."

Riana looked at her father. She threw her arms around his neck as they stood together, sharing the strength that family provides in times of trouble and despair.

"What can I do?" she asked.

"Eat. Live. Learn. Be ready for when she comes back so that she'll know we kept her world here safe."

Riana smiled and lifted a piece of sliced apple from the plate. She took a large bite, offering to share the rest of it with her father.

"Bite?" she asked.

As Dante took the apple, Riana was blinded by a flash that filled her with dread. She knew in that instant, if her mother was not freed soon, her enemies would discover her identity and she would be used as a pawn. Riana closed her eyes to hold back the fear that rushed to her heart—the horrifying fear that she might never see her mother again. She threw herself into her father's arms and held on.

"What is it?" he asked.

"She has to get out of there before they find her. She has to get out now!"

35

TWO WEEKS FOR ETERNITY

LAZER AND ELANA spent every moment of every hour of the next few weeks together. They talked over breakfast about their homes, families, schools, and friends. Elana shared with him the long years of growing up in the shadow of her father. The grand houses filled with servants and nannies, cold and empty until the warmth of her father returned home to rescue her from her loneliness. They talked about Lazer's growing feelings for her and Elana talked of hers for him. They shared how much they had wished for a brother or sister to grow up with and how hard it was to be an only child. Elana told him of her sadness for the mother she'd never known. A woman whose picture she had never even seen because of the pain it caused her father. Elana explained how her death must have shattered her father's heart into so many pieces he was unable to heal enough to ever love again. Elana found ways to be grateful for the shards of love represented by the extravagant gifts he so generously lavished on her, but they did not make up for the void left by not having a family.

Lazer in turn shared stories of his childhood, growing up in the barren outback lands of Atlantia. How he had seen death as a child of five when marauders murdered a young friend's family while he had been visiting. The pirates took what they wanted and killed settlers whenever they felt the desire. To this day, Lazer never understood why he had been spared that morning. The memories were still as vivid as if they had happened yesterday. Biodroids had been the Atlantians' only salvation back then; her father's Black Guard created a peaceful order for a troubled land, only to snatch it cruelly away when they attacked the temple and destroyed the mines. Lazer told her things he had only shared with Kyla and Cashton—the horrible arguments with his father his senior year and the haunting, painful memories of not getting the pass key back in time. The Black Guard had killed his father while he watched, and that he could never forgive.

Then there was Elana—the first glimpse of happiness and hope he had seen since his father's death. How was it possible that Elana could be the daughter of the one man responsible for his utter misery, and yet was also the one person who represented everything good in his life? This question pulled at him until he looked into her eyes or touched her hand or kissed her mouth.

In the afternoons, they took their lunches from the commissary and walked along the banks of the Silent River, so named because of its smooth glassy surface that hid a raging, treacherous current below. They followed the trails that led high into the foothills of the mountains and talked about everything from the grandeur of the universe to the essence of a kiss. They watched the sun fall behind the snow-covered peaks and counted the stars that glittered against the inky night sky. They shared kisses and hugged to keep each other warm. Lazer had seen nothing of the world; Elana had seen everything. They made promises to spend part of their summer together and travel to the underwater cities of Panazia, where they could explore the ancient wonders of Machu Picchu. They loved history, mythology, clever books, and the ancient writings of the great philosophers. Inevitably, the subject turned to Masta Poe. Elana shared how impressed Masta Poe was by Lazer's vast, untapped powers. Lazer smiled, honored and humbled by her compliments. He told her that Masta Poe had been his hero from the first day he saw her amazing abilities. They shared their dreams to be pilots and peacekeepers and make the world a better place.

They skipped afternoon classes that day and supper that night. Food seemed unnecessary compared to the feeling of oneness that satiated them. With night came a frosty fog that crept along the ground and danced at their feet. Time became meaningless as the moon reached above the trees to guide them. They knew they would be late for curfew, but rules didn't seem to matter much at the moment. They stood on the narrow outcropping of Vista Point, which overlooked the campus and the valley beyond. Lazer pointed out the place Cashton and he had found where they could scale the wall if they got stuck outside after curfew. Finally talked out, they walked back to campus in contented silence. Holding hands, they marveled at the rows of shadows that striped the barren orchard: a hundred horizontal columns that appeared each time the moon would peek out from behind the layers of wispy clouds to light their way.

"I want to have a family with you," Elana said. She revealed her heart to him, unable to contain the words.

Lazer stopped. He looked at her dumbfounded. He wanted to respond, but the words caught in his throat.

His expression sent a chill up Elana's spine.

He couldn't speak and he knew she couldn't read his aura and with it all feelings of inadequacy that must be registered on his face like day old egg. He knew she only saw his shocked eyes. Eyes that stared back at her with no words of explanation. She was a beautiful woman who had just professed her love and plans for a life together and Lazer was dumb struck. He knew it was because that life was his dream for him and Kyla. But Kyla has emotionally abandoned him and Elana was here; alive and beautiful and willing.

"I . . . I'm sorry, I . . . can't believe I said that, but . . . I can't help myself. I can't shake the feeling that time is rushing in to take you from me and I . . ."

Before she could finish, Lazer reached for her. He pulled her to him.

"I love you," he said, sealing it with a kiss. "I want to give the world to you, and when I've won my Rite of Passage and gone back to free Atlantia, I'll be someone. I'll take you to meet my mother and tell her you are everything I've ever wanted. I swear to you. I'll come back to get you and we will be together forever."

"Come back?" Her heart sank.

"I have to go home, Elana," Lazer said.

"I'll go with you. We'll go to my father and he'll help us defeat . . ."

Lazer loosened his hold on her. "Your father is the reason Atlantia is at war."

"But he's not the cause. He's not in control of the biodroids who did those horrible things. Let him help you. Let me help you," she pleaded.

Lazer turned away from her.

"Don't let this come between us, Lazer. Promise me," Elana said. An inexplicable fear overcame her. Her stomach turned, a bitter taste filled her mouth, and her head began to ache. Elana looked at her hands; they were shaking. She was afraid and no matter how hard she tried, she did not understand why.

"This is my battle, Elana. When it's done, I'll come back to you."

"You keep saying that. You'll go on your Rite of Passage and finish and come back to Tosadae and me . . . us," she said.

"Yes and then I'm going home to fight with the Wave and free Atlantia."

"I won't let you ruin your life," Elana said grabbing his hand.

"If you love me, you'll understand and not try to stop me from living the destiny I was born to live," Lazer said.

Lazer pulled away from her and turned to leave. She caught his arm and pulled him back.

"I'll go with you. We'll fight together. Atlantia's my home too," She said as tears flooded her eyes. "We'll fight together."

Lazer touched her face. He saw the determination in her eyes. His eyes closed as he searched for a way to make her understand. When he opened them, he knew in his heart he was losing her. He watched her search his eyes for the answer she needed to hear. She searched for a different approach.

"We'll take this one day at a time. We'll go to the dance and have a wonderful time. You'll leave for your first passage trials and . . . and I'll miss you, and think about you, and wait for you, and when you get back we'll finish the semester and figure out how to get home—together," she said.

He looked into her eyes. He wanted to explain, but the cold reality of what he had to do chilled his veins. The only promise he could make to her was that the next few days would be theirs and theirs alone.

"One day at a time," Lazer said and gently kissed her. The heat that had filled every other kiss was gone. He needed to talk to Cashton. To Kyla.

Elana was an empath and realized immediately that Lazer, whether consciously or unconsciously, was not telling her everything. He was lying, not to her, but to himself. She searched his emotions, but couldn't determine which were true and which were not. Elana kissed him again, demanding their passion warm his heart once more. He returned her kiss, unable to resist. The spark was there and it was strong.

"Promise me you won't leave me here," she whispered.

"I can't promise that," Lazer said.

The midnight bell began to toll.

"We're late!" Lazer shouted.

"I thought we were going to scale the wall?" She smiled, trying to push his words from her mind.

"Not in that." Lazer pointed to the tunic draping her lissome figure.

"Then kiss me and we'll levitate."

Lazer kissed her. Nothing happened.

"Guess we have to practice more, huh?" she said with a hint of mischief.

"Until then, hurry up or I won't get to take you to the dance. Move it!"

He grabbed her hand as they raced through the massive gates just before they slid closed. They ran across the main campus circle, laughing and teasing. Breathless, they raced past a lone silhouette, someone who watched from the arched shadows of Tower Hall. They reached Chopin dorm and, punctuated by a squeal from Elana, vanished inside. Their laughter faded away into the night.

The moon broke through the clouds and flooded the icy night with cold, white streaks of light that revealed the identity of the lone figure. Kyla stood motionless and watched their shadows pass by the windows of the lower hall, steal one last kiss, and go their separate ways. She was a voyeur to their promises. Elana's words pricked at her mind again and again—*have a family with you . . . have a family*. A single tear fell from Kyla's eye. It burned as it slid down her frozen cheek. It would be the last tear she would ever cry for Lazer, that she promised herself. The next tears would be Elana's.

36

SCORNED

THE MORNING SUN BROKE over the horizon, flooding the black hills with light and turning the landscape into a pallet of silvery gray and washed-out pastels. Cashton and Kyla jogged through a forest of naked tress and up along paths that clung to the rolling hills just west of Tosadae. Their breath danced from their lips and turned into curls of smoke that puffed out to the rhythm of their feet as they pounded against the still-frozen earth of the higher mountain paths. Kyla was a strong runner and easily kept pace with Cashton. Her eyes stared ahead with a distant glaze, her mind lost in thought. They ran in silence. They made their way past the narrow bends of the Silent River while the morning light sparkled off its smooth surface like a handful of diamonds.

Kyla frowned. Her mind was racing with a thousand thoughts. She wished Evvy were alive so they could talk about the thoughts and feelings that taunted her. She missed her now more than ever. Cashton was a good friend but he would not discuss her "girl angst" emotions, especially if they were about Lazer. She would have to decide how to handle

Elana alone. Each step she ran brought her closer to the same resolve. A look of determination fell across her face. Kyla signaled to Cashton that she needed to stop at the forum stables to check the status of her battle ranking. She veered off the path, and Cashton dutifully followed.

Inside the battle forum, the creatures used for third-level battle training languished, lazily sleeping or pacing in their cages. Kyla was startled when one of the archeops began screeching at its keeper. Something had her on edge. Using an eight-foot-long pole, the keeper tossed it a still living, sixty-pound capybara, which it killed and devoured with such accuracy there was little time to pity the animal.

"I wouldn't want to tangle with that one," Cashton said, as he watched the carnage.

Kyla said nothing. Her mind had been preoccupied with thoughts, which had distanced her from Cashton all day. He decided on a new tactic. "Hey, I'm really glad to hear you're okay with this Lazer and Elana thing."

"Lazer's my friend. I want him to be happy. No heat." She called up the digitized roster with a wave of her hand and searched for her ranking with the thumbprint recognition feature.

Cashton wanted to believe her answer. He wanted her to be okay. He wanted her to know she could have his shoulder to cry on if she needed it. He didn't need to be an empath to know how she felt about Lazer.

Kyla appreciated the cool, soft yellow aura that expressed his compassion, but today she wanted none of it. She entered some statistical updates to her ranking scores and started to jog away, but something made her slow at the prometheus' cage. Kippo was a lumbering female who had lived past her prime. She was easily the oldest creature in the stable and the most docile. Kyla studied its massive chest and ape-like arms as it stretched and flexed its paws, exposing its huge, bear-like claw that ended in a single toe. Several rows of broken spikes protruded from her thick neck, showing that a little porcupine had been spliced into the bear/lion/Komodo dragon DNA that made up the various strands of her genetic recipe. Even the saliva glands used to paralyze her prey had long been removed, along with most of her teeth.

"Gotta bounce," Cashton said, as he pounded a quick V salute and jogged away, heading back to the dorms.

Kyla again looked at the docile prometheus. She was old and useless and, other than Elana Blue, no one was afraid of her.

Without provocation, Kyla slammed her fists against the protective shield, startling the creature.

Kippo struggled to her feet and pushed lazily against the force field, trying to get through, obviously looking more for attention than to do harm. Kyla stared at the doddering old creature as a plan took shape in her mind.

37

CROSSING THE LINE

ELANA BLUE DESCENDED the stairs glowing with anticipation. She looked stunning in the iridescent blue, floor-length tunic that draped her amazing body. Her eyes searched anxiously for Lazer. He wasn't there. She checked her time band and searched again, suppressing the feeling of apprehension that had haunted her all afternoon. He would show up and they would have the best time she could ever imagine.

Kyla appeared next to her. "Oh, hey, Lazer just left here; he was looking for you."

Kyla smiled and hoped Elana couldn't read the jealousy that swirled in her head.

"He left! But I was supposed to . . .," Elana started to say.

"Yeah, something about meeting you by the creature chambers," Kyla added innocently. "I think it's a surprise."

"The creature chambers, but . . ." Elana blanched at the thought of entering the stadium and facing the rows of splicer creatures. It was a childhood fear set in place when she was seven, when one of her father's experiments tried to devour her. Her father's splicer labs produced more than enough deadly species to give her cause to be afraid. But that was years ago, she told herself, and besides, Lazer would be there; that was all that mattered.

"Well . . . I'll go meet him there then. Thanks, Kyla." Elana smiled bravely.

It was a warm, honest smile and it made Kyla feel uncomfortable.

"No problem. You look really nice," Kyla said as she walked away.

Elana Blue had never cared for Kyla. She didn't like the way Kyla glared at her, especially when Lazer was around, and she didn't like the milky aura that hung around her every time they spoke, except today. Today, Kyla's aura was a yellowish orange, which meant happiness and truth. Kyla was happy; the rest she carefully controlled.

"Kyla!" Elana Blue called out. "I . . . I owe you an apology. I thought you were such a . . . a . . . well . . . a snit when I first met you, but I see why Lazer thinks you are so ice." Elana smiled, then nervously checked the time on her wristsponder and ran off before Kyla could answer.

Kyla cringed. This was worse than the smile. How dare Elana be nice to her! Kyla's stomach turned. The guilt over what she had set in motion began to eat at her. Kyla tried to convince herself it was a harmless prank. The old prometheus was so tame no one knew why they even bothered to lock her up anymore. But Kyla couldn't take it. She raced down the corridor to Lazer's room, where she found Cashton, Skyler Bond, and a red-haired boy named Tisch outside Lazer's room pulling on the door. It was stuck.

"It's stuck," Cashton yelled through the door.

"I know it's stuck," Lazer called.

"Try the lock again," Skyler said.

"I tried it dozens of times," Lazer said. His voice cracked with frustration. "This can't be happening!"

"I swear it looks melted," Tisch said.

Kyla raised her hands, using one of the few kinetic powers she had learned since she arrived and heated the seal she had put in place to make him late. With a click, the door released.

"How did you do that?" Cashton asked, amazed.

"We didn't try that," Tisch said.

Everyone stood dumbfounded as Lazer burst through the door, beaming with gratitude.

Kyla gasped. She loved how handsome he looked in his dress white cadet uniform. Unfortunately, tonight he had it on to impress Elana Blue. Lazer planted a kiss on Kyla's lips and ran back to get the invitation and the corsage of creamy white palimander buttons that he had picked from the higher ridges of the forest earlier that afternoon.

"You are a goddess," he gushed to Kyla and ran by everyone.

"Tell me that after . . .," she said and ran in front of him, blocking his way.

"After what?"

Guilt reeked from her pores as she pulled him onto the escalator. She made him descend three steps at a time.

"After you find out I sent Elana Blue to meet you at the battle forum."

"The forum? Why?" Lazer was surprised and curious. His instincts kicked in. He wasn't a splicer or a clone, but he could read something in Kyla's eyes and it made his heart race.

"I told her to meet you in front of the old prometheus," she said, as she jerked him out of the building.

He tugged his arm away and stopped. "Elana's downstairs," he insisted.

"I told Elana to meet you at the forum. I hacked into the creature security system and programmed in a timed release to open the shield to Kippo's cage in three minutes. I . . . I wanted to . . . to scare her. I was gonna send you in to see what a chicken she was, but then she was so damn nice . . ." The words tumbled out with the speed of a machine gun blast.

"What are you taking about?!" Lazer said, his eyes widening with the realization that came with each word.

"She's totally afraid of every creature in there, and Kippo's older than dirt so I figured I'd scare . . ."

"No, Kyla."

"It was stupid and mean but Kippo's so damn docile, she'll probably nudge her to get her to pet . . ."

"Kippo died this morning!" Lazer cut her off. "Didn't you see the alert? They moved Deigen out of solitary and into that cage this afternoon!"

"Deigen! That's impossible. She's a killer! I . . .," Kyla said, not believing her ears.

"Change the security back!" Lazer commanded.

Kyla twisted her wristsponder, called up the access file codes and keyed in the command. ACCESS DENIED came across her screen.

"I can't," Kyla whispered. "I've been locked out."

"Universal God, Kyla. Do it again. Find a way and make it happen! Now!" Lazer said pleading. He turned and scanned the exits searching and calculating for the quickest way to the arena. The color drained from his face. Three minutes wasn't enough time. Lazer felt overwhelmed by the thoughts of horror that filled his mind.

"I can't get in," Kyla said after a second and third try.

He backed away from her and ran down the hall. "Do it, now!"

Lazer knew there wasn't enough time to get to Elana unless he tele-ported and he didn't have time to attempt such a feat and fail. Lazer bolted out the exit.

As he ran he could feel a trail of guilt emanating after him from Kyla like a hot wind blowing at his back because of what she had done.

"Help me, Kyla," he whispered to himself.

He saw her trembling in his mind's eye so hard he thought she might fall apart. He wanted her to stay safe but he needed her to come.

"Help me, Kyla," he whispered to himself again as he ran.

Lazer watched Kyla calm herself and override her fears and guilt. She hesitated for one brief second more before she raced after him know-ing the danger she'd accidentally put them all in.

38

DEIGEN

LAZER RACED toward the forum. He glanced back to see Kyla tracking in his footsteps that lay in the freshly fallen dusting of a late spring snow that still clung to the ground. He wished he hadn't made her promise not to use her wings. In flight, she could have lifted him and they would both have been there already. He ran faster. If he'd listened to Masta Poe, he could have willed them both there; teleported their particles the way she had done so many times, appearing from thin air anywhere she wanted. He had seen himself do it in his dreams. He knew he could do it. He knew he had the ability to teleport but some-how he couldn't make the connection between thought and matter. He could stop Deigen with his powers if only he could release his fears and trust his imagination. If only wasn't now. The battle dome was still sixty yards away. He wanted to teleport but couldn't.

Lazer pushed himself. He felt his body strain. Ahead, the forum door loomed closer. Twenty yards more. *I'm coming, Elana*, he thought, hoping she would pick up on his telepathic thoughts. *I'm coming.*

Inside, Elana Blue stood in the last shimmering rays of sunlight that fell through the high round windows and illuminated her. The light caught the dress and made it sparkle and shimmer with each breath and subtle motion. She felt excited to see the surprise Lazer has for her. It would be a special night. A night like no other. She felt it and it made her smile like a child waiting for sunlight at Christmas to race downstairs and see what the gifts awaited her. Elana looked around at the pens of the amazing creatures Tosadae had collected over the years. Her eyes followed the sunlight as it drifted past her and reached across the room shining brightest at Deigen's pen. The warm light bathed the sleeping monster in a soft, golden glow that made its pale, spotted fur glisten. She stepped closer.

Elana Blue checked her jeweled time band. She left the wristsponder tonight though with all its practicalities, but try as she might, she couldn't make herself detach from time. Time was too important. She didn't really know if being late was one of Lazer's chronic habits, but she noted it as something they should talk about in the future. *In the future*, she thought, liking the association with Cole Lazerman. It had a nice ring to it. She tried to imagine the evening, Lazer, the dance, all the other students dressed up and beautiful under the winter sky, but something kept pulling at her. She felt strangely uncomfortable. She looked at her time band again and then at the sleeping monster.

"I swear on the Collective you are about as ugly as they come," she said to the creature. Her voice was sweet, and she smiled.

At the sound of Elana Blue's voice, a single eye slowly opened. It was a drab amber orb with a vertical iris that expanded and contracted as it focused on Elana Blue. Nothing else on the creature's body moved. The creature was part large, predatory feline and some kind of chameleon. She had seen it shift from deep purple to red and emerald green when provoked.

"My apologies. I didn't mean to disturb your beauty sleep, because you definitely need it." Elana Blue made a face and laughed as she watched the creature shift her massive weight and stand. The cage was thirteen feet tall, which gave Deigen only ten inches of free space above her head. She was huge.

Out of instinct, Elana took a few steps back. She stopped and stared at the creature. She was doing her best to be brave.

"I'm not afraid of you," Elana said. She said it to convince herself that she wasn't afraid. *Thoughts into words into reality,* the words echoed in her mind. She stepped closer.

"See, I'm not afraid," she said.

Deigen made a low, almost unearthly sound that rattled with a threatening hiss beneath it. Elana Blue playfully did her best to mimic the sound back to Deigen.

"Not even close," she said.

Elana smiled suddenly feeling like a tiny mouse playing with a massive lion. Her playfulness gave her courage and, feeling a little braver, Elana Blue gave a roar and opened her arms to make her form appear larger and more ferocious. Her movement was too fast and too threatening. Deigen startled and out of instinct retaliated by shape-shifting into the vicious version of her docile self. Elana gave a gasp as rows of white, eighteen-inch spikes some as tall as Elana, fanned up along its spine. The boney projections rose along Deigen's back and neck and crowned its head. Elana watched amazed as the creature's skin turned from a light sand color to dark cocoa brown, the same rich color as the dirt on the battle arena's floor. The creature's eyes were fixed on Elana's. Its color darkened to a deep chocolate then dark ruby red. Deigen crouched, ready to stalk forward. Ready to attack. Deigen hinged open her immense jaw, bared her ten-inch canines and hissed.

Elana Blue felt herself flinched, but again, she stood her ground.

"I . . . didn't mean to startle you. It must be terribly sad being locked in there. I won't frighten you anymore," Elana said as Deigen hissed at her again. "I'm still not afraid of you, you old bully."

It was at that moment the subtle hum from the motors that controlled the protective shield ceased. Deigen's ears went back. Elana watched curiously as the beast sniffed the air to see if she could smell the scent of burning energy that held her inside its walls. She had tested the clear ball of energy that made up the painful and impermeable, translucent force field that kept her imprisoned inside. The creature understood instantly—she was free. Deigen again opened her mouth. Her gaping jaw protruded enough to revel the sacs above her fags. She spit her venom, drenching Elana in a silvery, clingy mist of paralyzing poison. It was only then Elana realized the danger she was in. The venom coated her and seeped into her pores. Within seconds, Elana's muscles turned to immovable clay. She tried to run, but could not. She willed her feet to move, her hands to lift from her side to throw an energy shield and shield herself. No matter how hard she tried, nothing moved. Time slowed. The colors around her brightened, the sounds grew louder as all her senses became more acute. Elana watched as the massive, blood red creature took its first step toward her. Slowly and cautiously she stalked forward, each muscle rippled beneath its skin and undulated the hairs. Deigen reached the rocks that marked the perimeter of her enclosure. She hesitated; sniffing once again for the smell of burning energy. Her nose told her there was none. It was safe and she stepped forward past where the now nonexistent shield should have been.

Elana's heart raced trapped inside her own body. Neither fight nor flight were options. Only die by being eaten alive. In three steps, Deigen was six inches from Elana Blue's face. The color drained from Elana's skin. She wanted to scream, but she could not will her mouth to open. Again she commanded her arms to rise, to create a shield, but they hung like iron anchors, immobile at her sides. She was paralyzed, unable to turn away from the nightmare of a creature that breathed its hot, foul breath into her face.

"Elana," Lazer whispered from the far end of the battle forum. "It'll be okay. Everything will be okay. I'm right here. Can you hear me? I'm right here," he said.

His voice was calming and almost hypnotic for both Deigen and Elana Blue. Lazer slowly inched toward the weapons vault, making sure his movements were smooth and controlled, and picked up a six-foot-long battle wand.

"I'm just going to get a weapon in case. Okay? Can you understand me Elana?" Lazer asked in the same calming voice.

"Throw a shield," Lazer said calmly.

Elana didn't move. Lazer saw the terror in her eyes and recognized the silvery venom dripping down her arms and face. His gaze went to Deigen. Lazer cautiously lifted the battle wand. He wished it were at least four feet longer. The wand's predecessor from the previous century had been the cattle prod. This one was a cattle prod on steroids. Once ignited, its tip was charged with five thousand volts of ionized electricity, but six feet was a very close distance to connect her and not hurt Elana Blue.

Lazer tapped the tip, igniting the weapon. A low hum vibrated faster and faster as it rested in Lazer's hand. He could feel it gathering and building the energy, pulling it from the air. The sound made Deigen's ears twitch. It was obvious the creature had felt the wand's biting sting in the past. Lazer had heard they'd used it to capture her from Passage Island. They'd used it to break her. It was a cruel necessity for the schools to capture her kind and use her to teach defense. Lazer didn't like the practice, but he knew she in turn had been taught in the wild to defend and even hunt and eat humans. Lazer turned up the amps with a twist of the throttle on the handle and extended the strike range of the battle wand. The shift in energy made an even higher tone. Again Deigen's ears twitched and its hackles stiffened standing straighter, but still the creature's eyes stayed locked on Elana's.

"Focus. Breathe and focus," Lazer said to himself.

As he moved closer to Elana, he continued speaking in the same calming voice.

"I'm almost there, Elana," Lazer said.

"Universal God!" Kyla said breathlessly as she burst into the arena.

"Shhhhh," Lazer said.

It only took a moment for Kyla to understand what was going on.

"She's been sprayed. Elana's paralyzed, Lazer. That means Deigen's still got her venom."

Deigen shifted her gaze slightly toward Kyla. Lazer could tell she recognized Kyla as a splicer, but still she kept one eye on her prey.

"She recognizes you," Lazer said.

"I feed her sometimes," Kyla responded.

"Talk to her," Lazer pleaded.

"It's too late for that. She's focused on her kill. You need to mesmerize her," Kyla whispered. "Whatever you do, don't use that wand."

"That's all I've got," Lazer said doing his best to hush Kyla.

"Use your powers, Lazer! Mesmerize her."

"I can't. I'm gonna distract her. When she turns to me, you get Elana."

"Are you crazy? You can't take Deigen on your own," Kyla said.

"Please. Just get to Elana, throw a shield around yourselves, and then pull her and you out," Lazer gave the order, but managed to maintain the same, calm, melodic voice.

Deigen snarled, and huge green drops of gooey drool dripped to the dirt.

"Look," Kyla said, pointing to the creature's teeth. "She still needs time to produce enough silver venom to paralyze all of us. We can take her but we gotta move now," Lazer said, stepping closer and lifting the battle wand.

"Lazer, I've seen her in battle, she's too big for that," Kyla whispered.

"Just throw a shield over you and Elana! Do it!" Lazer said.

"I can't throw a shield," Kyla said, her voice trembling.

"Yes you can," Lazer insisted. "I saw you at Vacary."

"Not this big and not long or strong enough to keep her out. I can't. She's too big. Trust me I can't!" Kyla said then took a courageous step forward. "Let me distract her."

"As what? Dinner?" Lazer said. "On my count, shield and get her and you out of here, please Kyla. Do it," Lazer said.

Lazer didn't have time to explain that Masta Poe had been teaching him—reality and the human mind cannot differentiate between what it perceives as real or not real and, in this case, as big or small; Kyla's shielded before and she could do it again. Believe. He leveled the battle wand. The electrical hum raised its pitch.

At the same moment Kyla grabbed another battle wand. She tapped the end and charged it to life.

Lazer lunged. He was three feet away from Elana as Deigen opened her mouth to snap off Elana Blue's head with a vicious bite.

Lazer stabbed Deigen in her right haunch. The burst of electric power slammed into the creature's body. Deigen twisted lifting her head up and wailing in pain. The massive creature expanded growing bigger, turned, and focused, teeth bared and hissing on Lazer.

Kyla raced forward to jab her again. Deigen's huge tail swung and slammed into Kyla, propelling her across the room and into a wall, knocking her unconscious.

Deigen's drooling mouth flushed a sickening pale green as the venom turned silver. Her massive jaws hinged open as she again prepared to express the glands that would spray and paralyze Elana Blue further, keeping her immobile, but alive while she devoured her.

Lazer leapt in between and shoved the battle wand into Deigen's face. Fingers of white and aqua electricity crackled and bit into the creature's jaw igniting the venom like dragon's breath. The charge held Deigen's face immobile. Deigen howled an ear crushing cry. Lazer could see the burning charge searing into its flesh. Deigen stumbled back a few feet as she choked on her own poison. She licked her face and snarled at the taste of the bitter charred fluid that hung from her singed lips. Deigen recovered, shaking its head violently from side to side. It turned its gaze to Lazer and lunged forward. Lazer lifted the wand and zapped her again and again. Half blinded by the jolt, she swiped her claws and missed Lazer's face by inches. Lazer ducked the swipe and jabbed the battle wand into her groin. Deigen bellowed and howled, shaking her head to clear the momentary blindness, and backed away. Lazer rushed to Elana, pushed her to the ground. He had no choice. To shield her, he needed his hands. He dropped the battle wand, straddled her, and threw out his hands. By the time Deigen recovered and turned on them, they were cocooned in a ball shaped, sheer energy shield.

The creature attacked. She repeatedly swatted and pounded at and on the shield, but the force field held. The bottom half of the shield went into the ground and anchored them solidly in one place. Deigen stopped. Slowly it circled Lazer and Elana, pacing and smiling as she searched for a way to get inside.

Lazer's mind struggled for a solution. Elana lay crumpled at Lazer's feet, shaking violently as her muscles tried to release from the hold of the venom. She looked like a helpless child left outside, alone in the ice and snow. Her skin was sheet white, her gaze fixed and unfocused. Lazer looked for Kyla and saw her in a heap across the room, fighting to regain consciousness.

Lazer had to face Deigen alone. The creature paced several more times studying its prey. It pounced, arms wide and claws extended, landing as it straddled the dome of the shield; Lazer could feel her pressing down with her full weight onto the top and sides of the force field. Lazer looked, her belly exposed as she pressed into the force field. Deigen's massive flesh and weight bowed the shield's form bending it from convex to concave. Lazer felt his arms bend under the weight. He pushed back and the field held. They were safe for the moment, trapped inside with no way out and no way for Deigen to get in.

Lazer knew someone would come. The question was when? He felt his arms tremble as he struggled to keep the shield intact. He took long, deep breaths, but it didn't take long for his arms to hurt from the constant pressure of the weight. He began to sweat. Then he notices, bit-by-bit, the edges of the shield walls getting smaller. They were shrinking, crushing in on them, compressing the force field inch by inch.

Kyla woke from her concussion. The world was spinning. She lifted her head and did her best to shake off the haze of confusion that clouded her mind. She searched for Lazer. From her vantage point in the shadowed corner of the dome, she could make out Deigen, but Lazer and Elana Blue were nowhere to be seen. Kyla watched Deigen expand and contract as if she were giving birth. In the midst of one contraction, Kyla glimpsed Lazer and Elana Blue under the belly of the creature; Elana's pale face flashed from beneath a skirt of skin and fur.

Kyla had to get a weapon. The battle wand lay on the ground fifteen feet away. She stayed low and inched toward it on her hands and knees. Her only hope was that she could get to the weapon without being seen.

Inside the shield, the force field continued to compress tighter and tighter above Lazer's head. He struggled, sweating from the heat and the strain. Lazer thought about his mother, alone in a captured country with no way out, and about his vow to avenge his father and Evvy. His eyes fell onto Elana. The venom was wearing off and her terrified eyes connected with his. He knew more now than ever, he couldn't die. Not now. Not like this. He had to hold on and live.

Kyla was one foot away from her battle wand. It was now or never. She leaped, and lunged, grabbed the battle wand and turned racing to attack.

From the corner of her eye, Deigen saw Kyla advancing. Deigen spun, ready to fight. Kyla sent a charge of electricity. At the same time, a single swipe knocked Kyla's battle wand from her hand. She stopped, unarmed, but exposed. Kyla looked around and Deigen recovered and charged. She had no place to go but up. Her wings tore through her shirt and unfurled, batting the air and lifting her from the ground. A second flap carried Kyla straight up–up–up. She looked over from above and saw Lazer and Elana. He was disintegrating the shield.

Lazer broke the shield and yanked Elana Blue up and over his shoulder. He raced to the side and set her by the door.

"I'll be right back," he said.

Elana looked at him through terrified eyes unable to move. Lazer turned and saw across the battle dome, Deigen after Kyla.

Kyla, wings extended, took off and flew straight up. She was desperately putting space between her and the advancing creature. In seconds Deigen reached the spot on the floor directly below Kyla. The creature squatted and leapt with the force of an erupting geyser upward into the air. As it rose, its mouth stretched open. Kyla glanced down and saw the gaping mouth, trimmed by ragged teeth and impending destruction. Kyla's wings, fully extended, caught the air and beat it back sending her faster and higher. She looked up and let her focus settle on the top most point of the battle dome. There was a small ring at the center of the window. Maybe it was enough to grab onto. She knew gravity would drag the creature down and if she could grab on she could stay alive. Kyla felt her hand reaching forward to grab the ring. It was there, five more feet away. Her salvation hung down from the center most point. Three feet. Two. One more flap and a prayer that she would reach it. It would be her sanctuary, too high for the creature to reach and devour her. Suddenly, Kyla felt its hot breath as one of her legs went inside Deigen's massive jaws. The heat of its fowl breath pressed against her skin and then, she heard the vicious steel snap and its jaws closing around her calf. She felt the creature's razor teeth sink deeper into her flesh. Kyla screamed, reaching desperately for the ring as if it could still save her. She felt the massive weight of Deigen, caught by gravity, pull her and the monster back to earth.

"No," she shouted.

Frantically, Kyla beat her wings against the forces that defied her. Faster and harder her wings fought against the air. She felt the flesh as it tore from her leg. Her back, where her wings connected, strained as the effort took every ounce of strength she had. Kyla kicked down hard with her free foot. It connected into the most vulnerable spot on Deigen's nose. It was hard enough to cause the jaws to unlock and unhinge. Deigen released her. Kyla flapped harder. She felt the skin and muscle in her calf rip away from the razor teeth that held on. Both legs free, she tucked, pulling them up and out of Deigen's mouth. Kyla arched back, swinging her feet above her head. Still falling, Deigen whipped its massive head and extended her neck in a last attempt to grab her prey. The creature snapped upward and this time clamped the jagged spiked teeth down into one of Kyla's wings. Kyla screamed as Deigen's teeth tore the flesh and bone wing from her shoulder and upper back. The crunching sound of the thin, delicate bones shattering inside the powerful teeth echoed across the forum. Kyla was falling again. She looked up and watched as the ring in the very center of the dome rushed away from her grasp. Deigen dragged Kyla back down toward the floor. Kyla flapped her one free wing and what was left of her half-severed wing. She could feel it wildly struggling to get free. Time slowed. Kyla heard more than she felt as she fell through space in what seemed like forever. She could hear the bottom half of her wing shredding and ripping on Deigen's razor teeth. They fell and then they crashed. She heard Deigen hit ground first with a thunderous crack. Kyla felt her body hit against the soft face of the Deigen. She felt herself arched and bent backward across the monster's lips and teeth. The world stopped. The perilous fall had left them both momentarily stunned. Slowly Kyla turned her head and looked into one, lifeless eye staring. It stared blankly back into hers. A second later, Deigen blinked.

Lazer raced across the room. He could see Deigen was stabilizing. The creature would eat Kyla alive in one, quick, gobbling bite. He had to act. Lazer dove, rolled, snatched the fallen battle wand, and plunged it into Deigen's ear with one hand. With the other hand, he grabbed Kyla and jerked her off Deigen's face and onto the dirt floor. The action ripped the rest of her second wing.

With the twist of the battle wand's controls, the wand ignited. It sent a thousand volts of electricity into the creature's head. Lazer dragged Kyla a few inches farther out of harm's way. He released the battle wand control leaving it on full blast. Lazer stood erect. He turned his focus back to the Deigen. As Masta Poe had taught him, Lazer cupped his hands and using his mind, gathered the forces of energy from the room into a ball. He jutted his hands forward and the ball unraveled, sending a stream of electricity into the creature. Lazer's field of energy fused with the power of the battle wand and the voltage surge quadrupled. Deigen's head blew apart like a ripe watermelon hurled down ten stories onto the cement street. The creature's blood splattered the dark soil of the battle forum and littered the dirt with chunks of flesh, fur, and a deluge of ruby blood. The creature was dead.

Lazer raced back to Kyla and dropped to his knees by her side. She lay in a twisted heap. Her body was battered and torn and covered in Deigen's brain matter and blood. Next to her lay a piece of Deigen's dismembered jaw; a row of broken teeth with pieces of her fleshy wings and shattered bones still caught inside. Kyla moaned. He knew she was alive. Suddenly, her eyes stretched wide from a rush of pain. Her back was arched and bowed like a broken rag doll that had been played with too long and then discarded. Lazer could hear her breathing was in short desperate sips. Slowly, she lifted one of her hands. He watched as she studied her fingers to see if she still existed. Deigen's blood had mixed with hers, blending into a thick goo that clung to her and caught the light. The image looked as surreal and unbelievable as everything that had just occurred felt.

"Stay still," Lazer whispered.

He wanted to sound calm, hoping Kyla wouldn't sense his panic.

"I'm . . . so . . . sorry," she whispered. The words caught in her throat.

"You're gonna be okay."

"Elana," Kyla said.

"She'll be okay," Lazer told her.

"Tell Elana . . . I never . . . wanted . . . to hurt . . . her. Tell her . . ."

"You'll tell her yourself," Lazer said, not sure what to do.

"Forgive me, Lazer," Kyla said. "I was jealous and stupid."

"I'll always forgive you just as I'll always love you. You have to be okay. I need you. Okay?" Lazer said. "I have to go get help."

"Don't leave me. Please," she whispered. "I'm so frightened."

Her fingers closed tighter around his hand.

"I gotta go get help, Kyla. Don't you go anywhere until I get back," he whispered and smiled bravely.

Kyla nodded. Again she grabbed his hand again and swallowed. Kyla tried her best to smile. She realized the pain had stopped and a strange calm washed over her, followed by a chill.

"It doesn't hurt, I'm just . . . so cold," Kyla whispered, surprised by the numbness that crept through her body. "Lazer," she whispered, "no matter what happens, finish your passage. Promise me."

He was torn. Now more than ever he wanted to get away from Tosadae.

"Promise?" she asked again.

Lazer leaned down and gently kissed her on the lips.

"I promise," he whispered. "You have to promise to be okay."

"I love you, Lazer. Always . . . have," she whispered, the last breath hissing from her lips. Kyla closed her eyes. She lay silent and motionless in Lazer's arms. Tears flooded his eyes.

"Kyla! Kyla!" Lazer screamed calling to her to come back to him.

Suddenly Masta Poe was standing next to him.

"Step away, Lazer," Masta Poe commanded. Her voice was strong and yet amazingly calm.

"Don't let her die. Please," Lazer pleaded, the words closing in around his throat.

Lazer didn't remember moving away, but in the next instant he was standing behind a kneeling Masta Poe.

Masta Poe gathered the lifeless Kyla into her arms and began to whisper into her ear, "*In gredia, lon fi tatum. Masi lai s tu. Che re fodu. Stali stamus, feritate.*"

Again and again, she repeated the words, "*In gredia, lon fi tatum. Masi lai s tu. Che re fodu. Stali stamus, feritate.*"

Lazer watched as a shroud of haze appeared from nowhere and encircled them. Through the curtain of fog, he saw Kyla lying on the ground and, at the exact same time, she was standing just on the other side of the haze, watching expressionlessly as the event unfolded. Lazer blinked, not believing his eyes. He looked down and saw her broken body still in Masta Poe's arms. He could hear the strange chant she spoke, but Masta Poe's lips didn't move. The sounds fell on his ears as though they were coming from a million miles away. Then, the standing Kyla looked directly at Lazer.

"I'll find you again," he heard Kyla's voice whisper in his ear. He could smell Kyla's scent and feel her hand brush his cheek and her lips press against his lips.

The ghostly image of Kyla turned to walk away.

"Kyla! No! I need you," Lazer shouted. He wanted to go after her, but his feet were stuck to the earth.

Again he heard Masta Poe repeating the haunting chant. Her voice became stronger and more emphatic. "*In gredia, lon fi tatum. Masi lai s tu. Che re fodu. Stali stamus, feritate.*" She was commanding Kyla to stay. Maybe Lazer couldn't understand the translation of the words, but he knew, with every fiber in his being, the exact meaning that lay behind the strange utterances. The chanted words were carried inside a siren's melody, so soft and hypnotic it pulled him closer without taking a step.

"*In gredia, lon fi tatum. Masi lai s tu. Che re fodu. Stali stamus, feritate.*" Masta Poe chanted the words again and again. "*In gredia, lon fi tatum. Masi lai s tu. Che re fodu. Stali stamus, feritate.*"

Lazer looked up at the vision of Kyla. It had risen from the ground and was now floating five feet off the floor. The tone in Masta Poe's voice became more intense. "*In gredia, lon fi tatum. Masi lai s tu. Che re fodu. Stali stamus, feritate. I lio ta univa. Tu vie. Tu vie. Tu vie,*" Masta Poe chanted. On the ground, her small, frail body was trembling.

Lazer dropped to his knees. Compelled by what he was bearing witness to, he reached out to Masta Poe, gently placing his hand on Kyla's shoulder. He joined his mind with Masta Poe's and with Kyla's.

"Kyla. Don't leave me," Lazer whispered inside his thoughts.

His ears were filled with the sound of a speeding train and he felt the rush of a warm wind blow as Kyla's spirit passed through him. It was filled with such love that Lazer gasped, clasped his hands over his heart, and opened his eyes. At the same time, he opened his eyes, Kyla opened hers.

At that moment, the emergency doors to the battle forum flew open. The creature crew entered in full white artillery, rushed in behind the head creature master, Captain Drew Janos, a scar worn, hard bodied man as he shouted orders to his subordinates. It took all of ten seconds for Captain Janos to assess the situation. Two men and one woman were wearing the familiar blue jumpsuits that signified their status as healers. Lazer listened as Captain Janos ordered one healer to see to Elana Blue. A second woman in pale blue and seven other men in a deeper blue rushed past Lazer to Kyla. They all stared at what was left of Deigen and then Lazer before turning their full focus onto Kyla.

"Get a floater over here, stat!" the captain shouted as he stood over Kyla.

The woman healer left Elana and rushed past the captain.

"That one's been sprayed. She needs a venom antidote. Get a call into trauma. Tell them she's in shock," she said spewing a list of medical terms, holistic and chemical words and amounts.

The woman pointed back to Elana as she spoke and one of the men raced away. She reached Kyla, dropped to her knees, pulled out a small device and did a t-ray scan of Kyla's body. Lazer watched helplessly as the healer pocketed the tiny device and gently moved her hands just above Kyla's skin to read Kyla's vitals through her auras. She frowned and Lazer could tell by her expression it was bad. He stepped farther back to give her more room as the healer called for additional help on her wristsponder. "Code Blue. Send me a mobile T-cell regeneration care unit pack for a . . ." She stopped and turned to Lazer. "What's she spliced with? Moth?"

Kyla's beautiful wings had been shredded by the teeth of Deigen and hung, frayed and tattered by the battle lying like ragged strips of bloodied cloth across the ground.

"Butterfly," Lazer said softly to the healer his eyes never leaving his friend.

The mobile emergency crew was there in an instant stabilizing Kyla in a series of vibrating ringed braces that hermetically sealed her into a germ-free force field. Before they switched the field on, Lazer could see them carefully doing everything they could, even as they moved her.

Lazer's thoughts went to Elana. He rushed to her side and took her hand. Her eyes were closed.

"Is she going to be all right?" Lazer asked.

"We were about to give her a sedative to slow the poison in her system down but it seems she's managed to slow her own heart and blood flow down. She's gone into shock, which is the best place for her until we get her arteries flushed and this anti venom into her veins," the emergency crewmember said.

"You'll be okay, Elana," Lazer whispered and gently kissed her cheek. "Everything will be okay."

"What about you? Are you okay?" the woman healer in the pale blue asked him. Lazer nodded yes.

"Then step back and give us room to help them, son," the woman said.

Lazer stepped out of the way. He watched as they loaded Elana onto an air floater. The other crew gathered Kyla's shattered body onto the next gurney and a third crew took the piece of jaw that held Kyla's torn fleshy wing and bits of bone. *Maybe they could clone or regenerate her wings using some of the cells,* Lazer thought. *Maybe she could fly again.*

Lazer saw one of the crew as he picked up the exploded battle wand from the pile of hair, ear, and mashed brains and brought what was left of it to the captain. The two men looked from Deigen's remains to Lazer in complete and utter awe. Lazer's eyes were on Elana and Kyla, but he could hear their words.

"There's not enough power in these things to do that," the crewman said to the captain pointing to Deigen.

"Yeah. Isn't that the kid that saved the transport?" the captain asked. "I'm guessing he didn't even need the battle wand to do that. What I want to know is how this cage field got shut down and what the hell is that chip?"

The captain picked up a small transmitter from a piece of brain matter and showed it to his crewman.

"Take that to analysis," the captain said. "Someone tagged that creature."

"That ain't a tag," the crewman said.

"Just get it analyzed. Somebody did this intentionally."

Lazer's attention was pulled back to the battle forum by the captain's last words. He was torn, he wanted to follow the two gurneys, but he knew they wouldn't let him ride to the emergency with either. He wasn't family and might not even be allowed into the ICU to see them. He'd have to get there on his own and take his chances. Lazer's ears perked at the sounds of sirens wail from the emergency transports as they faded away. He could smell the burnt flesh and hair that mingled with the leftover, ozone particle of nitric oxide gas that hung in the air like after a great storm.

He had been oblivious to everything else except Kyla and Elana Blue. His hands were steady. He had at no time felt any feelings of fear. Why? He pondered. One more person filled his thoughts. He stopped, his eyes searching for Masta Poe. She was nowhere in sight. When had she come in? When had she left? She was there. He saw her. She had called Kyla back from the dead and maybe she slowed Elana's heart to slow the venom. Had she stepped into him and helped him defeat the creature?

"Thank you," he whispered.

Lazer backed out of the battle forum and started to run. He wanted to find Cashton. He wanted to be with Elana and Kyla. He needed to speak with Masta Poe.

39

FAILURE

FIVE STOOD BEFORE THE HISS of white noise that played on the holoscreen as it floated before him. He stood for a long silent moment calculating the defeat. He along with his first team had been watching Lazer and the battle with Deigen. The remnants of the mechanical implant that had only a moment ago been functioning inside the living, breathing splicer were fried—useless— failed and once again Cole Lazerman, the human boy, who continued to elude him was triumphant and still very much alive. The team of clones, splicers, and biodroids who answered to Five stood silent. Two were terrified and one was trembling. All were waiting for the crushing blow of death that would befall whomever Five deemed responsible for, and yet, another failure.

40

ONE LESSON MORE

IT WAS MONDAY, one hour until the Rite of Passage transport arrived. Lazer reminded himself that it would be two weeks of basic survival and then he would find a way to get home. He wanted to be with Kyla and Elana Blue at Sangelino, but he wouldn't break the promise he had made to his mother and now his promise to Kyla. She had kept her promise and lived; he would keep his.

Lazer existed in his own private misery. He said little to Cashton. What had happened in the battle forum with Kyla and Masta Poe was an enigma he could not bring himself to speak about with anyone. He knew he had to see Masta Poe before he left. He knew, more than anything, that when he had completed his quest to rid Atlantia of the Black Guard, he wanted to come back to Masta Poe and study the Visionistic Arts under her tutelage. Lazer made his way through the serpentine corridors of the Visionistic Arts and Powers Building and headed down to Masta Poe's private chamber. He stood at the threshold for what felt like forever, trying to muster the courage to knock. He felt paralyzed. No matter how hard he tried, he was unable to raise his arm. A millisecond before he turned to walk away, the door swung open on its own.

"Come in, Cadet Lazerman," Masta Poe said, without bothering to turn from her experiments.

"I . . . wanted to thank you . . .," Lazer started.

"You already did, Lazer. I heard it in your heart."

"I want to understand what you did to bring Kyla . . ."

"I only did what you both wanted. I only showed her the way. It was love and faith that brought her back. And before you can lead others to that kind of love, you must first learn to love yourself, Lazer. Only then can you understand the powers that are the universal heart." She spoke to him in words she knew, but no matter how hard he tried, Lazer still was not willing to understand.

"There isn't much time. Come. I have a set of phaser cuffs on the desk." Masta Poe pointed. "Please put them on."

Lazer obeyed. He strapped on the double-barreled titanium phaser cuffs, complete with switchblade thumb triggers. *I can show her I'm ready.* The cuffs were designed for maximum speed and lethal power. They could be fired as an automatic weapon or, if used on another setting, they would produce an eighteen-inch laser bayonet hot enough to cut through steel. With a turn of his wrists, the narrow firing mechanism jutted into his palm. He pressed the laser blade release to send the seven hair-thin, fire-red laser points out around his fist to conjoin into the three-inch-thick bayonet. Lazer moved through a series of tai chi motions. He liked the thin hiss the lasers made as they cut the air.

"Is she well?" Masta Poe asked gently, finally turning to face him.

Lazer stopped. He retracted the blades. His disposition became somber. "Kyla was evacuated to a hospital in Sangelino. She's stable."

"And Miss Covax?"

Lazer looked up, surprised that she knew Elana's secret identity.

"They were both sent on the same shuttle to some special hospital in Sangelino."

"And what if that transport stopped in Atlantia?" Masta Poe asked.

"I'd have been the first one on it."

"That's all that's kept you from going?" she asked, turning back to her work. "A proton dome?"

"And a promise. I made a promise." Lazer straightened. He was proud that he was keeping his word to both his mother and Kyla.

"You still do not admit your limitations."

"What I lack in skill and weapons, determination can make up for." He held up the cuffs as a sign of his potential deadly force.

Masta Poe studied Lazer. He was arrogant and cocky, but that was partly confidence and partly fear. What he lacked, she knew, was the humility to learn and the willingness to exist in bliss and accept the remembering.

"It will take more than phasers and courage to protect you from your fate," Masta Poe added.

"You taught me that my fate is undetermined until I determine it!" he snapped back, using her words to emphasize his point.

Masta Poe swept the air with her arm. A shaft of white and orange fire streamed straight for Lazer.

Lazer reacted immediately. He ignited the phaser cuffs and fired directly into the fire stream, flattening it until it consumed itself.

Masta Poe sent a second blast, then a third and fourth blast flew across the room. Lazer counter blasted each one. She couldn't help but notice what a natural he was, that he had a grace and fluidity that made the cuffs act as if they were part of him. His form, his stance, his aim was that of a skilled master.

"You're draining all my power!" Lazer yelled, when he glanced at the power levels on his gun. There was a hint of panic in his breathless voice as the band flashed red then faded to black.

Masta Poe raised her hands and shot an even larger, more powerful stream of fire. Lazer's eyes widened. He closed the cuffs, dropped to one knee and, slamming his wrists together, threw an energy shield. The fire stream slammed into the shimmering force field that encircled him, heating the energy waves that protected him to a glowing white. Lazer began to sweat inside the shell, but he had learned from the prometheus that inside its cocoon, he could endure any onslaught.

The fire subsided and Masta Poe stared at him with unflinching, emotionless eyes.

"That's all," she said. "Stand."

"What was that about?" Lazer blurted, shaken and flustered.

"I wondered when you would realize the limitations of the weapons and draw upon your powers."

"You could have killed me!"

"Your death will not be of my design, Lazer; it will be your own." Masta Poe calmly turned back to her experiments.

"I'm not afraid of death," he said.

"No, Lazer, you are afraid of life."

There was a long pause before she faced him again. Her eyes were filled with a strange, gentle understanding, and Lazer felt her compassion and relaxed his stance. With her mind, Masta Poe called to his. Lazer opened himself and, for the first time, he didn't fight the tingling rush that occurred when he felt Masta Poe reading his thoughts and feelings. Through her senses, she reached for the hues of pure love that lay in Lazer's heart. She saw the light that still glowed inside the vast unconditional compassion he held for his family and friends. She saw his infinite depth of ever-growing faith that could, if he would open himself to it, become the power to manifest his every dream. But in each brilliant color that painted his emotions, she saw the shadowed walls of anger that hung like heavy velvet curtains and blocked the glow of all that was good. Potential bound by fear, innuendo, doubt, and, worst of all, by hate.

"Go, if you must, Cole Lazerman, but hear these words and heed their meaning. Trust in the knowing that you and the universe are one, and that all the powers of the universe are inside you at this very moment. But you alone must choose between the paths of love and hate, for each one brings a different destiny. It is the journey, Lazer, not the destination that frees the soul."

Lazer saw tears well in her eyes.

Lazer felt the wave of sadness that he had seen in Masta Poe's eyes crash into him and twist with the force of a turbulent storm. It was a cold knife that twisted into his heart and hung there heavy and dark. Why was she so sad? Was she so sure he would fail?

Doubt closed in like a cold, dark vacuum, taking the sweetness from the air and giving back only the stench of dread. The shadows of fear crept over him and rose up, pitch black and ghostly, creating a vision of darkness that surrounded him and filled him with the emptiness and horror of the unknown. It choked his spirit and blocked the way—not just of the journey he must take, but the courage he would need to succeed.

"I won't fail!" he shouted. "Why can't you just give me the secret of the knowing?"

"How can I give you something you already possess?"

"I don't. You told me I could demand it as my human right . . . then I demand it," Lazer shouted, commanding the universe and defying the ominous feeling that pulled at him. Lazer closed his eyes and, in the sigh of a silent prayer, he calmed himself. "I demand it."

"Ask your emotions, Lazer. They are your guides in these times, not me."

Lazer looked at her.

"Go in light, Cole Lazerman. The path that calls you awaits, and I will tell you only this: you have no time for fear. Let it go and the rest will flow to you," she said. In a gesture befitting a knight, Masta Poe leaned forward and kissed him on the forehead. Before he could say another word, she vanished into a silken mist.

Lazer was alone. He let thoughts drift and called to mind his most powerful emotions: the hate he held for himself that was sealed indelibly inside the guilt over his father's death; the regret he felt because he had abandoned his mother who, by all the signs, had been lost to him under the dome that encased Atlantia. Evvy's death also weighed on his heart. Lazer felt the pangs of his most trusted emotion—anger—for it above all had so faithfully fueled him. But the purest and most powerful of all was the hatred he held for the Black Guard, which burned like the blazing fire of a newborn sun. But in the exact same breath of turmoil and rage, the sweet memories of Elana Blue cooled the fever that boiled in his mind. Wasn't it his love for her that allowed him to save her from Deigen? Didn't that outweigh his fear that he might never hold her in his arms again? And, what of his vanquished homeland? Could it be the love of his friends—Cashton and his guardian angel, Kyla—that empowered him? Didn't his family and country matter in the greater scheme of life more than the black mark of hatred that covered his soul?

The questions pounded inside this wild, mounting cacophony of swirling emotions. Lazer let the feelings give him strength. He felt a warm rush of possibility flow through his veins and a knowing that once he chose his thoughts, he was capable of anything he could imagine.

Lazer's breath quickened with excitement. If he could hold onto this newfound power, he could not fail.

Could these feelings be his connection to his BAI—his personal key to the powers of the Universe? *This had to be the knowing*, he thought to himself. If this was the destiny Masta Poe spoke of, then Lazer was ready to face this ultimate decision between love and hate. He would take on his destiny like a welcome cloak—heavy with the weight of responsibility for everything he cared about. For the first time in his life, Lazer understood the power of choice. He had within his heart, mind, and soul the one thing that would carry him to victory against all odds; with one unspoken word, Lazer committed himself to the inevitable.

Lazer looked one last time around Masta Poe's office, gathered his bag, and left for the transport that would take him on his Rite of Passage and then . . . home.

CELIAN LANGUAGE

By Deborah M. Pratt

Lexicon Guide by: Dr. Katie Petruzzelli

THE CELIAN LANGUAGE is one of flowing words—one rolling effortlessly into the next. To those fortunate enough to hear and understand—every calming word is a peaceful song.

Let this guide to the Celian language help connect you to the oneness of the Universe. Go in light.

PRONUNCIATIONS AND TENSES

c—*c* is always pronounced as a *k* sound. Therefore, the word Celian is always pronounced with a hard C as in *Kelian,* and not as *Selian.*

x—*x* is always pronounced as an *s* sound, making the word Xhin pronounce as *S-hin,* and not *Zhin.* The one exception to this rule is the word *Xelian* which is still pronounced as *Kelian* as shown in the English spelling of the word.

a—*a* is always pronounced as an *au* sound, as in "trauma." Making the word *Alan* pronounced as *Au-laun* and not with the pronunciation of as the name "Alan."

e—*e* is always pronounced with the short vowel sound of *e* such as in "tender."

i—*i* is always pronounced as a hard *e*. Making the word *Garin* pronounced as *Gar-een* and not as *Gar-in.*

o—*o* is always pronounced as a hard *o,* as in "home." Making the word *lio* pronounced as *lee-O.*

u—*u* is always pronounced as an *oo* sound, as in "broom." Making the word *fodu* pronounced as *fo-doo.*

y—*y* is is not often used, and has the same rules as the letter *i.*

PLURALS

Removing the last consonant and vowel from the end of a word and replacing it with *-um* will make the word plural. Example: *Orah* (Gnorb) becomes *Orum* (Gnorbs). If the word ends in a vowel, only that last vowel is removed and the *-um* is added. Example: *Aliomi* (History) becomes *Aliomum* (Histories). If the word is two letters or less, *-um* is simply added to the end of the word. Example: *Ma* (Doom) becomes *Maum* (Dooms).

There is a singular use and a plural use of the word *the*. *Lai* (the) is used when the word following it is singular. Example: *Lai tatam* (The power). *Fi* (the) is used when the word following it is plural. Example: *Fi tatum* (The powers).

ADDING -ING

Adding *-wa* to the end of a Celian word is equivalent to adding "-ing" to the end of a word in English. Example: *Morran* (Know) becomes *Morranwa* (Knowing).

PAST TENSE

Adding *-ne* to the end of a Celian word will make the word past tense. Example: *Alan* (Unify) becomes *Alanne* (Unified).

CELIAN GLOSSARY

Celian to English:

A
Alan: Unify
Alanne: Unified
Aliomi: History
Aliomum: Histories
Am: Inside
Ank: Go
As: Incarnation

B
Bledash: Source

C
Cassim: Become
Cha: That
Che: Give
Chene: Given
Clay: Day
Clayum: Days

F
Fage: Our
Fan: If
Fatsi: It
Feriate: Perfection
Fi: The (*plural*—example: fi tatum/the powers)

Figgii: Part
Fodu: This
Fume: Longer

G
Garin: Fearful
Ghi: Human
Gighe: Call
Gighum: Called
Gleotopa: Let
Ganna: Pathway
Gredia: Command

H
Hane: Cause

I
I: Into
Ima: Have
In: I
Inu: Soul

K
Kachiti: Understand
Kilonye: Embodiment

L
La: Chose
Laan: One

Lanna: Single

Lai: The (*singular*—example: lai S/the Universe)

Leom: Look

Leitt: Real

Liageakiowa: Everything

Lio: Oneness

Lipa: Truth

Lith: Will

Loch: Be

Lochlaan: Be One

Lome: Way

Lon: All

M

Ma: Doom

Maage: You

Maagan: Your

Magien: Belong

Magium: Belongs

Mai: Physical

Manro: Find

Masi: Of

Maum: Doomed

Maya: Pure

Me: Vision

Morran: Know

Morranne: Known

Morranwa: Knowing

Morvaba: Mind

Morvabum: Minds

N

Nane: Allow

Naniba: Light

Ne: A

Nu: No

Nun: Not

O

O: And

Obana: Through

Obrdur: Held

Oloragi: We

Ommol: Elevate

Ommolne: Elevated

Onamm: Lonely

Ongam: Darken

Ongamna: Darkness

Orah: Gnorb

Orum: Gnorbs

Ori: Make

Orine: Made

Orinima: Energy

P

Pae: Keeper

Pug: Greed

Pasch: Gift

Paschne: Gifted

Paum: Keepers

Presg: Us

Q

Qua: Spirit

R

Rah: Every
Re: Back
Reage: Revenge
Reaom: Own

S

S: Universe
Sapharono: Great
Savi: Anger
She: Fault
Shovate: Each
Shum: Lost
Sho: Lose
So: Sensation
Stali: Life
Stamus: Breaths
Strat: Is

T

Ta: With
Taan: Future
Tash: Must
Tati: Are
Tatam: Power
Tatum: Powers
Te: Who
Ti: Secret
Titik: For
Tu: To

U

U: Universal
Umlin: Heart
Univa: Love
Uti: Wonderment

V

Va: Needed
Vi: Explore
Vici: Hatred
Vie: Eternal
Vioswe: Paradise
Vo: Solely

X

Xelian: Celian
Xihn: Do

English to Celian:

A

A: Ne
All: Lon
Allow: Nane
And: O
Anger: Savi
Are: Tati

B

Back: Re
Be: Loch
Be One: Lochlaan

Become: Cassim
Belong: Magien
Belongs: Magium
Breaths: Stamus

C
Call: Gighe
Called: Gighum
Cause: Hane
Celian: Xelian
Chose: La
Command: Gredia

D
Darken: Ongam
Darkness: Ongammna
Day: Clay
Days: Clayum
Do: Xihn
Doomed: Maum

E
Each: Shovate
Elevate: Ommol
Elevated: Ommolne
Embodiment: Kilonye
Energy: Ominima
Eternal: Vie
Every: Rah
Everything: Liageakiowa
Explore: Vi

F
Fault: She
Fearful: Garin
Find: Manro
For: Titik
Future: Taan

G
Gift: Pasch
Gifted: Paschne
Give: Che
Given: Chene
Gnorb: Orah
Gnorbs: Orum
Go: Ank
Great: Sapharono
Greed: Pug

H
Hatred: Vici
Have: Ima
Heart: Umlin
Held: Obrdur
Histories: Aliomum
History: Aliomi
Human: Ghi

I
I: In
If: Fan
Incarnation: As
Inside: Am

Into: I
Is: Strat
It: Fatsi

K

Keeper: Pae
Keepers: Paum
Know: Morran
Known: Morranne
Knowing: Morranwa

L

Let: Gleotopa
Life: Stali
Light: Naniba
Longer: Fume
Look: Leom
Lose: Sho
Lost: Shum
Love: Univa

M

Made: Orne
Make: Ori
Mind: Morvaba
Minds: Morvabum
Must: Tash
Needed: Va
No: Nu
Not: Nun

O

Of: Masi
One: Laan
Oneness: Lio
Our: Fage
Own: Reaom

P

Paradise: Vioswe
Part: Figgii
Passed: Cleh
Pathway: Ganna
Perfection: Feriate
Physical: Mai
Power: Tatam
Powers: Tatum
Pure: Maya

R

Real: Leitt
Revenge: Reage

S

Secret: Ti
Sensation: So
Single: laana
Solely: Vo
Soul: Inu
Source: Bledsash
Spirit: Qua

T

That: Cha

The (*plural*): Fi (example: fi tatum/the powers)

The (*singular*): Lai (example: lai S/the Universe)

This: Fodu

Through: Obana

To: Tu

Truth: Lipa

U

Understand: Kachiti

Unify: Alan

Unified: Alannne

Universal: U

Universe: S

V

Vision: Me

W

Way: Lome

We: Oloragi

Who: Te

With: Ta

Wonderment: Uti

Y

You: Maage

Your: Maagan

ABOUT THE AUTHOR

DEBORAH M. PRATT is a significant force in Hollywood. She's an American director, writer, producer, and actress. Ms. Pratt is a graduate from Webster University with a degree in psychology and theatre. She was co-creator, executive producer, and head writer on the iconic series *Quantum Leap* for NBC and *Tequila and Bonetti* for CBS. She also created for TV and became executive producer of "**The Net**" for the USA network. Ms. Pratt wrote for multiple television series including *Magnum, P.I., The Pretender,* and *Airwolf.* She is an award-winning graduate of the American Film Institute's Directing Workshop for Women and made her directorial debut with *Cora Unashamed* for the BBC, PBS, and Masterpiece Theatre's The American Collection.

Ms. Pratt is a five-time Emmy nominee, a Golden Globe nominee, and the recipient of The Lillian Gish Award from Women in Film, The Angel Award, The Golden Block Award, and six Black Emmy Nominees awards.

A published novelist, she breaks the mold of science fiction and creates a genre of science fantasy with the vision of a new, unified Earth and the keys to human empowerment. The books are intricately layered with scientific fact and imaginative fantasy. *The Atlantian, The Academy, The Odyssey,* and *Salvation* are due to be released this year. *The Vision Quest* series is a critically acclaimed, exhilarating journey into the future of our world. Ms. Pratt is a pioneer in trans-media entertainment and is developing the world she's created in her books and films across multiple platforms. Her latest book, "*The Tempting: Seducing the Nephilim,*" is book two in *The Age of Eve* novel series.

Deborah currently lives in Los Angeles, has two children, and considers herself a citizen of planet Earth.

Visit these sites to learn more:

TheVisionQuest.com • TheAtlantianVQ.com • DeborahMPratt.com

ABOUT THE SERIES

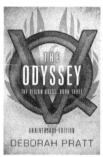
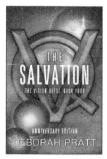

BOOK ONE	**BOOK TWO**	**BOOK THREE**	**BOOK FOUR**
TODAY AT AMAZON	**TODAY AT AMAZON**	**COMING APRIL 2017**	**COMING JUNE 2017**

THE VISION QUEST SERIES: In the not-too-distant future, Earth has unified into a brave new world. Humans have crossed their genetics with an array of creatures and these amazing new species have helped us to remember the powers humans forgot. But they also crossed their genes with machines, and our mechanical creations have become sentient and determined to change the world as we know it. On the risen continent of Atlantia, three friends—Cole Lazerman, Kyla Wingright, and Cashton Lock—are thrust into Earth's next evolution and forced to be part of the battle for humankind. Friendship, family, love, and a call to destiny, command them to find the courage to stand and fight or die. **This the journey of the Vision Quest and these are the heroes we've been waiting for.**

Visit these sites to learn more:
TheVisionQuest.com • TheAtlantianVQ.com • DeborahMPratt.com